THE CENTRAL LIMIT

THE CENTRAL LIMIT

a novel |

Andrew Davenport

Subsolar Press

www.subsolarpress.com

To my parents, for whom I am forever grateful

"Sir, are you expecting someone?"

I snapped from a heavy sideways slouch to an adultlike posture, taking off my noise-canceling headphones without pausing the audio. A helmet of crimson hair appeared suddenly, delivering a bake sale-friendly smile, not the usual gruff eviction.

"I'm waiting for a friend," I said, rubbing my eyes and focusing on the brightly colored patterns on her scrub top, goofy creatures that tried to calm terrified toddlers getting booster shots or having their blood drawn.

"If you give me their name, I can check their status in the system."

"She was going to meet me here," I said, immediately regretting the use of the past tense, implying that I'm still here pathetically waiting for a friend who stood me up. She nodded and smiled again, then walked back to the nurses' station at the front of the Foothills Medical Center Emergency Room. Her buoyancy implied covering a fellow nurse's night shift, not the typical thousand-yard stare during the second half of a double shift.

My phone showed 2:20 am. I was apparently one hour into a delightful long-form podcast episode on the fifth century BCE Greco-Persian Wars. Each episode was about four to five hours in length and frolicked in the deep end of palace imposters, heavy infantry tactics, and the convulsions of Greek politics where the hero of the Battle of Plataea Pausanias was starved to death for treason two years after the epic victory. I rapidly tapped the thirty-second rewind icon to return to the estimated last time of lucidity.

The Intensive Care ward sat adjacent to the Emergency Room and its public area tended to clear out later in the evening, leaving a selection of reasonably comfortable upholstered chairs with good views of the ER lobby. The rows of seats had shared armrests like airport furniture designed to prevent waiting passengers from taking horizontal positions, which was at first disheartening but later satisfying as it allowed me to watch the action while propping my head up with an outrigger elbow. Tonight's ER crowd featured a broken nose from a bar fight, motorcycle road rash, and the standard minor lacerations and inscrutable internalized troubles.

My seat offered an excellent vantage point, a wide visual field in reasonable auditory range to the action but far enough away to make being harassed or drawn into the arena of human desperation unlikely. I suppose my instinct to watch social interaction at a safe distance arose from a childhood spent in a formerly industrial Mid-Atlantic small town of closely packed houses for walkability to the coal mines. The wood frame homes often sported a modest front porch and sometimes a roof-mounted chair swing for sipping iced tea, engaging in short cordial conversations, and general neighborhood surveillance. It allowed one to be in a community but not be asphyxiated by it, a pleasant middle ground between sidewalk-less suburbia and hulking urban multi-family units.

I got up from the chair when the same nurse looked over in my direction again, put my headphones back on, and headed towards the ER exit. A bulletin board beside the coffee station caught my eye, serving up a platter of raw information for consumption like the always seductive Nutrition Facts labels. The flyers listed upcoming health events using words like *holistic*, *mindful*, and *practice*. A postcard-sized ad in the lower right corner said:

Join a nationwide psychological study
Novel treatments to increase individual thriving
Must be between 18 and 65 years of age
Participants paid $300 per week

I took a photo of the card, which included a contact email address and phone number, then hit the blue handicap button with a denim-covered knee to avoid the cocktail of bodily fluids glazed onto the panic bar. The clear sky-cooled air pushed back against drowsiness on the walk home.

The nonprofit hospital was by far the most expensive building in the area, a working-class neighborhood populated with asbestos-sided post-war ranches and other low-slung structures. I moved to the satellite city located seventy miles north of the larger metro center five months ago, in early spring when the days bled with abundant sunshine, nights were cool, and the high desert shortgrass prairie was as green as a golf course. As summer arrived, the south-facing room in the dark brick two-story apartment became a pizza oven, the carry-on sized window-mounted air conditioner woefully inadequate. The HVAC in the hospital, by contrast, maintained a solid sixty-eight degrees, unphased by climatic caprice.

Drowsiness returned after walking the two blocks back from the emergency room, the podcast narration decomposing into a soup of word fragments and verbal tones. The empty streets felt more honest to the area's barren landscape before human settlement. It must have been familiarity that drew me to the continental climate of the region, a setting similar to the Central Asian steppe where I lived before coming home, if home can be generously defined as the country of one's birth. Naked dehydrated expanses now felt more authentic than the jungles of life back on the East Coast.

My neighbors in the apartment building were a motley assortment on various forms of government assistance. A healthy contingent backed vehicles into their parking spots, pretending to be Steven Seagal ready for a quick escape. It was an entertaining crowd and an appropriate place for me given my own marginal economic status, though our communication was limited to head nods of masculine acknowledgment rather than conversation. Rusted wrought iron railings around the shared exterior walkways made the building look more like a discount motel than an apartment. Cursive letters on the eastern face proclaimed the structure as The Viscount but patches of dark dried wood on the peeling fascia boards and a tangle of competing company's satellite dishes cut into its former nobility. The unit faced the ever-growing hospital complex and would surely be consumed in the next decade to make room for a steel and glass cancer wing.

I tripped and scattered the pile of mail when opening the door – doggedly persistent Welcome to the Neighborhood promotions from furniture stores and letters insisting on my need for electronic home security. The air in the apartment hung heavy with heat slowly diffusing out of the brick walls while the air conditioner futilely gurgled in the living room.

It was only a few years ago when the idea of moving felt liberating, a chance for me and Jessica to have a fresh start in a new country. Our first meal would be street food eaten out of the wrappers while sitting on the floor. We would then blissfully collapse in bed after a tiring day of hauling furniture and setting up utilities in foreign languages, the intoxication of exhaustion making some tissues relax while others filled with blood.

While I improvised shelving and found the most efficient way to consolidate our clothes, she ventured out and would return with local discarded or threadbare objects, like a jumble of painted pottery pieces for a mural or segments of wire and thread for a hanging counterbalanced sculpture. I returned most of the salvage artwork to the dumpster when I vacated the Almaty apartment last March but stuffed the gritty kinetic art against a sidewall of my suitcase. Jessica stayed in the States after the winter holiday, our first Christmas apart in fifteen years. Even during the final stages of our disintegration, a part of me still considered marriage and children as some inevitable final causes of our relationship. This should have made the breakup harder. Instead, our firewalls of communication snuffed us out with surprising ease. She never asked what happened to the art pieces in our abbreviated email thread after the initial round of fateful phone calls. Our limited possessions didn't require a hostage exchange, our shared digital photos already floated around in the cloud.

I brushed my teeth, only allowing the electric toothbrush to beep once instead of the recommended three times, then stripped down to my undershirt and boxers. The windows rattled with the sound of a helicopter outside, a medical emergency being flown in for care. I found two foam earplugs under the bed, sometimes the choppers hovered around the block for five minutes or more, strafing the neighborhood. I pushed off the comforter but kept a sheet around my ankles and sank into bed, too tired to feel gross from a day's worth of passive sweating. I often struggled to fall asleep, unable to launch Task Manager to kill rogue neural processes, yielding fitful nights and requiring antihistamines to produce a slumber with the restorative quality of a night spent on a park bench. Utter exhaustion seemed to help. A free online course in cognitive behavioral therapy I took three months ago encouraged reducing sleep hours to condition the brain to associate the bed with rest rather than flopping around, which produced modest success.

After settling into a mummy pose, I pulled up a mental spreadsheet. My checking account would be depleted in a little over two years, at which point I would need to obtain a real job or produce another source of income. To continue coasting at my current rate required a supplemental revenue stream of six hundred dollars per month through deployments into the gig economy, which fortunately thrived here from the relentless growth of recreation-based tourism and incoming population pressure.

He entered the passenger side backseat of the car with deliberation, looking at the door hinges while lowering himself into the seat by firmly gripping the overhead grab handle with both hands. The slow but measured movement made me picture him placing forces and moments on various parts of the car and collecting their responses, like a building code inspector looking for points of weakness on deck railings.

"This is a nice vehicle you have here," he said in an Eastern European accent, where "this" became "zis." "Strong height above the ground."

"Thanks. The ground clearance is nearly nine inches," I said. Having done my research after imagining high pointing on snowpacks and rutted mountain roads, I bought the hatchback crossover SUV with cash four months back, the three-year-old car only depreciating thirty-five percent from the MSRP, but still offering a modest discount over new. The vehicle presented an anomaly given my otherwise spartan decision-making upon returning to the States. In fact, the choice to purchase a nice car over a sub $2,000 shitbox likely subtracted another eight months from my period of permitted laziness, an allowable indulgence justified by the fact that its fully collapsing rear seats could fit a 5'10" frame in case of a personal housing crunch.

The newer car also opened up an ability to moonlight as a ride-hailing driver away from my daylight occupations of library visits and early morning tennis matches before the heat really took off. I started driving two weeks ago, specializing in trips to and from the international airport, a good hour plus ride each way along the interstate, which could net about $40 or more with surge pricing. The ride-hailing app said his name was Victor and he needed a ride from the airport back to town.

He sat silently in the rear seat, dressed in a thin beige sport coat, plain white dress shirt, and grey checkered tie, looking like one of the salarymen that crammed into subways in black and white post-war videos. It was eight o'clock on Friday night as we drove northward in light traffic. I asked if he wanted me to turn up the air conditioning and he shook his head no, somehow impervious to the late summer heat. His right hand traced the door seal while the left hand held up some papers which appeared to be handwritten notes. I guessed him to be in his late sixties. He sported a four-day salt and pepper beard, deep-set dark eyes, and a series of liver spots on his forehead resembling a map of the Philippines.

The GPS software directed me to a neighborhood west of Old Town, towards the mountains and north of the university. I pictured him living in a tasteful mid-century modern house with large windows and heavy horizontal lines, the home of a college professor of some sort. Instead, we pulled up in front of a small Victorian bungalow with peeling grey-painted brick and ivy covering its north side.

"Would you like a hand with your bags?" I asked Victor. This perfunctory gesture was typically dismissed but in an otherwise terse ride, I figured it best to be polite at the beginning and end of each trip as these were the most memorable periods. I needed five-star reviews to maintain my elite driver status.

"Yes, take the one on the right," Victor pointed to a hard clamshell bag which must have slipped just under the forty-five-pound weight limit. He grabbed the smaller piece and we walked up to the house. Forbs and invasive weeds outcompeted what little grass remained in the dry late summer.

Victor flipped a switch to turn on a corner lamp in the living room, a largely empty space with original hardwood floors, thick crown molding, a comically undersized TV, and a slim beige sofa. I asked him where he wanted the bag. He said to drop it off in the basement, whose access door was located between the kitchen and living room.

The stairs to the basement had no kick plates which made them swing side to side on the way down under the eccentric loading of heavy luggage. On reaching the bottom, I could make out a set of upright tools and workbenches in the dim light from the dusty bare lightbulb. I reflexively checked the size of the single-pane windows near the ceiling to make sure they were large enough for a person of modest BMI to escape unless of course they had been painted, were rusted, or had otherwise been sealed shut. I laid the bag down and quickly went up the stairs, taking them two at a time.

"Vodka or bourbon?" Victor asked when I returned to the kitchen. "No beer, sorry."

"I really should be going," I said, pulling out my phone to check for new rides. Victor sat at the table with two tumblers, the one opposite him with a finger of brown liquid in it. At that moment, he reminded me of the patriarch of my host family in Thailand, offering us a glass of Coca-Cola Classic with ice at the end of each day, his elixir and universal gesture of goodwill. The lack of decorations and the matching length of Victor's neck and facial hair suggested that he lived alone. I sat down at the table which generated a tightlipped smile.

"How long will you do this, the driving?" Victor asked.

"History predicts I will burn out in one and a half years or so, give or take a year," I answered.

"I expected you to stop after midnight," Victor said with a weak laugh. "Long-term thinker."

Victor's laconic pause-heavy verbal style gave him a gravity that I found intimidating, unlike other passenger's bouncy conversations about pet dogs and the chances of making the playoffs. I half expected him to announce a drinking contest on the spot, like the hazing ritual of a Russian father-in-law. We each worked on our drinks, Victor providing an immediate refill when I finished.

"I like doing late-night trips to the airport; more intentionality with the passengers," I said, breaking the silence. "It's easier to fall asleep when I'm completely exhausted."

"What do they call this, side hustle?"

"Yeah, I guess," I said, not admitting it was my primary source of income.

"We were told that Americans lacked resolve. Too busy surfing and listening to rock and roll. Attention deficit disorder at a cultural level," Victor said, sipping his liquor. "Russians take pride tolerating decades of suffering."

"Is that where you are from?"

"Southern Russia. Family originally from the Ukraine," Victor answered. "Have you been?"

"No, only a few former Soviet states," I said while swirling my glass to create a weak whirlpool in the tumbler. "Unless you count virtual travel." I spent hours hopping around on street views of subalpine wilderness, then zooming out to continent-wide belts of green and beige, probing dark spots for isolated photos or roads. One website provided a random street photo and had the user guess the location based on the foliage and architectural cues, an easy way to lose an afternoon.

"Why the driving?"

"I usually tell customers it's about meeting people, being genuinely interested in their life stories, all that," I said, the whiskey warming my throat. "But honestly most people are forgettable and boring, which I'm sure is how they'd describe me too. I used to stay up late every night walking the streets listening to podcasts, waiting for something oceanic to happen, I guess. This seemed like a way to convert nocturnal habits into money. Be an actor, not just a spectator. Never shared a drink with a passenger before."

"I love the American mythology of open spaces and this fetish of movement," Victor said. "We got bootleg American comic books as kids, cowboys and outlaws on the open range. I would spend entire days out in the railyards with a homemade wooden revolver, hunting down train robbers and bandits in your sandstone canyons. There is too much history in Russia, the land is tired. Our proletariat superhero comics didn't sell too many copies over here I bet."

The alcohol's buzz arrived and words flowed out. "I find solace in the vast forests of northern Russia, the ones responsible for the seasonal sawtooth pattern in carbon dioxide levels, a single lane mud track road as the only sign of development in the satellite views. The towns and cities look a little tired though." The Cold War ended before I entered my teenage years, sparing me some nuclear anxiety but imprinting a nostalgia for the clarity of its worldwide ideological struggle.

Victor sipped his liquor and leaned back. "Roads in Russia, especially Siberia, are brutal. Endless. You do battle against the land, a fool pushing against the earth with a dull plow. I had many maintenance and retrieval assignments for the northern deployment of RTGs."

"RTG?" I asked. It sounded like a weapon from a first-person shooter video game.

"Radioisotope thermoelectric generator. Heat created by nuclear decay is converted into electricity when passing through thermoelectric materials. Energy conversion efficiency is dog shit, maybe three percent, but the heat source is free and off the electric grid. Each RTG looks like an air-cooled engine the size of a refrigerator. Same thing used on deep space missions, like the U.S. Voyager probe."

"What were they for?" I asked. I guessed that Victor was some type of scientist or engineer given his level of technical detail.

"Lighthouses along the Northern Shipping Route, the top edge of Russia. Each RTG only generated a handful of watts so each lighthouse had around ten of them. The nuclear honeymoon lasted much longer in the Soviet Union than in the United States, long after you stopped painting ceramics with uranium. Lots of these RTGs were built in the late 1960s and by the '80s had exceeded their design lives and required an increasing number of repairs."

"You did the service trips?"

"Volunteered. Our company inherited the lighthouse maintenance contract. I was placed there after trade school. I hated the office, a bunch of old guys obsessed with job security giving me stupid tasks like restocking office supplies or organizing engineering drawings. Me and Bogdan would fly out to Murmansk or another town where we kept a stock of parts and supplies. He'd get drunk the first night and I'd head out alone the next morning at dawn. We had a good arrangement."

Victor continued. "I somehow got a Sony Walkman, which was of course strictly prohibited, and then cassettes of books on tape. I started with the Russian classics – Dostoevsky, Tolstoy, Gogol – basically the stuff I was supposed to have read. Driving alone for hours to these remote locations made the stories resonate with me and I soon found myself driving slower, letting the words sink in."

"There is something about listening to stories when surrounded by stillness," I said.

"Escaping constant distraction." Victor finished his glass and spun the bottle of whiskey, inspecting the label and perhaps considering another round. "That was both the most depressing and most ecstatic period of my life. Your twenties and thirties will do that to you, and then you're forever hooked to recreate it. How old are you?"

"I'm thirty-seven. Just turned." I wanted to lie to him, make myself five years younger as if somehow this would make me seem less pathetic, an immunity granted to youth without clear direction.

"You look younger." Victor got up and put his glass in the sink, and returned the liquor bottles to their place above the refrigerator. The linoleum kitchen counters were entirely empty except for a sponge and bottle of yellow dishwashing liquid. He seemed like the kind of person who could survive for months on alcohol and a mix of canned goods, bulk grains, and other long sea voyage foods of high caloric density. "Come back Monday at 1 pm. I have a job in the workshop."

"You mean for pay?" I asked.

"You will be compensated, Mr. ..."

Victor should have known my first name from the ride-hailing app, though he was likely not savvy in its use given that I hadn't yet received a tip. He seemed to expect a full name, like a girlfriend's father in the old world, to judge the stock of my line. I wanted to give him something generic, like John Smith, and stalled a bit to think until I gave up.

"Martin Rasmus," I said, shaking his hand with an intentionally firm grip.

The smell of isopropyl alcohol drifted into the exam room where I sat on a cold vinyl chair. Rubbing alcohol typically precedes a blood draw or some other kind of needlework, which I didn't recall being part of the selection process based on the online questionnaire, admittingly signing the ten-page disclaimer after only reading the first paragraph. Someone ahead of me in line could be getting poked, though the only person I'd seen so far was a drowsy receptionist.

A young linebacker-sized man with a Hitler Youth haircut came in and escorted me to the hallway scale for weighing and took my blood pressure. He moved with precision and had a vaguely Sanskrit-looking tattoo on his inner arm, not something I expected to see on a nurse. A latex band above my elbow helped in the removal of two vials of blood. He mechanically stated that the doctor would be in shortly and left.

"Martin, right?" she introduced herself as Dr. Prisha Patel, the psychiatrist leading the study.

I shook her hand, which had the fingers of a piano player and matched her long, thin frame. A few gray strands snaked through her wavy ink-black hair, though other physical evidence pointed to her being around my age. She maintained a serene manner despite speaking very quickly and minimizing any silences.

"You indicated taking medication for depression and anxiety several years back, is that right?"

"Yes, I took sertraline for about two years maybe ten years ago. No prescriptions since then." This was technically true. All of my previous NGO, non-governmental organization, experiences had friendly local doctors which made getting under the table medications easy.

"Prior SSRI usage," she said quietly, taking notes. "Have you had symptoms of depression since then?"

"No."

"You marked no for any family history of schizophrenia or bipolar disorder, is that correct?

"Yes."

"No suicidal thoughts or significant social anxiety?"

"Nothing out of the ordinary." This seemed like a fair answer, as I sensed her skepticism in my prior unequivocal responses. Naturally, I had researched various methods of self-administered euthanasia or death by organ donation but I saw myself like a medieval scholar keeping a skull on their desk, a healthy reminder of being condemned to freedom.

"For the question of 'why did you join this study' you wrote 'malaise and money,' can you explain that?" she asked robotically.

"I guess it was a half-joke. I may have some periods where I lack motivation but nothing serious. More serious on the money side; that could be helpful."

Dr. Patel continued to fill out the form, pausing to ask questions and taking notes of my answers. At one point she kept looking at my forehead hairline instead of into my eyes, perhaps inspecting my general state of grooming. She asked me to stand up and took a few full-body photos.

"Have you ever been in an MRI machine?" she asked.

I shook my head no. She explained that an initial fMRI scan was required before I could be considered for the study. The machine imaged blood flow in the brain using magnetic fields, a powerful tool to map neural activity. After the scan, I would collect a check for $60 and be notified of their decision in a few days.

I felt like a snowboarder on an operating table, wearing non-magnetic oversized goggles which projected sets of images, presumably to check out my fMRI response. The pictures ranged from mathematical equations to soft pornography to early maps of the world to abstract artwork composed of geometric shapes to stark Western landscapes to aggressive interpersonal and interspecies encounters. I was proud of my neural engagement with each image, confident that the MRI operator would be impressed with the Doppler radar reddish-purple intensity of my cortical activity, but instead, she thanked me mechanically as I left the room.

*   *   *

I didn't have any way to reach Victor outside of showing up at his house, no cell phone number to text, and certainly no email address. Perhaps this was by design, an acid test of commitment. The idea of completely ghosting him crossed my mind as I extracted the crumbs from the corner of the value menu chicken nugget box. The man was interesting and presumably lonely but I feared getting trapped in his dark house, doing some menial task for a Mason jar of dirty pennies.

I grabbed a Diet Coke refill and walked back to my apartment. As I started reading from a library book on cultural anthropology, a child in the unit above broke into a tantrum which even the air conditioner's noise couldn't mask. I grabbed the car keys and left the apartment, bringing the book with me.

Victor's house looked even more forlorn in the midday sun. An older compact pickup truck sat in the cracked driveway, some meager evidence of life compared to the neighbors' treeless plot and daytime illuminated light next to the basement door. A solitary furrowed creosote-soaked lamppost presided over the street corner. I made a mental note to return at night to experience the setting under sodium vapor lighting, picturing some kind of Lynchian scene.

The front door swung open when I reached the covered porch. His brown wool pants looked virtually the same as before but now he wore a short-sleeve dark blue checkered shirt, the only non-greyscale or sepia-toned item I had seen him wear. He handed me a glass of water without ice with a joking assurance that it wasn't vodka.

"This is our opponent for this afternoon," Victor said as he pointed at a series of large cardboard boxes on the porch, some held down on a wooden pallet by steel bands and having the collective size of a dining room table. "It's got the weight advantage on us."

"What is it?" I asked. The customs labels implied an international origin.

"Vertical axis milling machine," Victor said proudly. Sensing my confusion, he added, "Precision machine shop tool. Weighs about 800 pounds assembled, hence the decision to move my shop upstairs and shore up the floor joists. For stiffness more than strength."

"What are you building?" I asked, picturing him making firearms or edged weapons of some kind.

"Some parts here and there. For fun." Victor moved a wheeled cart over the threshold to the porch. "Get it lifted onto this and push. Can you give me a hand with the hoist?"

We spent the next two hours taxing Victor's knowledge of mechanical advantage and my patience using an arsenal of engine hoists, ratchet straps, wheeled platforms, simple levers, door hinge removal, and Slavic curse words. Negotiating bulky masses of metal around the 100-year-old hallways and doors felt like parallel parking a battleship. For the coup de grace, we used the engine hoist to lift and position the machine onto its heavy base, which suddenly looked underwhelming when fully out of its boxes and its mystery removed.

"What do you build, Marty?" Victor asked. We sat down on chairs in the living room for a break, which, thanks to its north-facing windows, had returned to its more natural state of dim light in the later afternoon. The house was warm but surprisingly not sweltering, suggesting some judicious use of nighttime air exchange.

I should have objected to the nickname "Marty." My mother gave me strict instructions to correct adults and peers who shortened my name. Perhaps she had already sensed my weakness for being agreeable. "I've installed a new bike chain before, is that what you mean?"

"Maintenance," Victor said with a degree of imperiousness. "I was a few years older than you when I began fixing and building things as a hobby. One month off during a Russian winter in a small apartment will either make you an alcoholic, lecher, or give you a project."

"What made you start?" I asked.

"I chased women in my twenties and my career in my thirties. Both were futile. The wall came down in '89 and things started falling apart everywhere. Being freshly unemployed and single turning forty in a formerly industrial town made me obsolete. I moved back to my parents' home since they were now infirm and needed help."

"Tools and parts scattered around the second bedroom of their apartment, which became my room. When my father retired as a clockmaker, he took home his most prized set of tools, which was a rebellious act back then. His hands shook too much to use any of them by this point. After making their meals and running errands, I'd find a discarded fan or a toaster oven and fix it up. I'd worked for years in a machine shop before but it always felt like a job rather than anything inspiring. Something changed when I moved back," Victor got up from the faded emerald green chair and walked over to the basement stairway. "I'll show you one I've restored."

I followed Victor down the dark stairs, helping him grab the pull chain on the naked lightbulb. The basement looked different than it had three days before, sets of materials and hardware were now set out on the tables. He picked up a white painted platform with bronze gears and pulleys. It looked like an exploded view of a mechanical watch.

He flipped a switch to turn on a small motor the size of a C battery. The rotation of the its shaft set forth a dance of drivetrains, spokes, and linkages. At the top of the machine, a goose flapped its wings while its body moved up and down as the bird slowly orbited around the center of the platform. It was mesmerizing, the complex motion all driven by a single motor, some gears comically large and looking handmade, like twisting a coat hanger into shape.

"It's amazing. You built that yourself?" I asked Victor who smiled and we both watched the solitary flapping goose.

"Built it, yes," he said and flipped the off button. "These boxes go up to the porch, can you carry?"

A stack of six printer paper-sized boxes sat next to the stairway, each sealed with clear packing tape. Victor said they were extra materials, and did not elaborate further on their contents before he started making adjustments to the flying goose machine. The weight of the boxes implied a bulk substance, perhaps scrap metal. Victor directed me to put the final box into the bedroom with the milling machine.

The newly converted workshop had a bookshelf of dusty Russian language hardcovers, CRC handbooks of chemistry and physics, and a large collection of vintage National Geographic magazines. I picked up the oldest-looking one of the set and started flipping through the articles, landing on a Yosemite piece that marveled at the majesty of Half Dome and El Capitan with a dose of turn of the century wonder at the now ubiquitous slabs of granite. When I returned the magazine to the shelf, a picture fell out onto the floor, a small wallet size print with Cyrillic blue handwritten letters on the back. The photo showed a middle-aged man shaking hands with a military officer on some sort of catwalk in front of a large white canister the size of a school bus with a red hammer and sickle emblem painted on the side. The civilian must have been Victor, the body shape and stern expression seemed similar but the photo looked at least thirty years old. I pulled out my phone and took a picture.

Victor didn't notice my return to the basement, being too busy arranging tools and going through his stocks of raw material on the shelves. I propped myself against the foundation wall and waited. The exposed floor joists hung a few inches above my head, making it feel like we were in the belly of a large sea creature, looking up at its ribs. The cool basement felt good in the heat but working down here in the dark would be psychologically devastating in the winter. Victor pulled tools off their outlined homes on pegboards and loaded them into plastic bins and cardboard boxes, which I transported upstairs to the new workshop along with an extremely heavy stationary circular grinder. I slowed down after about a half-hour and stepped out on the porch, scrolling through useless news feed notifications on my phone.

"That will do it for today," Victor said, opening the door. "You're free to leave. I am taking a walk now." Outdated wired headphones hung around his neck and he put them on while he headed towards the sidewalk.

"Did you say I'd be paid?" I said, my elevated voice cracking into the wind. He turned back and smiled.

"You remember that small machine of birds on a wire?" he asked. I struggled to assemble an image. "Needs work, bearings are shot and the birds need rebalancing. Take it back with you and fix it up." Victor put his headphones back on and continued down the street.

There must have been some kind of cultural or generational disconnect. Perhaps moving a stranger's light industrial equipment was complimentary in the old country and my expectation of payment was a symptom of my position in the transaction-based gig economy. I went down to the basement and confronted the remaining hardware, searching for the machine. It was patronizing, to be paid with another project requiring even more investment of time, getting something from an eccentric Russian hermit's junk drawer.

Having no luck finding the birds on a wire machine on the workbench, I started opening up the boxes. One partially opened box in the corner had a 2x2 grid of cardboard dividers, like the ones used to keep Christmas ornaments from being crushed. The top layer held a mix of old machine parts: small pistons, gears, and motors sitting on a rigid wooden platform. I got to an edge and lifted the plywood separator, revealing a larger and more completed machine. It was a Ferris wheel-type vertical disk driven by some sort of smaller set of gears, making it look a nineteenth-century bicycle with a large front wheel. Small metal shutters like advent calendar doors were placed in two concentric rings and seemed to have colored glass windows behind them. Dust and oil fused onto the metallic parts leaving a dark matte finish, unlike the goose machine which seemed old-fashioned but of fairly new construction.

Choosing between a tall and grande café americano required careful integration of the marginal utility of additional caffeine, time of day, and gastrointestinal ballast. I often had to step back from the line to come to an ultimately random choice. However, some strange alloy of nihilism and Calvinist predestination produced an impulsivity when it came to larger life decisions, like moving to a Mountain West city based on a Wikipedia article. Previous bouts of *amor fati*, love of one's fate, were law-abiding – and only internally rebellious. I spun the wheel, back driving the motor. It needed cleaning and simple repairs that could be done without the use of customized tools, better suited for my skill set than fixing the birds on a wire machine. Fuck it, the old man's lazy description meant I could have any of them, and this one hadn't been touched this epoch. I stuffed the wheel into a smaller box and headed out to the car.

I awoke to the sound of a ringing cell phone. That meant it must have been after 9 am since I had the Do Not Disturb setting active from 11 to 9. The number had an out-of-state area code, not one that I recognized, so I didn't pick it up. A piercing voicemail notification arrived a minute later. The last week had passed like a holiday break; I relished the large chunks of time each morning before losing days as easily as hours playing video games. I signed up for massive open online courses on cryptocurrency and big data, getting into the second lesson on each before tuning out. High sodium snack breaks at the countertop between classes quickly transitioned into standing meals that demanded prostrate recoveries.

"Hello Martin, this is Andrea from Transcendent Health. We are following up on your application to take part in the clinical study. Please call us back at your earliest convenience."

Breakfast was 400mg of NSAIDs, two cups of coffee, and sourdough toast while listening to public radio news. I had gone to sleep around 2 am after two airport rides, the first with a power-suited woman buried in her phone and the second with three college *bros* taking a red-eye home after a *sick* mountain biking trip.

My relationship with sleep over the past decade had been passionate but dysfunctional, passing through seasons of relative calm interrupted by monsoons. I now took the proactive steps of wearing thirty-two-decibel foam earplugs, an eye mask, and installing 99.9% light-blocking curtains to combat waking up with the pre 6 am summer sunrises. Not giving a shit seemed to help with the initial drifting off, but days like today started in a potential energy well and required heavy doses of caffeine and physical activity to climb out. On lucky days, complete exhaustion bestowed quality rest and a transient hypomanic state the next day – a short layover in the sublime.

I pulled out my phone and scrolled through the recent banners, news stories about political convention drama and migrant crises, and stopped on a social network notification from my ex-girlfriend Jessica announcing her engagement. She looked to be either pregnant or standing in a conspiring tailwind. I expected her to cancel me as a friend after we broke up over the holidays but the connection remained. After scanning more celebratory posts and confirming that her fiancé was painfully cool, I closed the app and turned off my phone.

Victor's machine sat on the kitchen table, unmoved from where I had left it a week before. It required two nine-volt batteries to power up. I moved a chair over to the hallway and bedroom smoke detectors, removed their batteries, and pressed them into the housing at the base of the machine. When the silver toggle switch was flipped, the motor started spinning and the gear train engaged, increasing torque through gear reductions and shifting the axes of rotation until the vertical wheel turned at about one revolution every second. The spokes of the wheel supported a set of small orange translucent reflectors, like a bicycle wheel, blurring into an orange ring. All of a sudden, the wheel reversed direction and the advent calendar flaps opened on a different set of reflectors, creating a red ring. The two directions and speeds seemed to fluctuate at random, leaving a retinal afterimage. I sat mesmerized by the spinning machine for maybe twenty minutes, darkened the room, and took a video of it with my phone before switching it back off.

*   *   *

The heat smacked me immediately upon leaving the apartment in a desperate attempt to get Vitamin D and some UV light into my eyes for a neural kickstart. Chicken wing bones and empty vodka shooters were scattered across the tree lawn while oil stains and dried power snots dotted the parking lot. The empty streets made it easy to jaywalk diagonally through the intersection and into the convenience store.

The first drag of a cigarette was always liberating, a rakish middle finger to health and good decision making, but by the last pull, I always felt desperate, especially in the heat of the day. I invariably bent the top of the pack backward, breaking the remaining nineteen cigarettes in half and throwing the mess into the closest dumpster, concluding it was surely irrational to tempt myself further with such a large supply. A sequence of guilt commenced, visualizations of tar and fiberglass particles embedding in my lungs creating incipient cancerous sites, rationalizations that each day in a South Asian city was the equivalent to several cigarettes, and pledges to never smoke another. The habit started in college as a means of enhancing an alcoholic buzz by the touted fifty percent, and had continued in ebbs and flows ever since. Uncombusted fuel from a lawnmower two-stroke engine filled the air on the walk back to the apartment, snapping me back to reality.

I noticed that the egress areas of each sidewalk had grids of hardened plastic bumps, then remembered seeing these same structures across town. This universal upgrade must have occurred in the period of living overseas. At first inspection, the outside world looked essentially the same as twenty years ago, evidence for my thesis that despite the cheerleading of technologists, the change in the world from 1890 to 1920 was more dramatic than 1990 to 2020. Electricity, the automobile, and refrigeration were truly revolutionary compared with putting a computer on a phone. But maybe I was just blind to the changes, tuned out. In truth, I didn't have a mental model for how people spent their time outside of work, besides the obvious time suck of children and gardening. Tweakers spent days awake presumably doing something of interest, retirees stretched eighteen holes into a full day, and sportsmen floated around on pleasure craft. None lurched into a convenience store at two o'clock to buy a pack of cigarettes, smoke one, and toss nineteen.

I opened my laptop and sat on the living room couch I had purchased off Craigslist. The first of the month meant it was time for a financial summary, adding up expenses and checking current balances. My checking account had been in continuous decline since its infusion with the inheritance money six months back. The anticipated short time horizon until its use eliminated riskier stock market investments, instead resigning to slowly lose money due to inflation. I needed to increase cash flow somehow to buy more time until surrendering to steady employment.

"I'm calling about the study?" I asked the lady who picked up the line. "This is Martin Rasmus. You left a message this morning."

"Ah yes, I see you here. The team would like to see you for a follow-up," she answered. "What times are you available?"

"Does this mean I've been accepted?"

"Not yet, but you've been down-selected from a much larger group," she said positively. We made an appointment for the next morning at the same office as the initial survey. It would be an intensive three-hour evaluation with a $100 payment. I searched the Internet for their company name, getting only unrelated results.

The hourly weather showed a modest chance of afternoon thunderstorms which suggested walking the mile north to the library now and waiting out the rain there while reading a book. My right knee recently developed pain during long walks, a reminder of thinning cartilage and upcoming further degeneration with age. The proximity to the hospital offered psychic comfort in these bodily ailments, the knowledge that a mere block away witnessed sobering realities of the material world in contrast to the filtered images of happy couples and bouncing children on social media. The hormonal sunset of later years made life partners functionally health care providers and despite its lumbering bureaucracy and jungle of insurance, perhaps the hospital could do the same for me, close enough to yell out the window for help during an inevitable future debilitating back spasm.

Subtracting the first five years of life as they are without memory, I was likely less than halfway through the conscious stage of living, which should have been exhilarating but instead seemed overwhelming, having to endure four more long decades of accumulated pains and mental malware. The Hindu religion's goal of escaping the suffering of everlasting life, checking out of samsara, carried intuitive appeal rather than some interminable existence offered by Christianity.

Before leaving the apartment, I picked up Victor's machine, impressed by the heft of a contraption the size of a hiking boot shoebox. He had probably noticed its absence in the week since it was gone, and I expected a knock on the door. I lifted a corner of the machine and felt valleys and ridges with my fingers. The underside of the marble platform had scribed letters in Cyrillic and a date of twenty-seven years ago. Perhaps these devices were limited-run collectibles, placed on coffee tables or built in Eastern bloc university introductory engineering classes. I needed to know more. Its value sure, but also the meaning of the rotational instability, which seemed to be more than aesthetic. I created a new username with my junk email address and posted photos of it on an antique collector's website, explaining its discovery in an estate sale and my curiosity about its origin and value.

The exam started with a multiple-choice section testing spatial intelligence and was followed by several logic puzzles. In high school, I prided myself on an ability to get passing scores on multiple-choice exams without any prior knowledge of the subject, a highly lucrative skill in the era of Scantrons. One choice was always too easy, another ridiculous, which left only two possibilities often reducible to one given the test creators' inclination to avoid regularity and favor more specific and longer answers. My ability to hack these tests contributed to punching above my weight for college admissions but was of less use on term papers or problem sets once I was accepted.

The personality section of the test was more open-ended and I intended to use that freedom to paint an honest picture of myself. The test administrator, a short-haired and square-jawed woman, repeatedly reminded us of the importance of truthfulness, but I found myself intentionally selecting the more provocative choice. This resulted in answering "yes" to questions about making spontaneous travel plans and having bizarre fantastical dreams and "no" to questions of living in reality instead of the future and exhibiting empathy for others.

The only other person in the room besides the proctor was a woman close to my age. I finished the test early and noticed she did too and was now diligently rereading her answers, sometimes pausing to think by tapping a pencil against her lips, the slightly larger upper lip having a sharp ridge at the skin boundary. The helices of her hair, like stretched telephone cords, descended to her shoulder blades, their black color inconsistent with her milk chocolate eyebrows. Dark denim jeans with intentionally torn knees and bright white thread added to her overall punkish style, which was undermined by a loose unlabeled green t-shirt. I must have been consumed by the multiple-choice decryption when she came into the room.

I had sensed a presence behind me in the lobby when showing the same blood drawing tattooed man my driver's license. I kept a gold-colored condom in the interior pocket of my bifold wallet and it probably drifted down to expose its unmistakable serrated edge, likely visible to her and easily confining me to a maturity stunted fraternity brother always ready to copulate. We caught eyes after she finished double-checking her test and I quickly shifted my gaze to the window. This made her look out the window too, both of us staring at the staid parking garage.

The proctor picked up our tests and led us down the hallway where we each entered separate small rooms. The white-walled room was only furnished with a desk, two opposing chairs, and some type of helmet device. Dr. Patel walked in, wearing a long white lab coat but moving with greater levity than in our previous meeting.

"Welcome back Martin. I apologize for all the tests you are being subjected to. I can assure you it's an important part of our data collection process." She sat down on the chair opposite me and lifted up the large round black device, which looked like a motorcycle helmet. She reached into her lab coat pocket and pulled out a video game controller.

"Based on your responses, we know you've played the Z60 console before, so we'll use one of its controllers. Don't let the headset scare you, it's your basic wrap-around VR setup."

"Will I be playing a game?"

"Yes, a customized one. It will simulate different scenarios. We need you to be yourself, to act as you would act in real life. We find that video games are a good tool to focus attention," she said, pushing the controller and headset across the table. "Physiological data collection will tell us if you're fabricating your responses which will be cause for dismissal from the study. It will take about thirty minutes."

I looked into the headset before putting it on and saw several ports passing through the cushioning which must have hosted an array of sensors. The front screen suddenly turned on and displayed a large text box saying "Please Put On Your Headset." The game started with a round of cognitive exercises of short-term memory recall and brain teasers, then moved on to a series of virtual worlds exposing me to various interactions and prompts: at a party, arriving at the scene of a car accident, and going on a first date. The display followed my vision, re-centering the screen around the focal point once my eyes dwelled on one location for longer than a moment. Decisions were made by selecting options using the controller. Overall, the game design was reasonable if a bit dated. It felt like a corporate training video mixed with a role-playing game and I played it straight and boring.

Dr. Patel came back when it was completed and escorted me to the lobby, shaking my hand and assuring me I would have their decision in about a week. When I picked up the check from the front desk, I saw the black-haired woman coming down the hallway, accompanied by a graying older male doctor, the two engaged in close conversation.

"What did you think of the second round?" she asked when we left the office, picking up her pace to get closer to me.

"Not bad. I want to see the scores, or whatever it is they've figured out from these tests," I said, genuinely interested in the results.

"These guys won't tell us anything. We'll probably be in the control group."

"Still pays the same."

"At least they could have fed us. You hungry?" she asked while pulling out her car keys. The office building was at the far corner of the medical complex, at least a half a mile away from my apartment. I nodded and we got into her car, a late model Japanese station wagon with unrelenting reliability.

The stereo leaped into action playing a hip-hop song. The heavy bass rattled plastic joints in the dashboard and she punched the volume knob to turn it off. We drove to a new fast-casual sandwich shop which presented a rebellious anti-corporate image by featuring subs with names like "Cousin Susie's Mystery Meat Club" and "The 99 Percenter Square Meal." She ordered a salad with extra ranch dressing, extra croutons, and a local IPA. I got the daily special of corned beef on rye with shoestring fries, an economical 1,300 calorie selection that should carry me through until a late-night snack.

The restaurant had a condiment bar well-stocked with pickled items and the classics which could be pumped into large paper containers, immediately earning my respect. She walked up to the bar while I filled up a waxed paper soup bowl with a mixture of ketchup and barbeque sauce.

"You know you could just smother them," she said while grabbing a pickled pepper from the tank. I held back my horror at the barbaric thought of soggy fries at the bottom of the tray and followed her over to the booth.

"Oh, by the way, my name's Nina," she said. She ate like an ultra-marathoner. Large pieces of lettuce were folded to enter her mouth or canted to obtuse entry angles and this was done quickly, leaving residues of ranch dressing on her lips. The choice of a salad seemed odd given her enthusiasm for food but possibly came out of some voluntary or imposed dietary restriction.

"Martin Rasmus." I second-guessed giving her my full name, but she didn't seem to care. She gave off a nervous energy, a high frequency vibration that allowed her to drink a high ABV beer on an empty stomach in the middle of a hot sunny day and not collapse. The faint vascularization and forearm suntans on her sinewy arms suggested long duration outdoor cardio exercise or a lingering teenage metabolism. I found myself studying her sharp jawline along with a slightly visible left clavicle like a ying-yang symbol until realizing she said something.

"This corned beef is excellent," I said positively, hoping she didn't ask me a question while zoning out.

"How'd you end up in this study?" Nina asked, wiping off the ranch dressing from the corners of her mouth and taking a long drink.

"Responded to a posting on a bulletin board, you?"

"I was recruited. I've taken some psych studies and been on a bunch of different medications. This one showed up in my inbox one day."

"Do you have any idea what it's about?" I asked.

Nina leaned over the table and looked me in the eyes. "Do you know about Transcendent Health?" I shook my head no and she continued. "They are one of these stealthy human life improvement ventures. In reality, they're a project spun off from Xmundio. They were mentioned in an article by someone who traced back a whole set of trial companies to the media giant. Doesn't carry their name so they can play around in the sandbox with less risk to their brand."

"The same Xmundio as the apps?" I asked and she nodded yes. The company had an ecosystem of messaging, video, and social media applications, all of which had nebulous business models based on advertising and collecting personal information from its users. Their apps were free but had still managed to make their founder, Kory Gorman, absurdly wealthy. I never knowingly purchased anything based on their targeted advertising, thinking them reactionary and desperate, popping up ads to buy another pair of sunglasses right after you purchased one without any of their promptings. I was a castaway from the mainland of late-stage capitalism, a throwback to an earlier time when the peasantry aspired to be in the aristocratic leisure class reading books and playing yard games while remaining blissfully unaware of vulgar marketing.

"Gorman gave a TED talk two years ago on psychiatric well-being," she said, leaning back in her chair and resting each arm on the back of the bench seat, showing bicep shadows. "He basically said that we're just leaving the dark ages of mental health, finally ready to move on past bloodlettings and sledgehammer approaches."

"What do you mean? Everyone is so happy," I said and smiled. I viewed low-level depression as a sign of sanity.

"These billionaires often have messiah complexes. But he's probably right. In a hundred years from now, anxiety or depression treatment will be more scientific. There's a whole movement out there called transhumanism, it's pretty crazy. Sort of a techno-utopia for escaping our primate programming."

"Our study is a part of this?" I asked.

"I'm guessing it is, some sort of new technology or treatment. Did you read the disclaimers?"

"Some of them."

"There was a section on genetic data and their rights to use it but not sell your information or something. I'm wondering about the blood draw. Xmundio purchased that ancestry DNA website a few years back too."

"What about the hospital oversight?" I asked, suspicious of conspiracy theories. Most required a degree of coordination and secrecy impossible to pull off in large groups, though corporate plans would be easier to execute than governmental ones.

"Note where we were. It's a rented office on the edge of the medical campus but not actually part of the hospital," she said, reaching over towards my fries. "You mind if I have a few of these?" I nodded and pushed my plate to the middle of the table. She grabbed six at once and then dunked them into the soup bowl of ketchup.

"This is privately administered research?"

"Oh, they have some hospital doctors to give it credibility, but a large charitable donation does wonders with the Internal Review Board," she said.

"Will you accept if selected?"

"Oh, hell yeah, I'll take the money, and take on the challenge of figuring out who these guys are," she responded. "What do you do for fun?"

"Standard stuff. Hiking, reading, some travel," This sounded like every boring guy's dating app profile. I had expected the usual questions of employment and prepared a cryptic response that implied passive income but still presented me as having some value as an economic agent. Something like, *I'm financially lucky enough to be able to take long breaks but I keep coming back to my passion for teaching and helping people.* The passion for teaching was a stretch, though there were periods of genuine enjoyment working with children during the NGO deployments, especially older students who required less of an emotional connection. "But I just moved here, so I'm looking to get out more. What about you?"

"I get to blend work and play. Primarily pay the bills as a photographer with some freelance graphic design. The photos are mostly landscapes and some artistic shit," she said.

"You sell framed pieces?"

"That's the moneymaker, selling art at festivals and art shows. I have a miter saw and router in my shed and make the frames myself. Fortunately, this area has a lot of Midwest transplants who think a black and white photo of a mountain is genius but I'll take it. Where did you say you are from?"

"A small town in western Pennsylvania, sort of a rust belt place."

"I'd love to get some shots inside those old factories or coal breakers before they come down. You'll sneak me inside, right?"

I laughed. We continued talking about her photography, and she showed some of her pictures on her phone. Her online portfolio bounced between red rock formations to snowboarders carving powder down sheer mountain faces. I watched her hands while she scrolled through the album; most of her fingers had rings on them but none seemed to be in the wedding category.

"I could probably use the walk back to my apartment to prevent a food coma," I said when we got up to leave, wanting to make sure our meeting ended on a high note.

"Let's agree to keep each other in the loop on this study stuff. Deal?"

The message titled "PLEASE READ Re: Interesting Rotary Machine" stood out from the rest of the emails in my inbox about neighborhood lost dogs and pleas from non-profits for money. The previous few days had seen about a dozen inquiries into Victor's machine. Most were auto-generated emails advertising e-commerce ventures or online clearinghouses of seized property discounted to absurd levels. The few legitimate ones agreed on the Russian origin but couldn't add anything further to its provenance. The most recent email came from a very enthusiastic collector who hadn't hesitated to use CAPS-lock for emphasis. His message claimed the piece had *singular value* and should not be dismissed as a clunky garage experiment. He saw my location was in the greater metro area and asked for a meeting the next morning.

We met on the outdoor patio of the local coffee shop. He tumbled out of his older mustard-colored German luxury sedan only to turn around near the front door to retrieve a briefcase from the backseat. He was a well-fed specimen in his early sixties, with reddish cheeks that appeared even larger above a thick, graying beard. He walked with a pigeon toe gait and a degree of excitement, motioning some form of apology to the barista who handed him a house drip coffee. We locked eyes as he came over to the table.

"Thank you for meeting me on short notice," he said and continued without taking a breath. "The piece you posted is unique, completely unknown to most collectors. Excuse my excitement, I got up at five-thirty this morning to drive up here."

"Do you collect these yourself?"

"No, not really. I have one client in particular that likes these pieces. It is more of a demonstration than art. Can I take a look at it?"

I pulled the machine out from the box and placed it on the table. He beamed with excitement and clipped a jeweler's magnifying lens onto his glasses. He gently prodded the gears and pulleys with a metallic wand, occasionally tapping them like a dentist inspecting teeth. The etched writing on the bottom of the platform was of special interest. I could see his lips moving as he sounded out the words.

"Can I turn it on?" he asked. When I nodded yes, he jumped up from his seat and carried the machine over to a shaded table on the patio.

When he flipped the switch the mechanism spun to life, doing the dance between orange and red rings in a seemingly random fashion, alternating both its direction and speed.

"Is that what you expected?" I asked.

"This is gorgeous. It will really stand out with good backlighting in a dark room." He stood back and twisted his beard.

"Have you seen these before?"

"This is unique but I've read about it. The artist was a former Soviet engineer. He designed special mechanisms for their space program and military, a wizard type figure. After the Cold War ended, he created the most marvelous machines, not practical ones but devices exploring the nature of chaotic systems. They made beautiful movements through space, usually originating from a simple spinning motor."

"This is a famous piece of art?" I asked.

"Only in very small circles. Part of the appeal is his secretive past. A few machines got to some exhibits in Europe. There are photos out there of others but it's been completely quiet for maybe twenty-five years now. His reclusive nature only adds to the mystique."

"What's so special about this? The gears look cool and I like the rings, but it just spins back and forth."

"Have you ever heard of the Lorenz waterwheel?" he asked excitedly.

"I don't think so," I answered.

"It's a classic chaotic system. Basically, it's a wheel with buckets around the perimeter, each freely rotating to stay upright. Water is fed from the top and the buckets have a hole in the bottom. Depending on the feed rate, the wheel can reach a steady rotational speed. But at say a higher feed rate, the spinning will become chaotic, speeding up, slowing down, changing directions. The system's response is very sensitive to initial conditions. No two runs are the same. It is still deterministic but essentially unpredictable."

"And this device is like that waterwheel?"

"Yes, brilliantly so but with some differences. These magnets can be shifted around the perimeter and float radially on springs, moving to the outside when it speeds up. The magnetic changes induce an electric current in the sensor down here." He pointed to a small plastic housing at the base of the wheel. "This signal is combined with another input from an aft-facing sensor and the motor speed and direction are driven proportionally. At least that is how Ivantusky described it."

"What's his name again?"

"Leo Ivantusky. Did you know him somehow? Is that how you got this?"

"I went to an estate sale a few weeks back and they said their mother got it from a friend," I said.

"An estate sale ..., interesting." He stopped and looked directly at me, waiting for me to add something. "I have a hard time believing that."

"Maybe it's like this waterwheel here, small historical changes can produce dramatically different outcomes," I said and put the machine back into the box.

"Let me be honest with you. Though this device is unique, the market for it is very small. Not many people even know about these. My client is the only serious private buyer out there," he said, clasping his hands together on the table. "I gather that you value discretion; my client does as well. I called her this morning on the drive here. Provided its authenticity can be verified, she is willing to purchase the machine for $60,000."

"Sixty thousand in cash?" I suddenly wondered what was in the briefcase.

"I recommend against hard currency given the physical risks. She has structured deals where a set of payments are arranged, each deposit less than $10,000 to avoid federal tracking and also under the $15,000 annual gift tax limit, a steady flow of money for the next four years. It sounds suspicious but it's completely legal and very discreet," he said, sipping from the coffee. "Very discreet."

While $60,000 wasn't *fuck you money*, it was significant. The annuity-style payment plan seemed like it had been customized for my situation by enforcing some restraint. It could prolong my intentional under-employment or enable me to completely economically detach for an extended Southwest desert road trip this winter. Most of all it seemed to buy me time.

"I will have to think about it," I said, still spinning financial machinations.

"Sleep on it and let me know your decision by the end of the day tomorrow. No matter what you choose, I loved seeing the machine in operation after only reading about it." He reached across the table and we shook hands. "Others would have downplayed its worth and offered much less, but both my client and I value honesty and open communication."

As he walked away, I looked at his business card which read simply "Pierre Mercer, Collector" with a cell phone number and email address.

Late evening reality hung in the air on my walk to the hospital, the cicada's rattles weightier and the window-mounted air conditioning units more plaintive. More cars were parked on the street than usual, many badly in need of bodywork instead of duct tape and plastic bag windows, some with somehow still drivable T-boned concave doors, and others sporting piebald patterns from prior predicaments. I took the long route down Main Street, past the dusty tailor shops with 100-year leases and the vacuum repair business with a perpetual neon OPEN sign.

After a frozen pizza dinner, I tried reading a book from the library about a rogue journalist uncovering a public health scandal in late Victorian England but couldn't concentrate, my mind bouncing back to Victor's machine and the potential windfall should I sell it. The idea of total irresponsibility for several years seemed exhilarating, spread out like a seafood buffet on a cruise line, available with a single text message to Pierre. Each reverie into possibility snapped me back into a feeling of guilt, whether from a residual Protestant work ethic or playing with years like chess pieces. I spent the next two hours on the sofa, surfing around online articles on WWI dreadnoughts and naval strategy.

On the way over, I listened to an episode on Structuralism and its interpretation of signs, a free podcast on the history of philosophy marching chronologically from the pre-Socratics to the present day. My audio preferences swerved into philosophy the previous month. The innocence of ancient metaphysics brought comfort, earnest Greeks convinced that nothing could ever change or that alternatively, everything was always changing. All objects were made of water, no wait air, or maybe atoms. The deconstruction of grand narratives in postmodern philosophy was potentially liberating though I often found it incoherent and masturbatory. Not that philosophy or more generally "theory" came easily to me – as my college transcript would testify – despite the inordinate time spent studying introductions to the subjects. I did have a measure of genuine aptitude for math, my official major, although my comparative talent peaked in high school. My mathematical enthusiasm waned in college after I realized that advanced graduate school-level content was only intellectually accessible to me at a surface level, which felt fraudulent and scuttled my initial interest in pursuing a Ph.D. Compared to accomplished mathematicians, I was an entry-level user that knew a few hotkeys.

The activity at the ER was slower today than it had been the last time I came, presumably the lower dopamine levels on a Sunday night resulted in less reckless behavior, giving it a somber rather than frenetic mood. A concerned older couple without visible impairment huddled together and a family sprawled out in a corner, children pushed toys on the floor despite periodic scolding from their mother, but overall traffic seemed light. I hovered in the ER area for a bit, pretending to check for messages on my phone but really doing covert surveillance of the nursing staff to verify the absence of the ones keen on eviction. I grabbed a seat in the empty ICU area with the comfy chairs.

I was nine during my first memory of being in a hospital instead of the local urgent care clinic. I knew something was different when my mother gave me license to rummage through her purse, a bowling ball-sized cavity that seemed to contain everything from gum, loose change, diecast cars, tissues, and hopefully an individually wrapped jawbreaker. She kept crossing and uncrossing her legs and looking distantly in thought. We came directly to the hospital, leaving dinner in a half-prepared state, and sat for a long time, a church service length duration in near silence.

My reliably quiet composure each Sunday morning from 10 am to 11:30 am earned great praise from my father, a major source of pride in our three-person nuclear family. I endured the long summer services without air conditioning mostly through a fascination with the Middle East maps of Old and New Testaments on the inside covers of the Bible, visualizing the tribes inhabiting different geographic regions, fighting each other, and setting up defensive positions.

"Martin," my mother said as she reached over and touched my knee. "It's time to go back and see dad now."

"Has he woken up?" I asked, letting the 1970s muscle car I was playing with balance on the armrest.

She pulled me close for a tight hug, and I buried my face in her permed hair. We held the embrace for a minute until I felt a set of her restrained heaves. She separated from me and wiped her eyes. "Give me your hand."

We walked through the double doors into the medical area. I tell myself I cried when I saw his lifeless body on the hospital bed but this could be a wishful memory implanted at a later date given that all my subsequent experiences of loss were consistently asymptomatic. For me, the production of tears required months or years of gestation and sprouted when listening to music around midnight. We drove home that night to a cold casserole, my aunt coming over later and the two sisters mourning over a bottle of wine in the kitchen. Like on Christmas Eve, I snuck downstairs in search of the truth.

"Jean, I'm so sorry. David and I will bring over dinner this week," my aunt Clara said, kneading my mother's hands.

"Thanks," my mother said, taking a drink of wine. "I don't have the strength anymore. Martin is such an easy kid but you know, he's different."

"Martin really likes David since he doesn't treat him like a little kid. They talked about the differences between concrete and asphalt for like an hour at Easter."

The two sisters laughed, shook their heads, and pulled together in a sniffling embrace. David worked as a general contractor and had a large truck plus lots of power tools. He helped me get second place in the Cub Scout pinewood derby through the judicious use of dry film lubricants and undercarriage weights. They moved to Florida the next year, citing its more favorable weather for year-round construction and rosier economic forecast. I subducted myself further into the living room sofa as the conversation rocked between generalized grief and the many issues that needed to be taken care of, like life insurance and vehicles. It would be different.

Information about the accident leaked out from my mother over the next few years: the steering column, internal bleeding, the white oak tree, leaving work early. I retrieved the police report during the summer after high school which gave the cause of death as indeterminate. The extent of front-end damage implied that his car had been traveling at a speed above fifty miles per hour. This aroused suspicion as he rarely went more than five miles above the speed limit and enjoyed driving in the grand touring mindset of his father's Greatest Generation. There were also no skid marks on the road or the narrow shoulder. An airbag would have likely saved his life whether he wanted it to or not. Their standard inclusion started in the next model year.

We moved into the north half of a small duplex after he died, my mother extending her hours as a nurse in the local hospital to pay the rent. The new neighborhood was considerably more blue-collar than the planned post-war community we left, the streets filled with domestically manufactured cars and windows covered in aluminum awnings. I successfully avoided being bullied by attaching myself to a middle-status group of boys who spent their free time playing tackle football and stickball in vacant lots, stealing chrome tire valve covers, conducting abortive experiments from the Anarchist Cookbook, and sneering at academic overachievers.

Puberty and familial emigration dissolved the band during middle school, casting me out into the suddenly larger student body. I began spending the afternoons after school dismissal and before my mother's return from work at the town library, spurred on by an interest in the medieval period kickstarted by a History Channel series on the Crusades and the Black Death. At the time, ancient Greek and Roman histories seemed decadent and alien, like an old foreign movie, unlike gritty chain mail and Templar castles. I tried to trace back my lineage to find a gallant figure to connect myself to but only ended up finding three generations of uncomplicated laborers with presumably peasant forebears.

Scoring second behind Steve Rothstein in an eighth-grade math contest ignited a curiosity in me towards the subject. My teacher, Mrs. Ransom, a cold disciplinarian held in universal contempt, pulled me aside after class to hand out a stack of example problems to prepare for the regional competition in Erie. She introduced me to the other three eight grade math teammates, a nerdy group of alumni from the elementary school for gifted children.

I slowly worked through the problems on the long tables at the library, spreading out reference texts on probability and geometry, discovering the joy of finding the tens place digit of a huge number using the binomial theorem. Finding the key insight in the solution or proof laid the keel for a new kind of joy and power, something I had not experienced reading history. These small successes conjured a strange Maxwell's demon of dopamine, a selective gate filtering in neural rewards, even relishing getting stumped by hard problems and rationing their usage. I squeezed into first place in the regional math contest, getting my photo in the local paper. We were predictably slaughtered by a cadre of immigrant children at the state championship but I got to spend a night in a hotel, where I stayed up late watching Skinamax with the other two boys on the team. This modest academic success carried me through most of high school until senior year underachievement reemerged through contact with video games, alcohol, and awkward forays towards the opposite sex.

*   *   *

I felt vulturous looking across into the ER lobby from my seats in the ICU, watching body language for signs of relief or distress. Whenever someone caught me looking, I immediately dropped my eyes down to my library book. I was midway through an engaging and speculative chapter on the mystery of the Late Bronze Age collapse. The book contended that the risk of systemic failure was always underappreciated throughout history and that barbarians took new forms with each age. The author had predicted the most recent financial bubble and had cleverly sold stocks early, a fact he casually mentioned on several occasions.

An older man lingered at the ER counter, repeatedly rotating the entry paperwork back towards the attendant with mutual confused looks. This continued for several minutes, the front desk lady getting up to ask the nurses a question and returning to her chair. I discerned slurred syllables and nasal vowels which sounded French. This, combined with the man's dark skin and heavier build implied a French West African origin, which brought me back to Senegalese spicy bean street sandwiches.

Despite living there for a year, my command of the French language had been reduced to salutations, basic numbers, and whatever vocabulary was necessary to stumble through customs and immigration control. Still, I felt an odd compulsion to offer some assistance and walked over to help. At closer inspection, the man was much older than I had thought and suffered from a pronounced curved back, which took many inches from his former formidable height. Through our recruitment of cell phone screens, he was able to communicate that he wanted to check on his daughter, whose name he wrote out as Aida Giallo on the back of the admission form.

The letters had a consistent slant with beautiful form, a graceful throwback to an earlier age. My mother's handwritten letters, delivered through a logistical morass to me while I lived overseas, consistently installed a dose of warm belonging with an aftertaste of guilt. They usually contained clippings from the local newspaper, a sarcastic cartoon, or news of the marital/professional accomplishments of a high school friend, and had since been shoved into gallon-sized freezer bags along with my passport, Social Security cards, and diplomas.

A nurse reported that Aida had just entered surgery and the man would be taken to a waiting room near the OR. I groped at a translation but he understood their motions and followed the nurse down the hallway. The odds favored the man joining a multi-generational family waiting inside for news, but at a deeper level I knew he was alone, a solitary and handicapped caregiver for an adult child hanging onto life.

Victor's front lawn had now devolved into a plane of dirt and dried grass, only a few scattered thistle plants and other noxious weeds clinging to life. La Niña conditions caused by cooler waters in the eastern Pacific Ocean parked a stubborn high-pressure system over the Mountain Time zone, producing a Californian pattern of endlessly sunny and cloudless days. I placed the box with the waterwheel on the front porch away from view, tried the doorbell, and, receiving no response, knocked on the door.

While waiting for Victor to answer the door, nausea developed in my stomach. Since the brain observes the world a fifth of a second delayed from the current time, it always predicts the future, which is usually just a modest extrapolation of current events. But that morning my forecasting anticipated each small peripheral movement as a pending strike: an errant bicycler crossing in front of the car, the insufferable wind chimes outside the apartment as an intruder, waiting for cockroaches to emerge from cupboards. At that moment, I felt I was about to fall into some diabolical trap laid for me by Victor.

"Hello, Martin," he said, stretching out the syllables of my name. A dark oil highlighted his fingerprints despite his wiping them with a plaid patterned rag as he looked me over.

"I was in the neighborhood and thought I'd stop by," I said, debating whether I should just give him the box and dash back to the car. "How is the milling machine working?"

Victor smiled and opened the door further, backing up to let me in. When I crossed the threshold he asked, "Forgetting something?"

I followed him in, took a seat in the living room, and set the box down. We both looked at each other for a solid minute. It could have been the lighting, but his face looked older, more chiseled, and sculpted. It was obvious he knew about the missing machine, but maybe not its value. On the drive over, I toyed with the idea of purchasing or perhaps purloining more machines to sell to Pierre or even keep as collectibles to sell at a later date.

"I want to return this to you," I said, biting my lower lip and picking up the box. In terms of leverage, I had little reason to fear as my physical strength, while distinctly below the mean for a healthy man my age, certainly exceeded his and my economic position was in no way endangered.

Victor lifted open the flaps of the box and looked inside. "What did you study in university?"

"Math, with a history minor. But recently I've been doing some teaching." I said, feeling obligated to mention an actual profession.

"What do you know about computational theory?"

"Not much. I took some computer science classes, but none of the fundamentals like Turing machines if that's what you mean," I said. Victor walked into the kitchen and flexed a plastic tray to break loose some ice cubes. High school included introductory courses in BASIC computer programming, fun exercises factoring numbers and string manipulations, which made me think for a while that I might pursue a computer science major. The concepts of recursion and pointers in the second semester proved inaccessible to me, which put an abrupt end to that idea and sent me back to more familiar subjects. It felt like trying to understand Einstein's theory of general relativity, encountering a neural open circuit and taking the paved detour back towards differential equations and Renaissance political theory.

"Good, less baggage for this project," Victor smiled, returning with two glasses of iced lemonade. "You don't strike me as a teacher. Don't the farmers come back to school in the next few weeks after the summer harvest in America?"

"I guess you can say I'm on sabbatical since I moved here last spring," I said, expecting him to confront me on the waterwheel soon.

"You must be studying algorithms of ride-sharing. You teach secondary school, correct?"

"I've bounced in between grades, preferably geometry and trigonometry but also some earlier material too." Victor had quickly and correctly deduced I was too melancholic for elementary school and of insufficient intellect for college-level instruction. He wouldn't be the first to anticipate my endpoint as a socially awkward high school calculus or physics instructor.

"Why does a middle-aged teacher move across the country, surrendering their pension? Public employees still have those here, right?"

"I've mostly taught overseas, one or two-year type assignments."

"Where?" he asked, suddenly interested.

"Honduras, Senegal, Thailand," I said. "Most recently in Kazakhstan."

"What was her name?"

"The International School in Almaty," I answered, figuring he knew about the Central Asian former capital and assigned the feminine pronoun as a semantic convention, like naming a ship or the home country. Victor tilted his head skeptically and waited for a reply. "If you're asking about a girlfriend, I dated someone named Jessica."

"Ah yes, a woman. Humanitarian adventurism wanes after thirty unless you're a true believer or pair-bonded to someone that is," Victor said. "Right?"

I nodded in agreement and thought back to our early days in the country. The flight into Almaty was predictably brutal and interminably delayed. We arrived at our dingy hotel well past midnight, both of us exhausted to the point of giddiness, collapsing in the undersized bed without setting an alarm. Despite the other erosions of our compatibility, her scent was undeniably arousing at a primal level and lit up a corner of my reptilian brain, its pungency even greater given our two days of unshowered international travel.

"She loved teaching kids art, a real natural at it," I said, breaking out of the reverie. "We agreed that Kazakhstan would be the last stop before we headed home."

"End of the tour," Victor said and took a long drink of lemonade. "What did you think of Kazakhstan?"

"The land is dramatic, just like the architecture," I said.

Victor laughed. "Their buildings look like a science fiction movie. To their credit, the Eastern Bloc knew how to make you feel small: fifteen-lane streets, colossal statues of communist heroes, the repetitive geometry of apartment blocks. I admit that I like it."

"Always felt like an outsider though."

"Staring at foreigners is a popular pastime," he said.

"True, but also at an environmental level. In the beginning, we took road trips out of the city on weekends, away from the crowds with a borrowed dodgy two-door car. The emptiness of the mountains and plains made me think about Marco Polo traveling along the Silk Road, a more virgin landscape than you get here, despite Central Asia's long history. During the last road trip, the weather changed abruptly and left us stranded along the road for the night during a May blizzard. A native would have taken it in stride, their constitution tempered by the privations of the land. But I froze my ass off and couldn't walk the next day."

I stopped for a drink then continued, eager to talk to someone about my time in the country. "It's a dark spot on the map, most people still have no idea where it is. It's been that way throughout history though, both an incubator and target of invaders. The mounted barbarians from the steppe. Let's see, you have the Aryans, Scythians, Huns, Mongols, Mughals, and you can throw in the Black Death too. I like the concept more than the experience though."

"You visit Baikonur?" Victor asked.

"The space launch area?" He nodded affirmatively. "No, but that's famous right?"

"It's where Sputnik and Yuri Gagarin launched, the Russian Cape Canaveral. They picked the most desolate area possible, in case of failures. When the launch scaffolds pull away, the Soyuz rocket looks like a muscular arm pointing towards the heavens, with four flared booster engines." Victor moved his arms vertically in a cone, showing how the engines formed gussets at the base of the launcher. This was the most animated I'd seen him.

"You've seen a launch?"

"Many years ago, when I was your age. My brother received the Order of the Red Star by the Space Command and brought three people down to Baikonur as guests to watch."

"He was in the military?"

"A technical expert, bouncing between different projects. While the rest of us were stuck at our farms or factories, he flew in to solve problems or brainstorm new designs, sort of a celebrity."

"And the satellite?"

"He figured out a way to deploy enormous but lightweight structures in space, apparently saving a project from cancellation. The design used a network of shape memory alloys, metals that suddenly grow in volume above their self-actuation temperature. Distributed heaters controlled the deployment, releasing hinges to assemble into a large airframe, while other devices latched it firmly into place. Much cleaner than explosive actuators. He trotted a little demo around. It was like watching a time-lapse video of an antenna tower construction." Victor sipped his drink then cleared his throat. "You asked about the payload, well this mission was classified, the large fairing leaving much to our imaginations for what lurked inside. Who knows if it worked?" Victor finished by sitting back in his chair. I detected a low concentration of protective sarcasm in his overall tone.

"Is this an older brother?" I asked and felt a bit lightheaded, perhaps from the heat or only having an English muffin and a fried egg for lunch.

"Twenty-one minutes older," Victor said, swirling the ice in his glass. "Not identical. I can fault genetics for all the differences. Follow me."

We went down the hallway and into the workshop, which now had shelves stocked with medical tubing and fittings against the far wall. Victor drew out a length of tubing from a spool the size of a large coffee can.

"Consistent inner diameter is key. I bought thirty meters of it," Victor said, letting me flex the clear plastic material in my hands.

"What are you building?"

"For now, just the frame," he said, pointing to a stack of aluminum extrusions with an X cross-section. "Cut those to length and build some custom clips. The tubing and valves will take design work. You've studied partial differential equations, right?"

Fractions of Greek symbols and an engineering math tome with a satellite dish on the front cover came to mind, but I could remember none of its content. "Yeah, is this a quiz?"

"Take this heat transfer book, it'll come back," Victor handed me a dark-covered book with a broken spine. I flipped through the pages, relieved that the text was English and not Cyrillic. The yellow hue placed its likely last use several decades before. "The final chapter on analog methods will be useful."

"You know that computer simulation codes make closed-form solutions mostly academic. What are you trying to solve?" I asked incredulously, imagining Victor playing with high-energy physics experiments and running into thermal management challenges, something involving shock tubes or lasers. I glanced over through the first few chapters, which solved classic heat conduction problems. Heat transfer seemed like a banal choice since it could probably be easily predicted by any number of software packages, even free ones on the web.

"Nothing of practical value, but that doesn't interest me much anymore," Victor pulled out a hand drawing on grid paper and put it on the table next to the milling machine. "We're going to build a water integrator or at least attempt to."

"Water integrator?"

"A hydraulic computer. One of the first ones was built by Vladimir Lukyanov in 1936. I saw one of these machines at an exhibit in Moscow once. A network of tubes simulates a physical process, solving a differential equation in multiple dimensions. One of the first applications was the production of concrete blocks, which were developing internal cracks depending on their size, temperature, curing schedules, and so on. The water integrator actively simulated the temperature and moisture levels through networks of pipes, reservoirs, and pumps."

"Do you have drawings for this machine?"

"Of course not. Math is not my strength; you'll work out the details. I'm thinking heat transfer is a good place to start, very intuitive."

"Like how long it takes to cool off a south-facing apartment in August?" I asked.

"Good idea. We could play around with frost line depth as a test problem. I expect we'll end up modeling some physical system, and then struggle to figure out which one later." Victor smiled and flexed the tubing back and forth. "My brother would already be done with the design by now. For him, designing mechanisms came easy despite being a physicist by training. Everything was mechanical and analog back in the Soviet Union. We didn't have the integrated circuit technology of the West, instead relying on material solutions and simple electric circuits. While your F-16 has a heads-up display, our MIGs were cluttered with knobs and levers. We were trapped in the physical world so he worked in that medium."

"What did you study?"

"I went to a mechanical trade school, application instead of theory. I need to touch things to understand them, witness the work being done well and poorly. It's a lower form of understanding, seeing only part of reality rather than the essence behind it. Vulgar bulk manipulations of matter," Victor said.

"Sounds a lot like Plato's theory of forms with a side of Christian disdain for the body," I said, thinking back to a recent podcast.

"Exactly. I like the way you think." We left the workshop and moved out onto the porch, taking a seat on the wooden bench. He lit a cigarette. "It's hard not to see human development as an extended movement away from the physical and into the virtual. Real to ideal. I worked on a particle physics experiment at the university here that took over a decade to complete at enormous cost. If it confirms a few formulas, it will be a great success. But it may do nothing. The project employed ten people for a generation and funded my retirement. The best possible outcome may be a few academic papers – if they're lucky."

"A particle collider?" I asked, watching the ash advance on the cigarette which started to curl downward like a pool noodle. The initial smell of its smoke created a synaptic tingle which morphed into mild repulsion a few seconds later.

"A compact version. Don't ask me about the physics of it, I only built some precision instruments," Victor said. "A professor from Kyiv brought me over on a work visa after they struggled hitting tolerances and integrating the design. Apparently, Leo gave him my name a few years back when they needed an expert machinist."

"Leo?" I asked, thinking back to Pierre Mercer's appraisal of the Lorenzian waterwheel and its reclusive artist named Leo.

"My brother, of course," Victor said with a bemused look which was followed by a forceful cough. He locked the front door. "It's time for me to walk around the block."

"Sorry about taking the waterwheel machine, I couldn't find the bird camshaft one." I stammered.

Victor smiled as he thrust the dusty textbook into my hands. "You'll come back Saturday morning." He patted me on the shoulder and headed down the front stairs into the late afternoon heat.

The window air conditioner entered a high duty cycle mode, struggling to pump heat outside. The cooling immediately disappeared when it cycled off, the opposite of a car heater on a cold day. I laid on the sofa in boxer shorts after playing a tennis match in the afternoon heat, then treated myself to a one-dollar 32-ounce fountain drink diet soda. Ripping a one-handed topspin backhand passing shot up the line for a winner sat next to Indian food and sex as the greatest joys in life.

A string of plastic grocery bags sat along the hallway wall, containing non-perishable items like cans of refried beans and energy bars from a shopping trip yesterday, objects that belonged in cabinets but should be impervious to ground insects. I discovered a discount grocery store in the spring and imposed a goal of averaging a dollar per pound of purchased goods. Their selection varied based on the latest surplus or nearly expired products, the quality quite tolerable as long as you avoided the fresh produce or meat sections.

My phone vibrated with an email notification: the results from the DNA test had been posted. I submitted the saliva sample on a whim after a particularly profitable day of airport rides, well before Nina mentioned Xmundio's ownership of the biotech firm. I purchased the ancestry module, nothing good could come out of the health one.

I held out some hope that a half-sibling or unknown cousin would emerge, perhaps I'd find out I was adopted. At the least, it would identify ethnic groups on a brightly colored map and trace their journey across oceans. My parents were uncurious about their past, self-identifying as "American" rather than a fractional breakdown of various European origins. My last surviving grandparent, my father's mother, lived in New Jersey by herself and would occasionally send a Christmas card with a solitary signature on the inside.

The results on the screen showed smeared percentages across the lands bordering the North and Baltic seas, with one dot in southern Poland near Krakow, all ethnicities fully dissolved into American society without any sexy minority groups. Disappointingly, there was no trace of Ashkenazi Jewish heritage, whose genius essentially discovered modern physics and could provide me with some fulcrum for eccentric brilliance. The software listed a presumed second or third cousin named Alicia connected through my maternal line. The profile lacked a photo but a message could be sent. I closed the laptop screen and laid back down, scanning the room. I had unboxed two photos since moving in: one a faux weathered wood frame with a stock photo of a Buddhist monk sitting cross-legged at an ancient temple, the other showed me in a tee-ball outfit in the backyard next to my parents.

*   *   *

"Come on in boys, dinner is ready," my mother called from the open back door.

"Last at bat," I said and returned to pitching a tennis ball to Jeremey. He tightened his batting gloves and got into a hitting stance, peering over his left shoulder waiting for the pitch.

"Martin, listen to your mother," my father Ned said, closing the grill cover after piling up a stack of burgers onto a plate.

Jeremey smacked a grounder just inside the maple tree, which functioned as third base. We both played on the same Little League team, Kensler Equipment, a local construction company sponsor. Jeremey's father, Wes Clayton, coached the squad, naturally resulting in his son pitching and batting cleanup, though he had actual athletic talent. The Clayton family fully mobilized during baseball season, their mom Gillian worked at the penny candy concession stand and their legally blind grandfather argued with the home plate umpire on calls. I could throw well thanks to a masking tape strike zone on the garage wall, but couldn't hit much besides a dribbler back to the pitcher. My strong arm put me on third base, the hot corner, a terrifying prospect against bigger kids who pulled balls down the line. Jeremey and I became friends during the spring season, which now was coming to a close.

"Jean, I need to get this coleslaw recipe," Gillian said as we all gathered at the table. I sat next to Jeremey and his older brother Ryan.

"Of course," my mother said, beaming from the recognition. It took her a few tries to convince my father to have the Clayton's over for a Sunday dinner. He spent every Sunday afternoon during grass growing season tending to the lawn while my mother read thrillers. Not allowed to use any of the sharp landscaping tools, I usually threw tennis balls into the wall or accepted an assignment of weeding.

"What plans do you all have for the summer?" Wes asked.

"I'll be teaching Vacation Bible School the first two weeks of July," my mother said after a period of silence. The Clayton's were in our church but were classic Christmas and Easter goers. "Has Jeremey signed up?"

"It sounds great but we just booked an RV to drive around California, how many national parks again honey?" Wes asked.

"We're hoping for four before we fly back three weeks later."

"The boys insist on camping out under the stars. Until they see a bear, that is," Wes added.

"That sounds wonderful, take plenty of pictures to share," my mother chimed in.

"Not sure if Ned can spare losing his yard work apprentice for a weekend, but we're backpacking in the Allegheny National Forest in two weeks, maybe Martin can join us?" Wes asked. "Don't have to decide now of course."

"Worthy of consideration," my father responded which ended the line of inquiry. The remainder of the meal had us three boys peppering each other with baseball trivia questions and the two mothers exchanging cooking tips. Ned and Wes ate quickly and went out on the back deck to clean off the grill. I kept thinking about backpacking, a fuzzy activity filled with unknowns.

My father didn't need to ask if I wanted to go on the trip, he must have correctly assumed I had fallen under the Clayton's spell like his wife. He rose to his current job as lead insurance actuary by mining data and accurately judging risks. Sending your nine-year-old only child into the woods for his first night alone with a charismatic but unverified family didn't make any sense.

As I frantically blew on the second cup of complimentary green tea in the office lobby to cool it down, I regretted choosing punctuality over morning coffee. The same tattooed man, now squeezed into an extra slim button-down, tapped aggressively at a keyboard, bobbing his head up and down to look at the monitor and the keys. He made a smart choice in nursing, given the highly favorable gender ratios of subordinate medical work. I threw back the rest of the tea when he called me over.

We walked to one of the exam rooms along the hallway and I sat down on the chair, pulling out the only available reading material. The well-worn issue of Field and Stream featured an article on selecting a perfect camouflaged blind for hunting various ungulates. The magazine's cover date showed it was four years old, suggesting the room had been here longer than the spotless office would suggest or the magazines were lifted from another location.

"Martin, I'm glad we're seeing each other again," Dr. Patel said, sitting on a swivel stool. She swept into the room in a single movement, like a late arrival at a movie theatre. "Congratulations, you have been selected for the study."

"Is today the first day?" I asked, thinking about my subpar mental acuity and then wondering why I wanted to please her or Transcendent so much.

"Today is about setting expectations. Let's unpack that." She handed me a digital tablet that displayed a list of items, each one expandable into a set of rules and required actions. The sleek graphic design reminded me of Xmundio's applications, a functional minimalism I didn't expect to encounter in a medical environment.

"Let's start with the basics. The study will be twelve weeks long and you'll be paid at the end of each week." This was longer than expected but welcome. "The study includes a medication which shall be taken each morning with food. You are required to come to the office every other day, including holidays and weekends, for approximately an hour of tests which include but are not limited to: blood draws, fMRI scans, VR behavioral simulations, video games, and questionnaires. Any questions so far?"

I shook my head no and she continued. "You are required to install an application on your smartphone through which you'll record when the medicine is taken. It provides a quick interface for users to ask questions of our team and allows periodic check-ins."

"This is very important. You'll be given a set of motor ability and reflex tests each visit. If you notice any physical impairment or significant changes in sleeping, eating, sexual function, or any other side effects, you must notify us immediately. You also cannot take any other prescription or over-the-counter medication besides the multivitamins and pain relievers you previously listed. These will be detected in your blood tests and be a cause for dismissal. Finally, please do not discuss the study with other subjects at the risk of compromising the experiment. Do you understand?"

"Yes, I understand." I looked through the menus for any indication of the study's objective. "Can you say what this is testing?"

"I can only say that it is neurological and not tied to any particular disease. We need the participants to be themselves.

We realize that this requires a large amount of your time, and the compensation reflects that," she answered.

"Is this a double-blind study?"

Dr. Patel paused for a minute. "Neither the participants nor investigators know all of the conditions. But I will say that it is non-traditional and leave it at that."

"Is Kory Gorman sponsoring this?"

"The billionaire?" she asked in disbelief. "I'll ask about that, and demand a raise if it's true. I only know a little about Transcendent. This is a part-time assignment away from my primary work as a psychiatrist at the hospital. You'll see the documents there for your e-signature."

I looked through the text on the tablet until attention fatigue set in, then electronically signed the gauntlet of contracts, waivers, and agreements. After having my blood taken, I went to the distribution kiosk which I activated by scanning a code on my cell phone. Following the sound of small items impacting plastic, the door swung open, revealing a week's worth of white ellipsoidal pills.

*　　　*　　　*

"Are you going to be buried or cremated?" Nina asked me as we walked past a row of headstones in the cemetery.

"Haven't really thought about it. I guess buried but no idea where, haven't purchased a plot," I said. My parents were buried next to each other in their town cemetery in Pennsylvania but given our family's slow westward migration and limited progeny, they were the only Rasmus' on the grounds. "How about you?"

"Cremated, for sure. I have a friend that works in a cadaver lab. People donate their bodies to science to monitor their decay after death in the ground to help forensics. It's disgusting," she said without hesitation.

"There is something purer about cremation, dispersing yourself in the air. I've heard it said that every breath you take has a molecule breathed by DaVinci, Caesar, whoever," I said. "Part of me wants a headstone though, even if it's just a futile attempt at a legacy."

"Like Abraham Beggs?" she asked and we both stopped to consider the century-old grave. The stone sat on the outer orbit of the larger Beggs plot, a simple low-profile granite block bearing only the dates of 1880-1913. He didn't seem to have been buried with a wife or descendants. Nina touched the gravestone, staying in contact with it for a solid twenty seconds. I knelt down next to her, imagining Abraham as a God-fearing hardy pioneer escaping childhood diseases to arrive at the lower trough of the mortality curve only to get an infection from a farming accident, an utterly stupid way to die. When Nina got up, I chided myself for automatically sighting the upper horizontal edge of the gravestone against the surrounding blocks, gauging their parallelism and variable subsidence into the soil.

We had wandered into the cemetery after finishing ice cream cones in Old Town, lured in by the large shadows cast by the mature cottonwood and ash trees in the older area of the grounds. I suspected she had been here before, taken first or early dates to jointly contemplate their mortality, an existential version of the purportedly smart date choice of an amusement park. Not that our meetup carried any romantic implications. Our outing had been prompted by her text message insisting we get ice cream to celebrate our admission into the study. Even though we were essentially the only people in the cemetery, I felt like a tourist, blithely jumping between family histories, skipping past the mowed over recessed stones on the way to the larger and more unique monuments.

"You sure you don't want to get your name recorded, etched in stone?" I asked.

"There are enough headstones in my family," she said. "My clan homesteaded in a valley west of here a long time ago, sort of mountain royalty, I guess. They own lots of low productivity land far away from the ski resorts and tourist circuits," Nina said with a smile. "There is an obelisk monument thing with large block letters of our family name, always a pain in the ass to mow around."

We turned and walked down another row, this one a bit newer with more last names that ended in vowels. "Isn't it crazy how many last names there are?" I asked. "Most of them I've never seen before."

"I wouldn't consider this place a melting pot either," she said. "Do you mean that certain last names should be going extinct over time?"

"Outside of some wacky artists, I don't see people creating new last names based on their job, like Cooper or Baker, or changing them when immigrating. Once your name is on a Social Security card it sticks. I think the whole physical world is becoming stickier, or maybe it's just the US."

"I hate stickiness, especially on little hands."

"Like take a look at a map, I guarantee you it will look the same in fifty years. Maybe the yellow shaded metro area is a little larger, another set of roads are installed out onto the plains to create more subdivisions, the font sizes of the towns grow or shrink," I said as our walk slowed. "Take national monuments or historic places, which have basically stopped being created, really. And we add, what maybe another bridge or a new skyscraper every few years. The physical world is stuck."

"Are you one of these end of history people?"

"I was at the end of the last millennium. I saw humanity integrating into a single peaceful globally connected polis. But that view shattered, first with 911 and then the Iraq War, financial system collapse, populist leaders, etc. Despite this, it feels like material history has pretty much ended."

"Is that because you haven't changed since the new millennium, at least physically?"

This carried some linguistic stopping power and I nodded, thinking back to the final years of high school, a little less abdominal fat and no ear hair back then but, overall, I looked essentially the same. "I like that analysis, the way I see the physical world has been imprinted on me in my late teenage years and everything since seems gray or derivative."

"You know that your favorite music will be the one you were listening to in the period around when you first get laid," she said.

"And your sense of humor too. Ever watch a comedy from fifty years ago or recent ones? Never as good," I said, watching her calf muscles flex to form a curved hummock on each step. "Even with our biases, I think there's some truth there. The macro-physical world in the US has been set for a long time now, the advances have come in the virtual, the cloud, in language and ideas rather than airports and interstates."

"And hopefully the biochemical; isn't that why we're in this study?" Nina said, gathering her curly hair back into a bun and walking over to a shaded area. "I love the long summer days down here but could use some cooler evenings."

"Don't bother with anything further east or south. What made you move to the city?" I asked, picturing different stages of her rebellion.

"Not much of an art market at home for anything besides taxidermy. I still head back a couple of times a year for weddings and funerals, which leads me to a liquid diet of liquor and lager for a day or two," she said while the two of us sat down on a bench in front of a small reflecting pond. "Did you take the medicine this morning?"

"Yeah, haven't noticed any changes yet. How about you?"

"Took it first thing with a glass of water. Okay, check out my pills."

She pulled out a translucent beige bottle and her pills looked similar to mine, small white ellipsoids without markings. I poked at one of them, rolled it around in her hand, and started to take a picture.

"Stop!" she cried, clenching her fingers into a fist and hiding the pills. "Are you crazy? Don't you think the Transcendent Health app has access to our photos?"

"Wow, you think the app is surveilling us?" I never reviewed privacy permissions.

"I wouldn't be surprised if it did, even after I turned off all sharing. I'm in airplane mode now, the GPS or Wi-Fi geolocation would place the two of us together. Let me see." Nina took my phone and jumped into the phone's Settings, toggling the controls in a flurry of tapping fingers before jumping back to the home screen. She scrolled past the online dating applications which I had installed three months before.

"Do you worry about the microphone?" I asked.

"Oh God, why did you have to say that?" She punched me in the shoulder. "We may have to unplug these second brains when we're together. Do you see a difference in the pills?"

"No, they look identical. I suppose we could do a taste test. Most drugs taste bitter and the placebo may taste different."

"They probably tried to match them, but it could be worth a shot," she said. "I really can't be in the control group, seriously."

"Why's that?" I asked. "They made it sound like it wasn't a purely pharmaceutical trial, maybe something to do with those helmets and MRIs."

"I've been off meds for a year. That was one of the pre-conditions for this. I have this fear that my brain has been rewired, maybe permanently. Do you know that feeling when you get home and are still a bit drunk, can't focus, want to lay down, and have a simmering low-level headache? I wake up to that now."

"That sucks, I'm sorry," I said. I thought about Nina taking photographs, framing them, and trying to sell herself as an artist. Success as an independent economic agent was an internal and external confidence game, hard to fake. Making extra prints of a photo seemed pretty straightforward, but promoting them on social media must be brutally tedious.

"You know that these doctors still keep hardcopy notebooks?" she asked.

"Like pen and paper?"

"It has something to do with FDA approval and keeping records authentic, signing the bottom of each page. Plus, some of them are just old school," she said while pulling up the Transcendent office on the GPS mapping software, zooming in with two fingers like forcing open eyelids. "Is there any way we could get our hands on one of them?"

"Good idea, flip the spying back on them."

A wind picked up and brought with it a pocket of clear sky-cooled air. We got up and walked back towards Old Town, hatching hair-brained espionage schemes from hovering drones outside the windows to hiding out in the lobby bathroom ventilation ducts. A few lonely stars emerged in the sky, first from the east and then from the darker north, away from the urban pink hue.

We maintained a consistent spacing between us on the walk back to town. I tried to keep myself on the street side of the sidewalk and slightly downwind of her citrus-smelling hair product conscripted to combat the entropic tendencies of her curly hair. We reached the ice cream stand where we had met earlier in the evening. The well-lit location and wholesome families only permitted a relievingly quick farewell hug. I went in low with both hands, somehow defaulting to a slow dance position on her lower torso, and a second later awkwardly shifted my hands higher up her t-shirt in a bunching double-clutch movement. We parted with an agreement to meet that weekend for a strategy session.

I pulled up the ridesharing application once out of her potential view, flipped through the available pickups, and decided to wait for an airport drop-off. I loaded up a playlist of hip hop and other songs with heavy basslines and reminded myself not to let the upbeat music result in a speeding ticket or a front-end collision.

*   *   *

One of the older gangsta rap tunes conjured memories of sweet-smelling stale beer and excessively sized subwoofers in small spaces, later walking home from fraternity row with a liquor jacket on a mid-fall Friday night. Greek culture loomed large at the sprawling state school, the football team offering a reliable pretext for a weekend's worth of parties. The hundredfold increase in the size of the student body compared to high school and fewer classes released me into further comfortable anonymity, surely a bridge to an atomized adulthood spent extracting simple pleasures of takeout food and aquatic companions.

I acquired a Pluto-esque position in an outer orbit around a social group of engineering students in our junior year dorm. The circle sat in closer proximity to me along the nerdiness spectrum than my peers in the arts and sciences department. The fact that the group was predominantly male made it easier to arrange trips to the gym and join them for online first-person shooter tournaments. We remained a loose confederation and I only considered a few of them closer friends.

"You must be a good cook," I said as we got up from class. "Smells great."

"Tastes good too. It's all really the same stuff, just different ratios of salt, garlic, and oil," she said, gathering up her notebooks into a solid black backpack, paired with dark grey jeans and a black and white horizontal striped sweater. "Food trucks off Olive Blvd."

"But the glass bowl?"

"They charge you by the pound, get two or three meals that way. No styrofoam either. Are you new?"

"No, just not on this side of campus much. I'm Martin," I said, reminding myself not to reach out for a handshake.

"Jessica. I'm usually stuck in Glassman Hall until midnight." I had already found out her name from a brute force search of the school's primitive digital directory. We sat a few chairs away from each other at the back of a class on existentialist philosophy, the participation equivalent of picking grass in right field.

"Midnight? That's rough. Though I guess we've just learned we always have a choice. You want to grab a coffee and we can figure out this whole meaning of life stuff?" I asked.

"Okay. I live off campus, let's meet at The Grind tomorrow at ten." This was the preferred coffee house of smokers and malcontents, a dimly lit shop with distressed furniture. "PM."

"Cool, that'll wake me up," I said as we headed off to our next classes.

The day's lecture on Kierkegaard's leap of faith had provided the activation energy to break the ice. Jessica wasn't cheerleader attractive but had a conspiracy of freckles, light skin, dark hair, and what would later be called *resting bitch face*, all of which pulled me in. The visual and especially auditory experience of people eating had repulsed me ever since I was young; I even played music to avoid listening to myself chew and swallow. But Jessica was different, and I found myself drawn to watching her eat bowls of ethnic food during class like it was some sort of carnal act. I had developed crushes on girls from nearby dorms in the first two years of college, and had even had an alcohol-aided horizontal encounter, but nothing this consuming, this maddening.

We admitted over cappuccinos to taking the philosophy class due to an emergent dread of choosing our future after college rather than out of casual interest. The caffeine fueled banter about our majors: the peer pressure to be eccentric in her art school and the very true stereotype of math majors falling asleep into problem set booklets in the library. Cigarettes felt good in the crisp fall evening, and we took turns showing off our best impressions of neurotic smokers, from Keyser Söze to Tyler Durden in *Fight Club*.

She later confessed to not being initially attracted to me but the late-night instant message sessions of brooding remarks and sarcasm started a crack which I clumsily expanded through persistence. The university leased an art center two miles away from campus, the setup allowing me to deliver coffee and food supplies for her all-nighters, trudging through snowstorms fueled by narratives of overmen. Subtle signals of her interest gave me more confidence, creating a recursive pattern like my discovery of math back in the library during middle school, but included a new physical dimension for which I had no antibodies. By the spring we were inseparable, taking shoestring weekend camping trips and installing a dual nozzle shower head to the likely disgust of her roommate.

She came from a wealthy Main Line suburb of Philadelphia, her patrician parents funding a gap year in Australia after high school and reveling in their only child being an unemployed artist. Her mother inherited a large share in a limited liability family-owned company that leased vast tracts of land across the country to the fossil fuel industry. Her father had experienced a gritty childhood in the Bronx but was bequeathed with a cerebral advantage, starting out as a child chess prodigy and landing as a comfortably tenured physics professor. Her familiarity with nerdy male figures must have given me a backdoor to her heart. We quickly agreed that spending holidays at their estate made more sense than my mother's two-bedroom apartment, our days spent playing racket sports and sipping afternoon tea.

Her parental underwriting allowed us to take an NGO Grand Tour after college, spending around two years in each location, where we taught and facilitated community projects. She had a gift for the work, developing relationships with mother's groups in each village and playing with children, so we extended our foreign deployment well into our thirties, past the point we had expected to be entering graduate school and avoiding dirt under our fingernails.

I occasionally succeeded in doing something productive, like teaching math to variably interested students and working on local infrastructure projects. The public works efforts always seemed to involve delivering cleanish water separated from waste streams. For a while, I checked the quarterly posted drinking water bacterial levels after installing rural wells in Honduras, taking pleasure in plotting years of results using a spreadsheet. Jessica became lifelong friends with each local education director, cold messaging them to check in and share teaching ideas.

I lobbied for getting married after we both crossed thirty, cohabitating already being a fact on the ground. A small family affair in front of a justice of the peace would remove the burden of sending invitations and figuring out seating amongst mothballed college friends. She quickly demurred without offering a reason beyond the unnecessary formality of the event, no coy smiles that would tempt a spontaneous proposal.

The old school rap playlist ended as I pulled into the gas station. I thought about sending Nina a text message, something sarcastic about Transcendent Health or an odd news article about alien hybrids already living on Earth. I added and deleted several strange but unfunny articles in the message box, giving up when I got a notification for a client needing a ride to the airport.

The bedsheet shifted during the night, making me unknowingly fight the corner of the fabric for several hours until daybreak. I purchased the bed from a big box retailer after waking up in a teeth-chattering frozen state on an air mattress my first night in the apartment. I decided not to pursue a bed on the free and discounted online marketplace given the nonzero bedbug risk.

Through a process of hydraulic pressure, vacuum sealing, and folding, the mattress was squeezed into a cardboard box and then into the trunk, before leaping forth back to life like a crescent roll released from its sausage-like skin. The bed and basic steel frame addressed the temperature issue but created immobile vertebrae the next day, the firm surface making my body rest on a limited number of contact points. I added a two-inch-thick memory foam topper, a layer of soft subcutaneous fat over the hard body of the bed, which made it at least serviceable although it was still admittedly too small in the unlikely event of an overnight visitor.

I pictured the water computer like an old industrial chemical plant, tentacles of pipes, gauges, and pumps, venting steam like an animal breathing in the cold, calculating solutions in material terms by simulating a physical analog, a miniaturized Axis Chemicals from the original Batman movie. Victor's vintage heat transfer book sat on the nightstand, where I intentionally left it as reading material before bed two days before. I flipped through the pages after stuffing a pillow against the wall for back support. The interior section of the book dealt with finding exact solutions to well-posed conduction and convection problems. The rest of the text offered empirical correlations and engineering formulas for practical design work, making it a solid if dated undergraduate reference material.

The last chapter explored analog solutions, namely the creation of electric circuits to simulate real-world problems. Since voltage is analogous to temperature and electrical current similar to heat flow, the response of a simplified thermal network could be solved by converting a problem to its electrical equivalent and letting the circuit mirror the physical world. The technique was comically antiquated and had been entirely replaced with modern computational methods but I found it charming nevertheless. There was something obvious but elegant about the spatial gradient of a quantity – voltage, concentration, temperature, or pressure – producing a flow, and the spatial change of that flow must accumulate in time if it is conserved.

I pulled out some light green grid paper leftover from college, when I grabbed four tablets from an ambiguously complimentary stack outside the Earthquake Lab in my last semester. The crisp lines and squares projected a seriousness in the coffee shops and libraries where I most frequently put them to use, though I had rationed the pages and still had two full notebooks left seventeen years later. Sketching out differential equations took me back to standing in front of empty chalkboards stretched out across the wall while thirty sweaty teenagers watched me hack through deriving the Pythagorean theorem, using my fist to smudge out letters and make corrections. I could feel Victor looking over my shoulder as I transformed an electrical schematic into a series of pipes and reservoirs using gravity-driven flow.

The only reasonably interesting design I could come up with of a hydraulic system had a chain of five fluid reservoirs connected by tubing. Liquid diffused into the array based on differential column heights with a pump delivering water to the upstream feed tank, simulating transport from a source into an interior. It was a discretized solution, a crude approximation of the physical world, the power of analog computing perverted into distinct evaluation points without much likeness to Lukyanov's water computer. I folded up the paper and shoved it back into the book.

*   *   *

I took a few deep breaths in hopes that it would help me mindfully ignore the two free-ranging screeching toddlers scampering back and forth across the patio. Their parents, two upscale bohemians a few years younger than me, sipped coffee and discussed mountain biking. The children, named Auden and Ophelia, wore bright silly outfits and expressed joy in chasing winged insects. The place – a combination café, brunch, and market featuring hydroponically homegrown vegetables – projected a wholesome, hipster vibe. The rollup doors and high ceilings revealed its former existence as an auto garage.

I had walked over to the café to meet with Pierre Mercer again, after getting a text the night before requesting a meeting. It read:

> Bonjour Martin. This is Pierre Mercer who viewed the waterwheel last week. Another party is extremely interested in it. I would like to arrange a meeting. They already have representation. These matters can get quite complicated. You would benefit from an experienced broker like myself. Are you available to meet tomorrow at ten o'clock AM for a discussion?

My first inclination was to ignore Pierre, block his number, and forget it. But I wanted to see him again out of pity and curiosity. He was an eccentric hypertensive struggler who seemed straight out of a BBC Victorian era drama carrying a handkerchief and pocket watch, probably a Derringer for protection. It should be entertaining.

I arrived early and resumed a book on Roman history from Pax Romana to the fall of the Western empire. The current section explored the Crisis of the Third Century, a period of rampant usurpation and economic collapse that nearly ended the empire two hundred years before the infamous 476, an imperial midlife crisis. Out of habit, I brought my old white and black composition notebook which turned up while cleaning out the family home in Pennsylvania the past spring, its pages populated with notes and phrases taken from scattered non-fiction texts back in college. I found a set of fresh sheets and took down some notes on debased currencies and the growth of manorialism.

Pierre stumbled over to the table, his blue shirt showing stomach sweat islands which would certainly grow to archipelagos and continents with time. He sat down with a sigh. "A pleasure to see you again, Martin. How have you been?"

"Good," I said and noticed that Pierre's eyes were darting around the table.

"Where is the machine?" he asked.

"I didn't bring it with me, but you can attest to its function."

He kneaded his hands a few times. "I trust it's in a safe place. The group that's coming today is expecting to see a proof of life if you will."

"What type of buyer is this?" I asked.

"Not sure. I met the other agent at a roadshow in Chicago three years ago. He was looking for paintings and sculptures for high-end clients," Pierre said, tipping over to gain access to the smartphone in his front pocket. He stabbed at the phone's screen using a single, rigid index finger. "They are very close, much earlier than anticipated. Would you mind if we sat on the same side?"

I nodded. "Are you helping me to negotiate?"

"If we need to have a sidebar just tap my leg under the table," he said.

A large black and chrome SUV pulled into the handicap spot by the door, the only opening in the parking lot. A slender man in sharply creased blue dress pants and a light sport coat stepped out from the driver seat, followed by a tall blonde woman in athleisure wear and oversize sunglasses from the passenger side, and finally from the backseat came a middle-aged man with a Republican haircut and a heavily-unbuttoned blue and white checkered shirt and dark denim jeans.

"Is this them, the yacht club trio?" I asked Pierre who nodded yes. I adjusted myself to sit up straight in the chair and considered moving tables to put the three newcomers into the late morning sun but decided to be less adversarial since they clearly easily parted with money. The man in the suit held open the door for the other two. Only the woman purchased a drink, a single shot of espresso.

"Pierre, great to meet you again," the sport-coated man said, shaking hands with Pierre and then me. "Aldous Jensen, private sales director."

"Martin, or do you prefer Marty?" Aldous asked as he sat down at the table.

"Martin is fine." I didn't recall telling Pierre my name but perhaps it slipped out during our first conversation. The other pair sat down and introduced themselves as Roman and Irina.

"I believe Pierre told you we are very interested in seeing the machine; can you show it to us?" Aldous asked.

"I don't have it with me now." A look of concern crossed Aldous' face. He exhaled slowly. The other two sat in silence behind their sunglasses. "But it's safe, don't worry."

"You understand that seeing the article is critical, right?" Aldous asked.

"You have my word that it is legitimate, the inscriptions on the marble base are from Leo, without question," Pierre added. He then pulled out his phone and showed a photo of the waterwheel to the three. "The same markings as the drunken mouse from the Warsaw exhibit in 1994. See here?"

He showed them a website with photos of a figurine mouse balancing on the rim of a clear tank made to look like a beer bottle. The rodent's motion was presumably driven by some sort of linkage superstructure buried inside its upturned tail. The bottom of the marble base had scribed letters and a date of 1994.

"We believe you. Martin, are you able to go pick up the machine now? My clients have traveled specifically for this meeting," Aldous asked.

Irina scrolled on her phone, flicking the screen upwards like launching a bug off a countertop. Roman and Aldous waited for my response. "I wish I could but my schedule today is very tight," I said with feigned regret.

"You don't understand the seriousness of our meeting. This is a bit more important than reading history books," Roman leaned in as he spoke, seizing the bad cop role. In a show of support, Irina stopped swiping and took off her sunglasses. Her round face but slim frame reminded me of a mature Slavic model. She was quite attractive even if she likely had work done. "Do you know this man?" Roman asked.

He pushed a small, dated photo across the table. A man in a puffy, light blue winter jacket and grey scarf looked a lot like a younger, more clean-cut Victor.

"Hard to say. He does remind me of someone but I just can't put my finger on who."

"You know exactly who this is," Roman said, folding his arms and glaring at me.

"Look," Irina said in a calm voice, putting down her phone. "Leo Ivantusky was our father. We rightly own his artwork and designs now. It's a source of family pride. We must have the works returned. Our lawyer Aldous set this meeting up without getting law enforcement involved. To make it simpler for everyone, can we work together to return the machine?"

"What is the reward?" I asked, unable to help myself. Pierre tapped on my leg rapidly with his left hand and cleared his throat.

"Your reward will be the honor of returning something to its rightful owner," Aldous said. I turned to Pierre who was schvitzing aggressively in the sun. We excused ourselves for a moment and stepped away from the table.

"You set me up. This isn't a sale, it's some sort of weird shakedown." I didn't feel particularly threatened but I could see some type of legal action requiring the use of a printer and notary public.

"I'm sorry, I feared something like this but wanted to believe Jensen." Pierre paced back and forth, tugging on his beard. "It's best if you return it, but let's push back on the reward. You acted in good faith and purchased it for a significant sum at an estate sale, right?"

"I don't have the machine anymore, I gave it back to the original owner," I said, thinking about it sitting in a box in

Victor's basement. "I could try to get it back but definitely not to just give it away, especially to them."

"They'll never believe you if you say it's been returned," he said. "I'm a bit scared of the two of them. Roman and Irina may have declared Leo legally dead recently to acquire all his assets. We can't let ourselves be intimidated, though."

We walked back to the table which now sat in direct sunlight, baking the black powder-coated metal top and chairs while the three of them sat in the shade.

"I wish I could help you out. In truth, I never really owned the machine in the first place," I said.

"Exactly!" Roman snapped.

"It was only borrowed, and it's been returned."

"Fucking Victor, I know he's in on this," Roman told the lawyer.

"Martin, I'm afraid this will have to move into a legal stage. Depositions, court orders. You can avoid all of that by working with us. Please tell us who you returned it to," Aldous said.

I picked up my vibrating phone from the table – it was an ESPN notification about the final week of preseason football. I casually took a photo of them while flipping through the screens, then slowly put the phone back on the table. The Plague of Cyprian, a pandemic of hemorrhagic fever, ravaged the Roman empire from 249 to 262, further destabilizing the economy and fragmenting the empire into parts, which would be sort of like if the US returned to the Articles of Confederation and was invaded by Canada or Mexico. I couldn't survive under such an upheaval with its loss of legal and police protections, although the testimony of my inherited DNA must have provided some adaptive advantage in previous lives, perhaps a slow and efficient metabolism or some epidemiological benefit. Pierre tapped my leg again, reeling me back to reality.

"If you're not receptive to compensating my client for the piece, our time here is done," Pierre said, sitting up in his chair. The lawyer got up first and the others followed suit, clicking their hard sole leather heels in defiance against the stone patio when walking away. I smiled at Pierre and shrugged my shoulders.

*   *   *

The cool air caused my whole body to shiver when I left the apartment in running shoes and mesh shorts. A stream of moisture from the southwest had finally broken through the high-pressure dome in the afternoon, delivering two tenths of an inch of rain and dropping the temperature down to the tolerable dew point. The water drew an earthy redolence out from the ground and created puddles along the curb rich with solutes and particles from the road accumulated over the previous parched month.

I ran westward towards the foothills, crossing into a large tract of open space, an area turned over to nature to remediate the environmental effects of a WWI-era chemical weapons factory. I expected the carbohydrate cannonball in my stomach to produce an abdominal cramp any minute; it was, in fact, the cooking and eating of yet another prodigious quantity of pasta that had led to this sudden bout of exercise, a guilt-laden several months' worth of hovering at the basal metabolic rate supported by refined sugars and starches. I felt a sense of relief when the collar of my t-shirt darkened with sweat, a confirmation that I had actually engaged in vigorous activity.

I failed to achieve stable cardiovascular output in the thin air and had to stop along the trail which happened to run through a large prairie dog colony. One of the little animals periscoped around on its hill and barked at me, warning the others of an incoming simian. How these hyperactive rodents survived in such arid environments and through long winters made no sense. I walked for a few minutes, hands on hips, before I decided to head back to the apartment a mile away.

It felt good to be midway through the run and crossing into the second half of the activity. The way I wholly embodied the concept of the *middle* struck me: the middle of my actuarial life span and in the middle of the country, midway between the Great Lakes and the Pacific. I balanced on the anatomical average for height and build, and only expressed the phenotypic dominant genes, a weighted average, an index fund. My income level as a secondary school teacher would certainly be close to the country's median, and each end of the political spectrum seemed tribal and reductive to me. My default position was a regression to the mean, a comfortable equilibrium. Being in the middle meant I lacked closeness: to people clearly, but also spatially to anything personally significant, and temporally to anticipated events. Perhaps proximity and a movement towards closeness could create happiness, close enough to raise hope but never arriving. Joy could be the slope, the change, the derivative, not a static absolute value.

The prairie dog mounds stretched out like a flattened egg carton, with a plucky rodent on some of the bell-shaped humps. The central limit theorem states that when independent random variables are added together, the resulting population will exhibit a normal distribution – the famous bell curve with a weighty central lump and thinning tails – a shape that if known in antiquity would have been worshiped for its symmetry and grace like Mt. Fuji. Normally distributed traits like intelligence shows they are a sum of many sources. The present emerges as the weighted sum of the past. As I ran, I began to vocally catalog my lifetime list of random events and relationships, their sum which now inexorably pushed me back towards the fated middle, the calculus of mediocrity. My heart rate increased as I fought the light incline, choosing the longer route, the one with more hills and valleys back.

A black luxury SUV sat outside of Victor's house. It must have been his brother's children and their lawyer, applying pressure to get Victor to release the machine. I parked a block down the road and approached from the gravel alley before deciding to cut through the neighbor's yard to get past the cedar privacy fences.

Victor and a stocky man in a maroon suit and newsboy hat stepped out into the back yard, absorbed in conversation. The man pointed across the yard, turning his head and scanning the area. I ducked behind the neighbor's bushes to avoid being spotted and continued watching the house after the two went inside for about five minutes. There was no sign of dapper lawyers or rich kids ransacking the place.

This was the first time I saw Victor interact with another person. Clearly, the two were friends of some sort. Each gave off a bookish Old World vibe, one consistent with Victor's older house but incompatible with the sunbathed high plains. I had increasingly come to believe that the Mountain West had a pervasive, youthful amnesia, likely aided by the thin air, an obliviousness to history that manifested itself in sunny dispositions, an abundance of megachurches, 4,000 square foot houses, and an avoidance of introspection in favor of endorphin-addled pursuits like skiing and mountain biking. Victor stood as a counterexample, building machines without an audience apart from the unexamined masses. This felt compromised by his new friend.

I knocked firmly on the front door and then realized that I had forgotten the heat transfer textbook, bringing only an empty notebook with my sketches tucked into the front flap.

The door swung open and Victor invited me in, noting my punctuality. The stockier man rose up from the sofa to shake my hands. His face looked like unmixed dough. The listing of his nose to one side and the rounding of his ears suggested a history of wrestling or other grappling. He introduced himself as Sergey with a less nasal accent than Victor's but one that was still solidly Slavic.

"Victor said you two are designing something?" Sergey asked. "Don't let this guy fool you, he's more than just a machinist."

"Just putting the new milling machine to use," I said. "Have you worked together?"

Sergey laughed. "He did most of the work, I just wrote out some equations." He adjusted his hat and moved towards the door. "I'll let you two get to business. About two weeks to get that upgraded Vic?"

"Depending on parts, yes. Helical gears can have long lead times."

We walked out to the porch with Sergey and watched him get in his SUV, the driver's seat shifted forward and raised close to the steering wheel, making him look like he was driving a school bus. We went inside after Victor smoked a cigarette.

"Let's look at those designs," Victor said and went over to the notebook I left on the table. "Are they in here?"

"Just some sketches," I stammered and looked to change the subject. "What are you upgrading for Sergey?"

"One of his toys." We went to the workshop where a light green bullet-shaped object the size of an adult golden retriever sat on the workbench. Four black fins in the aft section appeared to have the ability to rotate; it was some type of underwater craft with a propeller at its aft end. A clear window on the nose of the vehicle made it look like a mouse with an eye mask.

"He's working with one of his former grad students on this. They want a long duration, low noise, inexpensive autonomous undersea robot for deepwater remote sensing. It's a proof of concept for a dispersed web."

"You're fixing this one?" I asked.

"Changing out a burned-up transmission. Spur gears are very loud. Will change to a set of helical gears, like the ones in your car. There isn't much noise a thousand meters down, Sergey thinks that grinding gears may scare off the creatures. Adding a propeller shield for protection and further noise reduction."

I stepped closer to the streamlined body. The side of the dorsal fin had decals of the local university and various governmental and public-private partnership science foundations which included the emblem of my ride-hailing app employer, Kinetix.

"Is this a joke?" I pointed to their logo, a K made to look like a highway interchange on a map.

"They have a lot of money to throw around. Sergey said they sponsor many other projects." Their parent company was Incrementum, Inc for short, another tech titan with hegemony in search and mapping, a rival to Xmundio. I didn't expect an Internet search provider to be interested in finding exotic deep ocean creatures. This must be a public relations move, lending their data analytics skills to college research projects. The company ingested massive amounts of information stored in servers around the globe, often without a clear business application.

"I guess data is the new extractive industry. Is there much down there?" I asked

"Outside of a geothermal vent, the energy density is very low, though occasionally a weird crustacean squirts by. I'd rather keep some areas of the world dark though."

"For future generations?" I asked.

"We should keep some of the world unknown, even though it's futile. It's psychologically rewarding to be on the edge of a frontier. Everyone in this country wants to be along the coast, against the semi-infinite ocean knowing there is another largely unwatched world underneath the surface."

"You can get lost in the infinite and finite from a single location. What about us?" I asked.

"On the edge of the Rockies, enough open land to believe it's still wild, still has animals, rivers, things that can kill you. People like that, buying into the mythology but in reality, everything is well known."

"Unlike the depths of the ocean?"

"GPS doesn't work down there. There is still the possibility for discoveries. The rest of the physical world is filling in the pixels, increasing the resolution and explaining relationships. All of which is set aside for experts, the new high priests," Victor said with a smirk.

"Hence the flat Earthers, the new apostates," I said.

"Non-experts still need to discover something in the material world, more than just tinkering with their own psychology or exploring virtual reality."

"That's a real burden." I thought about the recent surge in superhero movies, which had now evolved into gangs of superheroes fighting each other, a second-order simulation completely detached from reality. In seventh grade the true scale of the universe sunk in – the impossible light years of distance effectively confining humanity to our solar system – I experienced this as a betrayal. "What are you working on now?"

"The new gearbox is volume constrained and requires a custom design, probably a hundred to one reduction for best power matching with this motor." Victor picked up the electric motor from its mount, a gray cylinder the size of a can of beans. "That's for next week. You will take some of the final cuts on this angle support."

A block of aluminum sat on the milling machine, held in place by a vice. Victor pulled up a hand drawing of the part, an angled piece with flat flanged areas on either end. Three of these blades supported a tube that would form a collar around the propeller, protecting it from impacts against the seafloor or coral.

"Touch off with the end mill using the X axis and then point five cuts to take a total of five point two from this side," he pointed to a set of digital readouts for the position of the table, which could be advanced in either the X or Y axis with a handwheel. I assumed the numbers were millimeters. "Feed it slow and use plenty of lubrication."

I braced for a sexual reference given prior single-gender work experiences but instead, Victor gave macabre safety advice regarding wedding rings and long hair, then started up the machine. I took the first passes exceedingly slowly, generating hair-sized fibers of aluminum. The final pass landed exactly on 5.20 millimeters from the initial position.

"Isn't machining aluminum a joy? I could fall asleep to the sounds of it," Victor said, clearly in his element. "The last step will work the Z dimension, thinning out the support in the center."

"It makes cutting metal with a bandsaw seem barbaric," I said, thinking back to middle school shop class.

Victor released the part from the vice and rotated it around, then pulled up the drawing and talked through the next set of operations. These required using the vertical feed to determine the depth of each cut. He left the workshop and went into the hallway bathroom, coughing vigorously. I eased into the passes, taking my time to enjoy them but also hoping he would return to set up the next round.

The Transcendent Health office had been predictably empty that morning when I arrived on time for the appointment thanks to their frequent phone app reminders. The day's fMRI focused on solving more difficult spatial problems as opposed to the session two days before which seemed very remedial, with simple language analogies and word associations. Ten days into taking the pills, I didn't feel any dramatic changes except for a slight headache. This appeared immediately on waking, and my brain felt impatient, like it had already been shifted into third gear. In a way, it felt like a milder version of the all-natural multivitamins I had purchased from the crunchy local grocery store. The pattern of yellow hexagons on the box conveyed a molecular level of precision, which persuaded me as much as the bouncy saleswoman to opt for the 100-count bottle for the best value. After two days, I acquired a nervousness that was coupled with a persistent headache, my sympathetic nervous system on a constant state of alert. I gave up with 97 pills left.

I flipped the part around and finished the next set of cuts which were symmetric with the other side. Victor complimented the progress and we moved into the living room to discuss my design. As we walked down the hallway, I noticed that he seemed weaker than in our previous meetings, walking with a bit of limp in his left leg. I picked up the notebook and handed him the grid paper sketches. He tapped the sheets with a pen, making small checkmarks as if grading it.

"Is this your frost line depth calculator?"

"A five-node model of one, I guess. I pictured the tank on the left being filled and drained by a pump." In my sketch, five tanks were placed in a row and connected with tubes. The height in each tank represented the temperature of that node. The difference in height between the tanks moved water between them, just like a temperature gradient creating heat flow. The heat capacitance of each node could be adjusted by changing the diameter of the tank, producing a faster or slower accumulation of liquid height.

"Maybe use a gear pump – easily reversible and consistent volumetric flow rate to simulate the seasons. Let me get something." Victor went down to the basement and came up with two wallet-sized white plastic parts the size of hockey pucks, each with an LCD screen and buttons. "Programmable power switches, cheap and easy to adjust, powered by twelve-volt DC."

"This will provide a nice triangular input for the height of the first tank which will be the mean daily surface temperature of the ground," I said, picturing the pump filling and draining the upstream tank over time.

"Triangle? Not a triangle pattern outside for the last two months," Victor said. A triangle wave has a sharp peak and trough, unlike seasonal average temperature changes which are more gradual, hanging out on the extremes for several months.

"I suppose we could change the speed on the gear pump, some probably have a setting for that," I said, watching Victor who squinted and furrowed his brow, waiting for a better solution. "A curved tank with a variable diameter, maybe an hourglass shape so the height change is less at the extremes!" I said with excitement, feeling immediately embarrassed.

"Perfect. Turning long and deep internal surfaces is a challenge, so how about we invert that, create an insert in the tank, displacing the water and producing the same variable height over time?"

We agreed that this was the best approach since it also allowed us to easily swap out different input functions. I started hashing out the design, sizing each reservoir given the already purchased tubing diameter. The simulator's reservoirs and transition pieces would be made of transparent acrylic and connected with clear plastic tubes, allowing for easy flow visualization.

"Pipe flow on page 150." Victor dropped a dusty fluid mechanics textbook on my lap and went back to his chair to continue sketching on the tablet, leaning forward in his seat with excitement. "Pick out a gear pump when you get home, twelve-volt DC. Cheaper the better. Buy two or three, we'll probably burn up a few. Also, get tonic water."

"Tonic water?"

"Glows light blue under a blacklight. Diet, no bugs." He flipped the tablet around to show an isometric drawing of the apparatus, which looked like glass beer samplers connected with tubes. Embedded track lights ran along the base platform. "Not sure it's the water integrator but we'll be simulating something. What's it called?"

"Water network analyzer?"

"We've got the water integrator but this one acts on height differences," he said.

"Hydraulic difference engine," I offered and he agreed. We went back to sketching out aspects of the design. I kept picturing the nest of tubes and valves in Lukyanov's device, a more generalized machine of reservoirs and adjustable flows. It must have modeled the response of a process variable in a system of inputs and outputs, rather than binary logic gates, fully leveraging the analog abilities of a fluidic system. I started to sketch out a schematic with a central mixing reservoir with branches and then scribbled it out.

"Do you ever wonder how far you could advance civilization?" I asked, a thought experiment that recurred in my head often.

"This machine won't be a technological leap."

"No, I mean with your innate abilities. Say that you reproduced asexually by generating clones of your personal genetic code, without mutation. That was the design for all time. However impossible, could this version of humanity discover agriculture? Fire? Make bronze tools with tin and copper?"

"Do you believe that progress requires heroic inspiration?"

"I don't see myself making it past antiquity. I could scratch my way into some basic Euclidean geometry, simple levers, maybe an arched aqueduct – some Hellenistic stage of development. Quantum mechanics or general relativity? Not happening," I said.

"On principle, that must be false, though Einstein was a singular figure," Victor responded. "It may take ten or a thousand times as long, and we might flail around in some dark ages for a while, but eventually knowledge will advance, even when not fully understood at an individual level. No one truly understands quantum mechanics for instance."

"There must be a cognitive threshold though," I said. "Some minimum level of intelligence necessary to have profound insights."

"Only in having the toolbox of spoken and written language needed for knowledge to accumulate. Sergey and I talk about this. He says that the human brain is a Turing complete system at a minimum, a computer able in theory to solve any computational problem given enough time and storage. Of course, there are limitations of memory and processing speed.

Memory is now supplied by written information and culture, processing speed by the parallel activities of many actors at once. Progress may be incremental, like diligently recording the orbits of planets and eventually realizing the Earth goes around the sun or it could be revelational, like Einstein."

"So, dolphins could take over after we exterminate ourselves? They have a language, right?"

Victor laughed. "Not recorded, though. You need to get to the level of abstract computation, otherwise, it's only limited lifetime agents with biological programming. Your premise is that knowledge needs genius just like evolution needs mutation. But I think of it like the speed function of molecules in a pure gas, they are all the same material but it's the collisions that produce a range of speeds, with the outliers being extremely fast. For a while at least."

"But what about unique acts of creation, like us trying to create a water computer or something?"

"That's what I love about this country, the mythology of the individual, the self-made hero. Which is persuasive, just like the concept of free will. Genius is just an intersection of genetic, temporal, and environmental collisions. Some intrinsic ability matters but the external conditions have to be right. Do you think that Florence lurched around for centuries and then suddenly produced a bunch of Renaissance geniuses in a few generations? It was the system of patrons and shifting cultural incentives, not lightning bolts and comets," Victor said and paused to think. "I'm exposing myself as a reformed Marxist, a historical materialist. But I do believe that once the initial conditions are established, knowledge will grow interminably when viewed over a long enough time period."

"Technology raises the temperature of the gas, speeding up the system, faster particles and more collisions," I said.

"New technology is exciting but nauseating. I checked out of that world twenty years ago, stopped caring about the latest gadgets and instead tried to find things that are simpler, more fundamental, or just enjoyable, like machining aluminum or reading history," Victor said.

"Do you work on projects with other people?" I asked.

"Just Sergey. He still has a lot of connections at the university. I only work two or three hours a day, so the projects drag out. I'd rather work with machines than people," Victor said and he flipped through sketches of the hydraulic engine. "We need to draft these designs."

We spent the next hour sketching out design features and enhancements, running subscale flow rate tests in the sink, and discussing the correct time scale for entertainment purposes, settling on a goal of a season in about ten minutes based on the average millennial attention span. The landline phone rang, and Victor picked it up, talking about an upcoming appointment and answering some questions. He laid down on the couch and told me he needed to take a midday rest, and I left. I started reviewing the hardware checklist when I reached the apartment, soon realizing I had forgotten to ask him about his niece and nephew.

I pushed on my bladder to confirm its emptiness, a rigid finger thrust above the lower pelvic ridge. Riding in the truck for an hour would have us arrive at the job site right when the coffee kicked in and before any strenuous work that could prove dehydrating. An eighteen-foot box truck pulled up in front of the apartment, "Two Men and a Truck" written in bold letters on its side over a recent white overcoat. The indentations and scuff marks along the galvanized corner rails testified to either a long service record or aggressive driving.

The truck must have had a first life as a rental given the large seamless molded plastic dashboard and gray vinyl bench seats, the smooth surfaces making the cab spill-proof and easy to clean. Edgar nodded in silence when I entered the cab and then returned to sipping a large Mountain Dew, wedged in between his thighs due to a puzzling lack of cup holders. He appeared to be around medium height, stoutly built, and cube-shaped. He had a layer of muscle and visceral fat that swelled each body part, a thick stump of a neck that merged into his skull and jaw without inflection, a large head requiring using the last plastic snap of his Dodgers baseball hat, and a shiny silver watch embedded in his meaty wrist. This sturdiness reassured me. Since I was serving as a last-minute replacement helper, I assumed Edgar would anchor the lower position when moving bulky items up stairwells.

I wandered into the help wanted ad when looking at various gigs the night before, and I called the listed number directly instead of sending an email. Edgar explained, in a laconic manner that resembled a verbal text message, that his partner had called out sick and emphasized the simplicity of this in-town move: no pianos, pool tables, or other oversize items. I would be paid $120 for maybe six hours of work, much of it driving which sounded good.

My longest sustained conversion of outright manual labor into money had taken place the summer after my sophomore year in college back home in Pennsylvania. I managed to last two months at a paperback printing factory. The offset lithography machine rapidly printed, folded, cut, and delivered "signatures", or roughly thirty-page booklets, fed horizontally onto a table where the operator used wooden end blocks, a hydraulic press, and lacing cord to bale and load the paper onto palettes for later binding and finishing. The unrelenting output of the press required consistent productivity. The repetitive cadence of compressing, tying, and lifting bails of signatures onto the skids became hypnotic. Romance novels and self-help books comprised the bulk of the printed material and classic rock ruled the air. My muscles ached and I relished the two well-defined breaks, subdividing each workday like an uphill 5k race.

The job occupied a slot of memory next to camping in the rain and sleeping in airports, a Type 2 fun that can be painful in the moment, but enjoyable on the drive home blasting emo music. Something about the repetitive manual work appealed to me. Jessica astutely noticed this predilection for perseveration and reminded me of it after listening to my analyses about the perfect ways to dice salad ingredients.

The previous few years saw an increase of connective tissue ailments which I ascribed to age, inactivity, and an inertia against trying physical therapy. My lower back protested after more than five hours in a horizontal position despite OTC anti-inflammatories and various imported ergonomic foam under knee supports and pillows. My right knee flirted with tendonitis every few weeks. A pragmatic solution involved the use of a rainbow of elastic bands but I preferred the economics of a more strenuous approach. Moving would give me a blue-collar satisfaction after a few hours of moderate lifting and stacking of boxes, and I would finish with a happy soreness from an honest day's work.

We started ascending the evergreen spotted foothills about a half-hour into the trip. I asked about Edgar's family and history in the job, each question receiving a simple answer until he turned up the volume on the Spanish radio station, ending the conversation. Perhaps I needed to earn his respect through hard work. My pallid complexion didn't exactly exude vitality and likely gave him a rational fear that he would be forced to shoulder the load all day.

"Keep coming, keep coming," the homeowner stood waiting for us in the driveway and immediately started directing Edgar to back up the truck alongside a sprawling house. "Now cut it hard to the left!"

The box swung into the oval-shaped pavement facing the front door. The single story ranch had an abundance of rough-hewn lumber and square footage. I walked over to the side, scanning for basement windows but thankfully finding none. Two toddlers, a girl and a boy, burst out of the front door and ran towards the back of the parked truck and peppered Edgar with questions while he unlocked the rear roll-up door.

"The wife gets back in about two hours, so let's start with the big stuff. She gets nervous we'll crush something," the man stated, leading us into the house. His cargo shorts, a golf visor with swept-back sunglasses resting on the hat's brim, and an extra eighty pounds matched the style of the house – spacious rooms for living large. Thick, rough-cut timber trusses hung overhead in the sunlit great room, decorated with vintage skis and wooden snowshoes. Large landscape photos and a TV the size of a horse blanket covered the walls. The multi-piece leather sectional looked especially imposing, but at least the house had wide doors. I pegged him for a real estate broker or marketing executive of some kind.

"Are you moving?" I asked Brett after we exchanged names.

"Nah, just clearing out some stuff," he said and took us into the rec room. "Putting some of this into a storage locker, along with a bunch of the tools in the garage. Gotta start the reconquest of the home office."

"What line of work are you in?" I asked.

"Consulting. Content management and brand development," Brett rattled off. "Until the algorithms take my job," he added with a forced laugh.

Edgar slewed from item to item in the room, getting a read from Brett on each one's destination. The ping pong table stayed but the foosball table in the corner went; the wine refrigerator stayed but the recliner went to storage. He placed a blue sticker on the items that were going. The attached garage hosted a large number of boxes and some oversized kids toys as well as the aforementioned tools.

"By the way, the pool table goes too. Can we start with that one?" Brett asked at the end of the tour. "I've already removed the bumpers and felt, just need to load the three slates and the foundation."

Edgar exhaled in disappointment and went to the truck, returning with hump straps – a device with two slings mounted over the shoulders to create a saddle at waist level that can be looped under heavy objects – for the two of us. We slowly humped the first slate out to the truck, taking wide turns like a tractor-trailer and trying to get the kids to not stand in the middle of doors they held open. Lactic acid arrived suddenly when moving the heaviest center slate up the ramp into the box. I suddenly knew for a fact that the Pyramids had been built by aliens, as moving ten-ton stones with human power was clearly impossible. Brett kept checking his phone and ineffectively policing his children, who swarmed around us like bees. The girl took an interest in the ratchet straps and insisted on helping advance them a few clicks. The boy jumped into the cab and managed to turn on both the radio and headlights. The last slate moved at a glacial pace and a hernia felt imminent, my abdominal wall straining under the pressure like a blister. Edgar didn't break a sweat.

While he tied down the bulky items to the wooden slats, I shuttled cardboard boxes and translucent bins stuffed with clothes and decorations to the box, regaining my composure and breath by slowly loading them up on a dolly. Brett took a phone call and walked out to the back patio, spreading out his legs like he was peeing over the edge, talking loudly with a mix of vulgarity and laughter.

Nina should sell him one of her landscape photos, I thought, maybe one of a lone, pensive twisted pine beneath an approaching storm. Our text messages over the previous few weeks were sporadic and breezy, settling into several hour or day-long pauses. I threw out some ideas for infiltrating Transcendent Health but received only an emoji in return. She could be knee-deep in an artistic endeavor or underneath a new boyfriend in Durango. Since moving in the spring, I remained largely on the dating sidelines, occasionally swiping through glossy profiles before bed as more of an attempt at unwinding than an earnest effort of finding a partner. The few matches I had made ghosted me after the first or second exchange. My opening lines suffered from a homespun friendliness, like greeting a barista at a coffee shop, and I suspected that getting a response required more ribald tactics. That seemed like a lot of effort.

One night I took a mental detour down the path of calculating the number of compatible partners, multiplying the fractions of childless women, eligible, modest intelligence, appropriate age range, a few physically attractive attributes, reciprocal interest, shared values, and so on, and the denominator rapidly grew out of hand. The result was two potential matches given the population of the mid-size town. This romantic version of the cosmic Drake equation, a similar series product for the probability of finding communicative extraterrestrials in the universe, sobered any excitement generated by waking up to dating app notifications on my phone.

My general passivity could have landed me in Nina's friend zone, I probably even subconsciously steered myself right into it. I didn't feel prepared for dating or any serious engagement. Even with Nina's smaller frame, my double bed would be punishingly narrow. I usually awoke in the middle of the night to find myself splayed out in the center of the bed like a crime scene chalk outline. The sole bathroom in the apartment lacked an exhaust fan, easily getting blown up after a visit following my morning coffee. My lack of restraint when it came to flatulence would also be problematic. This is before considering the actual mechanics of dating, which now that the weather was getting colder would move away from free outdoor pursuits to costly indoor activities. Despite her artist sensibilities, she would ultimately demand a well-resourced long-term mate.

While I loaded the last box from the garage into the truck, Edgar shifted the items around to create rigid modules, adding ratchet straps and army blankets for cushioning. I reached a cautious armistice with my lower back, resting it for the final round of large items. Brett and his two urchins came up to the box to inspect our progress.

"The boss is running late. She'll need a final walkthrough before we leave, make sure I'm not including a wedding album or something," Brett chuckled and slowly shuffled down the ramp.

I threw on the hump straps again and joined Edgar to move the foosball table from the rec room and table saw from the garage. Once we had those securely in the box, we moved on to the sundry gardening tools and badminton nets, nesting them in the truck like battlefield anti-tank hedgehogs. Brett brought out cans of flavored seltzer water to celebrate the end of the loading, the five of us taking a break on the back patio deck chairs overlooking a canyon of ponderosa pines. The two kids played a sort of checkers game on a nearby table, while Brett regaled us with stories of his San Juan River trips. After receiving an audible text message ding, he announced that he'd deliver any leftover items to the locker himself when meeting us there later. His wife had more errands to run in town and wouldn't be back for a while.

The necessity of large-sized value meals became obvious when we stopped for lunch, my body craving carbonated drinks and calorie-dense foods. The remainder of the trip went well, we moved the slates and other large objects into their final position in the storage locker, Edgar slowing his pace on my account. Brett gave me a $20 tip which seemed both perfunctory and generous at the same time.

I anticipated the trip back to be triumphant – like getting off the second shift at the paper mill had been – collapsing in utter exhaustion and sleeping for ten hours. Instead, we drove in near silence and I spent most of the ride rubbing my knees and lower back. Edgar dropped me off at my apartment and paid cash for the day. I lowered myself out of the truck like a beaten boxer slinking from the ring.

*   *   *

A lanky man came on stage, shook hands with the host, gave a wooden wave to the crowd, and then shoved his hands back in his black faded denim pockets. Kory Gorman, the founder of Xmundio and one of the world's richest people, diffidently moved from one side of the stage to the other as if getting ready to breakdance or freestyle rap.

"We've trained an algorithm to predict my entire talk here at TEDxAustin by feeding it hundreds of speeches from tech company leaders over the last decade." Gorman pulled out and unfolded a dot-matrix printout on green and white striped tractor paper from a briefcase, getting a laugh from the crowd. "Says here that I'm destined to start off with a nerdy joke, thank my significant other for tolerating my work schedule and never-ending awkward stage, mention disruption in a positive way with a historical reference, tout our programs for diversity and empowerment, announce the launch of a new charity, and wear an indie band t-shirt to not look like a billionaire." He crumbled and tossed the paper off the stage. "Now that's out of the way, let's get to it."

"I recently went through a lot of old photo albums and scrapbooks when cleaning out my parent's house. There were three generations of memory boxes." He flipped through a few photos on the screen. Shirtless men sat on naval guns, sepia-toned families posed with tight-lipped smiles, a woman held a baby in front of a tail finned car. "As I went through the pictures, it struck me that everyone looked more or less the same: the same clothes, the same haircuts, the same generally trimmer body shape – basically looking like less attractive versions of Jimmy Stewart and Ingrid Bergman. Now, of course, society back then was less diverse, lower resolution photos mask differences, long exposure times forced everyone into dour expressions, and a lack of options made clothing more homogenous. We're programmed to notice variation along the current cultural axes, the narcissism of small differences thing. But I don't believe that is the whole story. Outside of the idle rich and a few wandering seducers, appearance and more generally physical identity were not curated like they are today. The center of the bell curve curated character," he said, dwelling on the final word.

"I can sense the mental eye rolls now: a social media CEO sermonizing about the importance of character while his company makes money on the endless churn of selfies, the superficial economy of likes and shares, the covert production of consumer demand in your daily feed." Gorman stopped the end of each phrase, flipping through collages of Xmundio content. "The changes in the last half-century weren't flying cars or moon stations but in our minds. Our reality now gets filtered through a series of user interfaces that morph and flex to our desires, leading to a Copernican return to the individual, placing us back squarely in the center of the universe. Your minute-by-minute choices fertilize the digital ecosystem around you – personalized media instead of mass media. This endless feeding of the ego has consequences."

"We know that depression and anxiety are rising around the world." He showed plots of increased anti-depressant usage and suicide rates in developed countries. "Our digital landscape bears some responsibility, and we need to be part of the solution. We've become very good at recognizing behavior patterns and marketing products, with the user's consent of course. We know your new favorite movie before you've watched the trailer. But this is all like watching the shadows on Plato's cave wall, we're gleaning the blurred forms of our user's personalities, only tracking their interactions with a screen."

"Ultimately, each life can be understood as a sequence of mental states. Every experience, every thought, every feeling of joy or despair is an electrochemical condition in the three pounds of wetware between our ears. One hundred fifty years ago we created consumer products from raw materials, seventy-five years ago we created the entertainment and culture sectors, now we will create well-being."

"While I hope the human brain continues to be a mystery well into the future, the mechanics of mental states can be subjected to the same machine learning that diagnoses diseases and recognizes faces. Think of this technology like a life coach, informed by your genetics and neurology, a form of data-driven therapy. You will exert more control over your mental states, strengthening them like physical therapy does for hips and knees. Pharmacological assistance could play a role, but more like a protein shake than steroids; it will open up pathways rather than take shortcuts. There is still this persistent belief that a pill will be a panacea. After all, they are easy to administer and monetize. But to fully utilize our brain's plasticity requires experiential training, something that religions have long accomplished using ritual and practice, like meditation."

"This effort requires baby steps, starting with gathering large amounts of data from diverse demographics. The first deliverables will be modest, maybe a customized wellness schedule based on your genetics and life history. Someone suffering from excessive rumination and mild depression could get a personalized program of interior and exterior activities. The current therapies for well-being – religion, work, social participation – are imposed in an entirely contingent manner, dependent on the specific instances of where you were born, your parents, random friendships you developed in high school. We'll never fully erase that, but maybe we can empower people to reach the summit of a local peak in the landscape of fulfillment in a few years instead of a lifetime."

Gorman held his head up and strode back and forth across the stage. "Xmundio is a large company with lots of resources but we see ourselves as a partner, a minor player in this endeavor, lending data services and analytics to scientists and doctors. We've begun collaborating with labs across the country and funding experiments to shore up the most basic science." Gorman flipped through several slides showing the seals of major universities and excerpts from peer-reviewed publications. "In the same way that we advanced from bloodletting and being victims of devastating disease to modern medicine in 100 years, we're embarking on this century's quest to unlock the mind and decrypt human well-being."

He answered some softball questions and left the stage to modest applause. My knees ached as I got up from the couch to forage in the refrigerator for a snack before bed. I copied the video link and sent it to Nina, then turned on my Do Not Disturb feature and collapsed.

The phone bleated on the ground next to the bed, the horrible sound from the arrival of multiple text messages crashing me out from dreams of liquid reservoirs and tanks, adjustable valves, and water levels beating up and down like a heart. I thrust my left arm out laterally to check the phone, attempting to unplug it with a one-hand maneuver. My left shoulder shouted in pain and met resistance, the joint capsule engaging an inflamed area.

I recognized the pain from fifteen years before when a shoulder impingement required three months of tedious physical therapy. It happened when hanging out with high school friends over Christmas break, the four of us heading to the local gym to play basketball. I had responded to an online post polling those in town for the holidays, which opened an inclusion to a peer group above my normal social level.

We headed down to the rec center basement to lift weights until the church league basketball games ended. Angle iron racks of dumbbells and cracked vinyl benches sat on the industrial carpet, giving the place a prison-like feel. We immediately went over to the flat bench press, setting an Olympic bar across the supports. The weights jumped from a thicker and smaller twenty-five-pound disc to a thinner and much larger diameter forty-five, a dramatic increase in apparent size designed to boost the ego. Hulking figures, likely firefighters or policemen, occupied the rest of the musty room, clanging multiple plates onto the bars with gusto. I knew I had to keep the forty-five-pounders on the bar for the first set, before the onset of muscle fatigue. I squeezed out eight reps for respectability, then shifted to lighter weights. Pain in my shoulder awoke me the next day.

Transcendent Health texted me reminders for my appointment that morning, inserting the requirement that I take my medicine before coming in. I tried to move my elbow laterally out to the side but retracted it quickly because of the pain. The injury would eliminate me from impromptu employment opportunities, but, in reality, driving paid the best, and besides, I drove with a single hand in the six o'clock position anyways. I pulled up the rideshare application and checked the current rates. Business travelers flew on Sundays, making the day ideal for landing drop-off and return trips to the airport.

Fatigue sunk in after the second ride back to the city as dusk arrived, well past the half-life of my morning coffee. The stiffness in my shoulder ebbed and flowed during the day, and I was able to hold it back to a manageable level by keeping my left elbow against my hip in a kind of virtual splint. The pain further complicated my pledge to join a local gym, perhaps one catered towards younger bro culture in an abandoned warehouse or something. A mix of frugality and calorie awareness historically resulted in an ability to reasonably control my body weight, though the upcoming decline in free testosterone and this latest imposed inactivity would accelerate the distribution of mass towards a *skinny fat* physique with a growing soft equator.

After parking back at the apartment, I walked to a recently opened arcade bar, a homey place with a solid selection of local IPAs and several classic cabinet games. The bartender greeted me upon entry. She was uncomfortably gorgeous in a casual sporty way, which felt out of place on an early Sunday evening when the bar was full with the board game crowd. They sat at tables opposite the bar spreading out Magic the Gathering decks and Settlers of Catan expansion sets.

"The arcade games are all free," she said after dropping a pint of hazy IPA on the bar in front of me. I sat on the far end of the bar to maximize my distance from her and reduce accidental staring which ironically gave me even more time to watch her and her yoga pants walk back towards the main section. "The fried pickles will be out in a minute."

A plexiglass window in the bar top revealed a small screen and joystick for an emulator with several early Atari titles. I loaded up Pitfall and advanced to the crocodile stage before landing in the jaws of one of the reptilians. After sensing several phantom vibrations, I stopped checking my phone for Nina's text message reply to the TED talk link I had sent.

"This place would have saved me a college fund's worth of quarters back in the day," a man who looked like an ex-Marine said, placing his amber lager on the bar next to mine. "Mind if I sit here?"

I nodded and paused the game. His tech shirt and garish sneakers suggested he wanted to be some type of athlete. I judged him to be around fifty, give or take ten years. He introduced himself as Oscar.

"Space Invaders challenge?" Oscar asked and got up, sat his beer on top of the arcade cabinet, and started the first game. While the figures looked familiar, I grew up in the later Nintendo era of Tecmo Bowl and Super Mario Bros. He played with a feverish intensity and a degree of talent, judging by the duration of his game. "I feel sorry for kids these days."

"Why's that?"

"They're spoiled by high resolution, plus too many choices in games. I reach a Zen state at some point with these old ones, start seeing through the screen. You're probably too young for pinball or arcades, right?"

"The roller rink had a few before they closed when I was in middle school. Video games became an at-home thing around then," I said, thinking of my generation of atomized individuals obsessively competing against the computer.

"I've got my own war story from the video game crash," he said after getting knocked out by the final fast-moving alien. "I spent the summer of 1983 interning for a company called Imagic in the Bay Area. Tested out some games, made coffee, that sort of thing. The atmosphere back then was electric, a sense of speed and change. Like other bubbles."

"Do you still work in software?" I asked.

"No, I wish. Maybe now I've calmed down enough to sit behind a non-video game screen," Oscar said, bringing over two fresh pints from the bar and placing one next to my empty glass. "Two ACLs ended my dream of becoming a professional skier after college. Bounced between corporate gigs, now semi-retired as a consultant. How about you?"

I told him I was a high school math teacher, but currently taking a sabbatical. After he successfully evaded questions about his work, we settled into a comfortable reminiscence about the history of video games, which got us through the second beer. I asked for ice water, anything over two drinks with only a dozen fried pickles on board would render me prostrate for the evening.

"How are the winters here?" he asked.

"Moved in last spring," I said. "Hopefully the rain shadow keeps the snow in the mountains."

"Where it belongs," Oscar said. "To tell you the truth, my wife has me on a mission scoping out neighborhoods. Her checklist is walkable to a coffee shop and ethnic food, bike trail access, less than ten minutes to a hospital, local art scene. I should have written these down, probably missing a few."

"Not a bad area for that."

"You live around here?" Oscar asked.

"Yes, over near the hospital."

He pulled up a map on his phone, a quilt of green, yellow, orange, and red. "She's into these crime maps. Looks like some petty larceny but not too bad. Do you feel safe?"

"Bit easier as a guy, but yeah."

"What block are you at? It's showing a big difference between the north and south side of the hospital campus," he asked.

"I'm around here," I pointed to a yellow area on the map near the apartment building. "I wouldn't leave my car unlocked but I feel safe."

"Thanks, thanks," Oscar said. "She wants to retire away from Chicago, somewhere she can bike into the foothills but close enough to town for a book club. I'm flying back in a few days. Do you recommend any hikes around here before I leave?"

"The reservoir trail should be less crowded on a weekday. I haven't been but it seems to be popular," I said, hearing this some several riders. Oscar pulled up some photos of it, nodding his head in approval while scrolling through them.

"You want to exchange numbers? Text you if I decide to go?" Oscar asked and gave me his phone number.

I texted him a *yo* message to keep it simple and nonchalant. We shook hands after getting separate checks, Oscar left a $20 tip on the bar on his way out. When I left a few minutes later, I saw him sitting in a cobalt blue crossover SUV, taking notes on a digital tablet and tapping on his dashboard cradled phone before accelerating away.

I opened the door after two rounds of aggressive knocking. Victor's truck sat in the driveway and the mid-morning time was well before his constitutional. After reconfirming that yes, today was the day we agreed on the previous week, I pictured him entangled in the milling machine or otherwise incapacitated, only capable of guttural noises. The number of motorized pieces of equipment available to the man made essentially anything possible.

"Victor, are you home?" I asked as I stepped into the living room. The house looked more cluttered than I remembered it, three used coffee mugs with evaporated syrup rings, unopened letters, and loose hand tools covered the dining room table.

"Out in a few minutes, Martin. Look at the reservoirs in the shop," Victor said from the bathroom, turning on the tap water for noise coverage. "Don't get old."

In the workshop, I found clear acrylic pipes fused onto slightly oversize circular bases, creating mortar-looking cups about the size of sixteen-ounce tallboys. I picked one up and went back to the living room and flipped through the mail. Outside of a phone bill, they all appeared medical in nature. I pulled out a page from an opened one, seeing a table of services quoting endoscopies and some types of scans with acronyms I didn't recognize with a date of two weeks before. I pulled out my phone to take a picture when the bathroom door started to open, quickly jamming the paper back into its envelope.

"Need to add ports on the bottom for barb fittings," Victor picked up the reservoir and rotated it against the light coming in from the kitchen window. "The first container needs an overflow drain for protection. Now we start thinking about this platform."

I unzipped my backpack and pulled out two gear pumps, black plastic housings with D cell battery-sized motors on the back. Victor's face lit up and he asked for a datasheet, then started muttering about how to connect the tubing to the ports on the pump housing. I pulled up a grainy image on my phone with a few numbers that stood out above the Chinese characters, implying the pump worked on twelve volts DC and pumped a half-liter – which was likely per minute and hopefully not per hour. I found the cheap pumps online with free next-day shipping from an industrial supplier.

"Beautiful, probably for metered liquid dispensing. Not food grade," Victor said. He sat down at the table, free-falling the last few inches into the chair and looking towards the door off the kitchen. "We need the digital DC power supply from the basement. Small grey shoebox with a vented housing. Wire strippers too."

The basement looked the same as it had last week, and I wondered if it had been touched since Victor brought up the electronic timers. I went over to a set of boxes on the ground that reminded me of the one with the magnetic waterwheel, then pushed against a few, trying to gauge their contents. Two seemed very heavy, almost cemented to the floor, probably filled with tools and heavy motors. The exterior of several boxes darkened to a deep caramel by infused dust and slow oxidation over decades, like an old newspaper, and these had one or two-digit numbers indelibly marked on each side. The shelf of electrical equipment contained mostly grey boxes with different LCD front panels. I grabbed a long narrow one with voltage and current knobs, then headed back upstairs.

We benchmarked the pump flow rate with a stopwatch and worked through the best way to gravity prime the pumps. Victor stayed remarkably calm with me spilling water on the kitchen floor in the process of setting up the tanks and the hasty assemblies of clamps and couplings. We agreed that the water source, pumps, and reservoir tubing connections needed to be buried inside the base platform but somehow had to avoid turning it into a shallow dog bowl prone to spill. The only connection of the pumps and holding tank to the upper containers would be through a hidden inlet and outlet on the bottom of the first reservoir.

"Is this a new design?" he asked after picking up a few pages that had spilled out of my backpack when I pulled out the gear pumps. I went to the hospital two nights before after feeling guilty about spending three hours hopping around Wikipedia entries on the Eastern Front, bringing a pad of grid paper. I sketched out hydraulic networks on the chair in Intensive Care without disruption. "Is there a regeneration path in this one?"

"I keep thinking about a more general liquid computer, adding in some return flows. Or somehow communicating the error back like a negative feedback control system."

"The most interesting machines involve some level of recursion, an internal awareness looping back on itself. The water integrator probably did this in some manner," Victor said and looked at the rest of the drawings. "What is this design, a rotary sprinkler?"

"It's one of those spinning carousel chairs little kids ride, the angle gets more horizontal the faster it spins. I pictured some cups of water, fed by the central spinning post, being raised and changing their feed and emptying rate, maybe generating complicated patterns."

"Turning simple rotation into complexity," Victor said and sketched lightly on the pad. "The problem is that the changing weight of the cup acts on both the centrifugal force and gravity making the angle stay the same, but perhaps the rope – the feed tube in our case – is stretchy. Both the supply and emptying rate would depend on the mass in different ways, perhaps creating some storage and release dynamics. We'll call it the Martian carousel."

I gave a nasal laugh. "Is that how your waterwheel works?" I asked, realizing it was time to learn the truth about the machine.

"Malkus developed it in the 1960s so he deserves the credit. I only built it."

"What about the magnetics and the circuit? That's a big change."

"I'm a philistine when it comes to electronics. It is clear why electrons were recruited for computation by evolution and later Silicon Valley. Some materials conduct electricity with ease, others are near-perfect insulators, others pass current when you apply an electric field. What other property spans over this many orders of magnitude?" I shook my head quietly in acknowledgement. "Control is ethereal and exact, superior to any mechanical system. But I would have gone with an actual waterwheel."

"Then why did you build it?"

"I needed to see it in the real world, not just a concept," Victor said. "What are you trying to find out?"

"A lot of people want that waterwheel." I waited for a reaction.

"Including you, until you returned it," he said.

"An art collector made a shady cash offer and two siblings have come forward saying it's theirs. Does that ring a bell?"

"A well-dressed brother and sister?" he asked.

"Those are the ones. They claim it's an inheritance."

"Well, they've earned it through hard work, and their lawyer has to justify his retainer too," Victor said. I could tell his brain had shifted gears from the faraway look in his eyes. "Irina and Roman, my niece and nephew. Something has changed."

"What?"

"They are in control now, and more professional and litigious than their mother's family who settled matters by force. Someone tipped them off." Victor looked directly in my eyes after saying this.

"I posted a picture on a collectible website to get more information."

"The fetishes of the art world move in unpredictable ways, some interesting feedback loops there," Victor said.

"Two-dimensional art is a tired static medium and people want something that shows movement like a living thing but is still sufficiently eccentric, I guess. You can see it in architecture too, designers now show off ventilation ducts and trusswork in the ceiling rather than sealing them off. People like the old stuff, the nineteenth century gears and pulleys," I said, long ago concluding that framed fine art was the domain of old people with too much money on their hands.

"What do they call that, steampunk?"

"Yeah," I said. "Leo designed the waterwheel? It's his machine?"

Victor got up from the table and came back with a large brown notebook, its edges curled over with use like ski tips. Some of the green pages had sets of incomplete sketches while others contained detailed cross-section views and equations. Victor turned to the page with the waterwheel and flipped the notebook around to face me. It was less of a polished design than a collegiate physics problem set – arrowed vectors showing the gravitational, rotational, and spring forces on the magnetics – and an electrical schematic of the sensor and amplifier circuits driving the electric motor. The author tried to predict the rotation speed and direction of the wheel over time, plotting exponential decay, periodic oscillation, and a third curve that moved chaotically, adding an exclamation point next to it. A date of April 14, 1992 was scribbled on the lower left corner of the pages.

"These are Leo's designs for the waterwheel," Victor said. The next page had more incomplete equations. By the following page, the sketches were of a different machine, one with a linkage driving the movement of some underwater creature.

"You built these?" I asked.

"Some of them, like the waterwheel and drunken mouse. Leo created these designs between early 1991 and late 1993. The first set of sketches are simpler and heavily mechanical like industrial art. Later designs are more abstract, block diagrams with calculating modules. Some are nonsense, indistinguishable from doodles."

I flipped to the middle of the notebook, to a web of boxes connected with arrows, annotated with Cyrillic script and numbers. The last entry was dated December 1993. I kept flipping through the empty pages and came across another set of sketches. These had sharply drawn lines and dimensional callouts with exploded views like engineering drawings. There were no dates in the footer.

"Not up to ISO dimensioning and tolerancing standards but still readable. It's more forgiving when the machinist and drafter rent out the same head space," Victor said and explained that some of the callouts were datum lines. These references enabled defining locations of precision holes and features. "Leo had the inspiration and I delivered the perspiration. In reality, he could have done both but he didn't have the time. It was more of a hobby for him, a way to step away from the madness of post-Soviet Russia. We coped with the changes in different ways."

"What was it like, living through that time?" I defaulted to a view of history as something that happened primarily in books.

"When you're young or sufficiently intoxicated, the world vibrates with possibility. Bizarre scenarios condense out of the atmosphere: maybe you wake up on a stranger's floor with a tattoo or sleep with your high school gym teacher after an underground heavy metal concert. We felt the same level of tenuous excitement after the end of the Cold War, everything moved at a feverish pace that no one could predict. The honeymoon period didn't last long. Galloping inflation drove people into poverty, like our parents."

"How did you survive?" I asked, picturing bread lines comprised of babushkas in large hats bracing themselves against the Siberian wind.

"We all reinvented ourselves to some extent. My friend from the RTG maintenance work had a rich uncle who purchased millions of state-issued ownership vouchers from citizens desperate to buy food, which allowed him to grab a majority stake in a newly formed oil company in Tatarstan," Victor said slowly, using the edge of a letter to sweep away spilled salt on the table. I wanted to get up to get a drink and down an Ibuprofen to combat the headache I knew was coming, but this moment seemed special, like I was taking a confession. "The company had issues with the local Kazan gangs. Most were just street-level thugs looking to make some rubles through simple extortion or grab trucking supply contracts. My friend hired me as a handyman, someone who could get things to work. I installed a set of surveillance cameras around the refinery and the offices, simple closed-circuit television networks which Mikhail, the owner, became quite obsessed with. He later asked me to tap the phones and set up microphones in the break rooms."

"Leo had a hard time with the democratic revolution. Being a favorite son of the old regime and the huge cuts in defense programs put him out of a job. Since much of his work was classified, the retirement of the old guard removed most people who could vouch for his brilliance. These black projects were never acknowledged in the public. He briefly thought about coming to America, a few of his engineering colleagues were gobbled up by US defense contractors like the German rocket scientists after WWII, but his wife Alexandra wouldn't have it, her roots were too deep in the Motherland. Having a wife and two children raises one's level of risk aversion, making it harder to move to Kazan for a year or two."

"Is that when he started designing the machines?" I asked.

"Yes. Scheduling freight movement for a trucking company was a letdown after dashing around the country solving puzzles. He got bored," Victor said and asked if I was thirsty. I jumped at the opportunity and got us each a cup of tap water, choosing two beige mugs with university seals instead of cloudy glasses.

"I first saw the notebook when visiting our parents over Christmas in 1992. Leo and I were working together fixing a toilet and sink in their apartment. Getting tools and materials for plumbing in those days took an Apollo 13 level of improvisation but we figured it out. He said that the freight logistics only took about half of his time and Alexandra didn't want him hanging around the house. She and her sisters liked having it as their domain. He started sketching out these machines then, in the office between phone calls to warehouses and cargo companies."

I flipped through the pages and Victor gave a commentary on each design. He attempted to build around half and only about half of those produced a viable outcome. Some remained undecipherable and others, once built, proved uninteresting or simplistic. "Are only some of the machines chaotic?" I asked.

"He added an instability to some of them, those were his favorites," Victor said. "Mechanical automatons have been around since the Greeks. The genius of the ancients is lost to history: self-opening doors, moving statues, that sort of thing. The pinnacle of mechanism design is Harrison's clock. You need to read his story, a self-taught carpenter who built an accurate marine chronometer and won a British prize for figuring out longitude at sea. Leo's linkages are not the grasshopper escapement but their instability makes them unique. The chaotic elements feel more natural, a potential for emergent complexity despite simple origins, like starting with a single rotating motor. I suppose they were a reflection of his own life which narrowed into regimen but had a looming macroscale instability, both a threat and a potential for escape."

"Why did Leo stop designing these?" I asked.

"The situation got worse in 1993. The trucking company went into bankruptcy and Leo was out of work again. We started talking on the phone more often and I could tell it was eating him up to feel useless." Victor spun the book around and looked through the last pages of Leo's drawings. "I helped get him a job out in Irkutsk, Eastern Siberia. A new division in my company got a contract from Gazprom to develop a drilling method to bring the massive Kovykta gas condensate field to market, an actual engineering position with decent pay. Alexandra didn't want him to go, she thought he should keep pressing to get his old satellite job back. He couldn't resist having something to design by this point and told her he had to take it."

A reflection of the late morning sun off the roof of a cobalt blue SUV through the front window caught my eye. The car was slowly rolling down the street. The model and year seemed to be the same as Oscar's, the gregarious guy from the arcade bar. I jumped up and headed over to the window above the sink to watch it stop next to my car and then speed away, the sunlight too bright for me to make out any occupants. The license plate ended in 343, an easy-to-remember cube of seven.

"Sudden bout of dehydration?" Victor asked.

"Would your niece and nephew hire someone to follow me?"

"Probably to gather information to use against me or you," Victor said. "They prefer to solve problems with legal and economic leverage. Their mother sought a more personal form of justice. I don't blame her for kicking me out of their family after Leo disappeared."

"Disappeared?"

"I flew to Irkutsk after Alexandra called me crying. She hadn't heard from Leo in three days. There remains a fear about the dark interior of the continent: the gulags, the bears, and the punishingly cold weather. After finding his apartment empty, I searched the area, driving from Lake Baikal out to Tulun with hopes of spotting him at a gas test rig. I mentally prepared myself for a kidnapping or finding him hospitalized from an exploded gas well. After looking for a whole week, I convinced the landlord to let me back into his apartment, took the notebook, and repacked his suitcase," Victor said and put his elbows on the table, holding up his head with joined hands under his chin. He continued at a slow measured pace like he was giving a deposition.

"I thought of ways to leave the suitcase at their front door without speaking to them. I could drop off the luggage and later claim a pressing return flight to Kazan. In the end, I told her what she already knew, that he was missing without any clear reason. It is the most terrible kind of absence, the one that holds you hostage and wondering for years. You doubt your marriage and blame your suspicious brother-in-law. She never accepted his death, refused to file the paperwork to declare him dead. I suppose there were also tax benefits to claiming he was still alive."

"What do you think happened to him?" I asked and couldn't help but wonder: an unreported hunting accident, ankles chained to concrete blocks on the bottom of Lake Baikal, an escape to Southeast Asia.

"Part of me waits to get a letter from him each Christmas but I know he's gone. I can get leaving Alexandra, but he cared about the children too much to disappear." Victor said, the silence hanging in the air.

"I'm sorry, it doesn't make any sense," I said, struggling to find a non-religious condolence.

"It should have been me that disappeared."

"Why is that?" I asked.

"I already accepted the risks of working in that environment, the hostile rivals, the bribes. It's like inviting a friend on a hike above the tree line in a thunderstorm, the air is charged and lightning is ready to break it down."

"Couldn't it just be random?"

"It's like everything else, a biased randomness. I understand why Irina and Roman are vengeful."

"What is special about now though?"

"I suspect Alexandra is out of the picture. They know I live around here or at least can figure it out with a little work. They are now the rightful heirs."

"To machines they know nothing about. Why didn't you put your name on them?"

"It didn't feel right and I didn't want to incite more ire from Alexandra and her side of the family. I submitted the first machines anonymously which created some interest, then added Leo's name to the bottom of a set for a traveling exhibit called *Behind the Iron Curtain*, along with a short description of each," Victor said, ending with a phlegmatic cough. "I sold a few of them to raise money to move to America. A single middle-aged man with an estranged family is even more pathetic in Russia than here; I had to leave. I think some of these devices are in private collections, the owners probably afraid to turn them on and risk damaging them. I stopped maintaining them until two years ago when the college pushed me into retirement."

"Will you hand over the machines if the two of them confront you?" I asked.

"Not if they come with a lawyer and demand it," Victor said. "I'm sure you've read enough novels to know that Russian families are always complicated."

"Do you ever travel back there?"

"I went back once after my mother died. I expected a flood of memories and emotions but everything seemed cold, like watching it through a window or something. Enough of my monologue, let's get to work."

We walked back to the workshop, retreating to the sweet smell of cutting oil and ozone from starting up the mill and wood lathe motors.

I began to suspect a psychoactive component to the little white ellipsoidal pills I was taking each morning. My drug use history was comically pedestrian, limited to nicotine, alcohol, trace amounts of THC, and a few one-night stands with study aiding amphetamines. This new effect was subtle and more of a mindset than a palpable sensation – no euphoric feelings or hallucinations. In the previous few days, I had felt a greater degree of immediacy with the world, an inquisitiveness neurally mothballed since my youth, and a felicity juggling free associations. My mental models still skewed towards the technical but now occasionally managed to escape from a default state of self-absorption. A walk around the block became an expedition into front lawn biomes and musings on post-war architecture. This buoyancy was not totally foreign to me, but now felt more easily triggered and sustained.

I increased the temperature of the shower to amniotic levels, reaching the end of travel on the single handle valve. An ideal thermal fluid, water boasted a high specific heat, low viscosity, high surface tension, and accessible freezing and melting points – any one of these being potentially critical to the proliferation of life. A water main break quickly crowns the fluid as the king of the essential utilities over electricity and natural gas. I watched the eddies around my feet collect and accelerate towards the drain. No current computing machine could predict the exact turbulent effects of this open channel flow created by the real-life water computer, a beautifully chaotic system.

I watched an online video of a simulated Lorenz waterwheel, showing a constant rotation for low filling rates but turning into a chaotic system at higher flows. Despite the apparent chaotic motion over short time scales, the center of mass traced out two distinct lobes over time, the system hypnotically evolving towards these attractor structures. Biological and cultural attractors created planes of behavior, each agent moving in a locally chaotic fashion, feeling the illusion of free will as their center of mass passed through the center of rotation and briefly stopped the wheel, like an inverted pendulum waiting to fall to one side. The upper bucket fills and the wheel plunges down, tumbling back into the attractor's orbits.

I started to feel guilty about the wanton length of the shower, flippantly using potable water carefully diverted from forest streams into man-made reservoirs several thousand feet in elevation above the city in this arid land, not to mention the ancient carbon required to heat it up and now floating in the air in an oxidized state, blanketing heat against the planet. Despite the waste, the literal and metaphorical flows of material and energy humbled me and made me realize that even the most revolutionary technology will eventually become routine.

A surprising number of hairs hung onto the angled rear wall of the tub beyond the reach of the falling droplets. I didn't recall there being so many before, the two-inch-long fibers assuming a range of curves under the light mist: a woman's lower buttocks, a single eyebrow lifted in excitement or anger, the catenaries of hanging chains, and the kind of smooth non-letter forms used in corporate logos to represent smiles or birds in flight, the visual equivalent of easy to pronounce vowel ending drug names.

I distinctly remember my maternal grandfather having wispy white hair on the top of his head, but no visible bald regions. This offered me some solace but my thinning was already noticeable and now required an intentional randomized dispersal of the upper follicles using a clay pomade to cut down lines of sight to the underlying white scalp, whose crest I saw a few months ago, the hair collimated and easy to see through like a stand of trees after a forest fire. My hair was still serviceable when viewed at a professional distance, especially from port and starboard. I stepped out of the shower when the water started getting cold and splayed out on the bedroom carpet to air dry.

*   *   *

I stared up at the peak of the thatched roof, where the bamboo and grass stalks spread out radially from a single point, scanning for defects in its symmetry. We were three minutes into a ten-minute silent meditation, past the body scans and visualization prompts from our guide, a Southern California surfer turned shaman named Slade. He secured the use of one of the village elder's huts for Sunday late afternoon and invited Jessica and me to one of his sessions, advertised as some amalgam of meditation, gestalt therapy, and general mysticism. Slade ostensibly performed some type of community outreach in Senegal though his real talent seemed to be avoiding work.

I tried to breathe through my stomach, forcing it to rise and fall with each inhale and exhale. The neutral position of my abdominal wall had now sunk to well below my rib cage. I lost about fifteen pounds during the year and a half in country, the earth-colored one-pot meals having no gastrointestinal residence time despite heavy Imodium use. This returned me to a college-level weight but instead of rangy I felt angular and atrophied. I would lobby for someplace cooler with bland food when we superimposed the results of my humanitarian and Jessica's artist-in-residence applications the next week.

"Isn't it magnificent to experience ourselves expanding into this space, our boundaries lifting away?" Slade asked, which caused Jessica and me to sit up and face forward. "I hope you enjoyed that practice."

"Really good," Jessica responded as she wiggled to sit upright at attention. Slade's use of the term *practice* annoyed me, one meant to signal humility and continual improvement but instead conjuring images of grab-assing Little Leaguers and smug low expectations.

"Jess, please open up about where you're at," he prompted.

"I love it here, love the kids, love the community, but I feel stifled. I used to be moved to tears over a beautiful landscape, capturing an idea with art, making love. But now it's just one day after another." My first instinct was to reach across and hug her, as this remained a reliable form of affection. "Our relationship feels like a friendship and it's eating me up inside."

"Having a friendship instead of an intimate connection?" Slade repeated back in the form of a question.

"I feel selfish for saying this but I don't feel special. A childless thirty-something woman bouncing around the third world pretending to be an artist but instead being dirt poor and invisible."

"Invisible?"

"As a recognized artist, what my parents wanted."

"My girlfriend Olivia likes to talk about the dominant narrative," he said, sweeping his Kurt Cobain-esque dirty blonde chin-length hair behind his ears and pausing in thought. "The dominant narrative of Western society says artists need to be shown in galleries rather than inside the minds of thousands of little kids."

"That's true," Jessica admitted.

"And your relationship?"

"I feel invisible there too. He's always busy watching documentaries or reading history books. It's like he's eighty years old or something. The most emotion I get out of him is when I cut the tomatoes too big for a salad."

"Martin, how does it make you feel when Jess says that?" Slade asked. I had expected a guided meditation and casual therapy, not couples counseling. No one called her Jess except me and close friends.

"It makes sense, I suppose consuming information is a coping mechanism of some sort."

"Tell me more," Slade directed.

I went on to lay out an abbreviated history, highlighting the death of my father and refuge of intellectual status-seeking in high school, then late-blooming into substance use and one main romantic pursuit. We talked about my narrowing social network, the fading nodes of high school and college friends living across an ocean. The personal account ended with us as international itinerants.

"Do you like being a stranger?" he asked.

"I guess it gives me an excuse to be anti-social," I said.

"I still love the adventure of it. For me, it's a social challenge," Jessica added.

"But it makes Martin retreat further into himself," Slade said. He waited for me to agree with his insight but gave up after twenty seconds of silence. He pulled out a worn paperback from his Baja jacket-looking drawstring bag. "Olivia gave me this book. You should read it."

He handed me *Don't Ask Me About It: Escaping the Tyranny of Masculinity*. I glanced at the back, which touted the book for decrypting outward emotional detachment, workaholism, and anger as attempts to avoid confronting male depression.

"I think you'll connect with it, I did," Slade said. "You and Jess are a team. She needs you to open up emotionally."

"Shouldn't team members get married?" I asked.

"Marriage is just a piece of paper, a construct," Slade said.

"The dominant narrative," Jessica added.

"Exactly," Slade said. "The book talks a lot about the false idols of a patriarchal society. It will take a lot of rehabilitation to break free from it, but that's what Jess needs you to do. Have you both decided what's next after Senegal?"

"Hopefully a residency for me and some high school teaching for Martin," Jessica said. "What about you?"

"Back to California, maybe starting a mindfulness practice. It's time to head home." Slade sat up and started rolling up his mat. "I'm leading a sunrise meditation tomorrow, you interested?"

"Of course, stop by your place for coffee ahead of time?" Jessica asked as we both got up. Slade nodded then greeted the wizened village elder who entered and started arranging pots on the stove. We walked out into the early evening heat and dusty streets. Life thrived in the smoke and coastal humidity but I craved seeing a clear night sky, that precise cold vacuum.

I read Slade's recommended book over the next few months, generally agreeing with its diagnosis of male depression. Like alcoholism or original sin, complete elimination was impossible, at best it could be continually managed by something equivalent to a twelve-step plan. Kazakhstan could be the first step.

* * *

I shifted back into the reality of laying naked on the bedroom carpet. Victor had a long-term relationship with the brilliance of the mechanical world, the joys of intelligent creation. I could lean into my weaknesses without guilt. He offered a pursuit of pure knowledge, something to transcend narcissism and the irrelevant in-fighting of humanity.

A text message from Nina dinged on my phone:

Gonna escape the city for a hike and overnight camp after the appointment tomorrow morning. Got an extra sleeping bag – lemme know.

I gave it a few minutes to respond to avoid looking overeager.

"We'll swing south to pick up some traps," Nina said over the post-punk music on the stereo. "You'll like this area, right at the tree line."

"Traps?" I pictured a bear gnawing at its leg which was caught in one of those spring-loaded jaws of metal.

"Camera traps. They sense motion and take photos or video," Nina said. "A friend and I adapted some used commercial traps with better cameras. They are strapped to some trees up there and camouflaged. Forgot to record the GPS coordinates, but I might have a picture of a few."

"Trying to catch Bigfoot?" I asked.

"Uh, he goes by Sasquatch in these parts," she answered with a smile, taking sips out of the gas station coffee we got on the way. "As a kid, you think the world is crawling with animals but these cameras get mostly ptarmigans and squirrels but today's a bear day, though, I can feel it."

I worked on my nasty Colombian dark roast coffee, its inky color unphased by cream. I moved her wallet from the central cup holder to a shelf under the console, compressing a set of receipts and hot sauce packets to make space. The handsewn rainbow trifold didn't quite close all the way, showing a stack of thick stock papers that looked like either loyalty rewards or business cards. I considered engineering her driver's license to accidentally fall out for some gentle teasing but decided to reserve that as a future option.

The rear seats were folded down flat and hosted a set of unmarked plastic containers next to my two cloth grocery bags. I had stuffed a change of clothes with extra socks into one, while the other carried pretzels, sunscreen, a headlamp, a large Ziploc of various travel-sized toiletries, and a polycarbonate water bottle. I felt blithely unprepared without knowing the altitude of the campsite, but showing up with an international travel-sized expandable suitcase was unthinkable.

"Was your fMRI different this morning?" Nina asked.

"Were they trying to hypnotize us?" I returned. The prior uses of the machine were goal-oriented, asking us to solve puzzles or conjure scenes in our minds. But that day's test used soothing music and gave instructions for controlled breathing, putting me close to falling asleep.

"Some sort of meditation thing," she said dismissively. "I'm too restless for that stuff, like trying to take a border collie on a slow walk. They mentioned something about loading a meditation module into our app, probably getting a baseline measurement."

"I could use it, limit the constant processing," I said.

"This is my meditation, escaping the city and hitting the cold air of the mountains," Nina said, cracking the window and gripping the top of the door with her left hand. "Ideally, we'd have taken off at like five o'clock in the morning, still tired but ready to kick the shit out of ourselves with a few thousand feet of elevation gain before the herd gets on the trail."

The all-wheel-drive station wagon developed a throaty metallic whirl on the uphill climb. We joined the state highway heading west and traffic became competitive, wolf packs of pickup trucks with recreational equipment passing the slower motorhomes and trailers. Nina slid between lanes easily, only slightly depressing the turn signal without making it click into place, as she moved back and forth like a skier in a giant slalom race. She must have driven this route through the mountains before.

"Are these pills doing anything for you?" she asked.

"I was agnostic until a few days ago. I'm finding myself more interested in the beauty of mundane objects, like marveling at this dead tree outside my apartment for five minutes. It must have stood there for thirty years, the bark now completely removed and bleached by the sun like driftwood," I responded, which was completely honest and not said to appeal to her artistic side. "Maybe I'm just sleeping sounder, not unconsciously disturbed every five minutes by the cycling of the air conditioner."

"Have you dropped acid?" she asked casually.

"No, never. Just the vanilla drugs."

"I'm not feeling shit with these pills, at least not yet," she said, raising her eyebrows and shaking her head. An irrepressible body language made it easy to gauge her feelings, and I could tell this was a sign of resignation not desperation. "You remind me of my friends who take acid or mushrooms. They say it dissolves your default programming and you see beauty in everything, plus some mind-warping aspects of course."

"How does it feel to you?"

"Oh, I haven't done it. My oldest brother developed some mental health stuff that could be genetic. The thing is I think I need it or some type of rewiring."

"I'd be afraid of the bad trip," I said, thinking back to smoking schwag in late high school and driving home going fifteen miles per hour, convinced that the cops were in hot pursuit.

"A guide is necessary to create the right setting," Nina replied. "I'm wondering about this drug trial. From what you're telling me and after watching that TedX talk by Gorman, I wouldn't be surprised if it is working on the same neurochemicals as psychedelics, but somehow suppressing the perceptive distortions, keeping you functional but still seeing the sublime. I'm totally jealous."

"I could see that. Though Gorman implied that any chemical solution would be only part of the treatment, more about just gathering data," I said, thinking back to the talk. "Whatever it is, it's very subtle. Maybe I've climbed up the happiness scale from a four to a five."

"You notice how you get a new bottle of pills every week?" Nina asked and I nodded. "They could be alternating between the drug and placebos, maybe micro-dosing for a week and then off, some sort of training."

"Hmm, yeah, yeah." Nina was clearly more invested in the outcome of the trial than I was, working out possible scenarios and subversive motives. I wondered if she had been truthful with Transcendent about her family history of mental illness. "Like sleep medication. You take that long term and develop a dependency, the quality of sleep deteriorating over time. Better to use it temporarily as a reset and reinforce the connection between laying horizontally and sleeping."

"Douche bag!" Nina yelled and smashed a palm into the center of the steering wheel to blare the horn. A raised pickup truck with double back wheels cut us off in a large sooty cloud of black smoke from their illegally modified diesel engine. The side mirrors extended outboard like horns and hung into the other lanes. "Hate that guy. Probably my damn cousin."

"Huh, looks like his truck nuts haven't descended yet," I said, picturing the hanging plastic scrotum attached to the rear bumper of similar vehicles.

"Oh my God, yes," Nina said, struggling to gulp down coffee before bursting out laughing. "I forgot about those things. Feel free to DJ on my phone."

We talked about camera traps and photography over the music, which had shifted to upbeat indie-pop. Nina conceded that while framed landscape photography still sold, anything novel would require a new medium or different modalities like the use of UV light or insect vision. She handed me her phone, which showed a photo of green, beige, and blue particleboard terraces for a 3D topographical map.

"Tons of outdoorsy people here would eat that up," I said, zooming in to look at the piece which seemed to be the island of Kauai. "Maybe include ski hills, prominent mountain peaks, something like that."

My phone dinged loudly. It was a text from Pierre Mercer, the collector. He wanted to set up a "three-party talk about the artwork." It sounded like the two of us were one party; Irina, Roman, and their attorney the second; and Victor the third. He must have figured out that the estate sale story was a lie and looked to broker some agreement between Victor and his nephew and niece, but his incentives weren't clear.

"Your girlfriend?" Nina asked.

"She just sent over some nudes," I answered and turned off the phone. This produced a small laugh. "Someone I met a few weeks back. A collector straight out of central casting."

"Oh, really?"

While Nina would probably appreciate the drama, I knew better than to draw her in, perhaps out of a selfishness towards the machines. "He's an odd duck. We met at a Meetup during a film festival over the summer. Nice guy, maybe we'll grab coffee."

She pulled over to the shoulder, the change in speed causing the seat belt strap to clamp down. This jogged her t-shirt up, exposing a tattoo of a winding serpent around a twisted staff, a medical symbol of some sort. Tattoos are seldom orphans and I tried to scan around for others.

"Sorry, hold on," she reached her right arm across my chest, like holding back groceries or a dog, as we lurched onto a rutted gravel road narrowly cut between the pine trees. "Not on this for too, too long."

I had doubts about the legality of the unmarked road but presumably it was some sort of National Forest easement or a utility service road, hopefully rarely patrolled. Nina had found a campsite here a few years back over the Fourth of July when all designated sites were booked. We headed towards a green area on the map which suggested some type of public land.

*   *   *

When we reached our destination, Nina changed into leggings and a flannel shirt. The trees by now were stunted and bare on their windward side, the vegetation becoming more clumped and sparser. I offered to carry her backpack but she refused so I followed her along a nebulous trail swinging my water bottle by its plastic hook.

"Two traps are along the edge of the forest here and two up at the lake. Keep an eye out for thunderheads," Nina said as she sliced through the woods at a quick pace. I didn't understand my exact role so I started scanning trees for camouflaged bricks strapped onto their trunks. The midday sun had heated the pine trees, producing a pleasant evergreen smell. This feeling of serenity drew me off task until I wandered into a subalpine meadow. A few cumulus clouds peaked over the ridge but their bottoms remained white.

"Found one!" she exclaimed and I headed over towards her. "It took one hundred and twenty photos, good sign, good sign."

"This must be what hunters feel like when an elk finally wanders past them," I said. "Maybe I'll just look for the salt lick you set out?"

Nina laughed lightly and moved on ahead, clearly much less affected by the thin air than I was. For the next hour, we swept back and forth in the woods like mowing a field. She identified wildflowers and cautioned against trampling delicate areas. After analyzing a photo she took in late spring, we finally located the second unit, which sat about seven feet off the ground over what must have been a snowdrift the past winter. Only thirty-two pictures. She would go through the smart card later with a laptop.

We left for the lake after a lunch of peanut butter and jelly on dark rye, now getting firmly above the tree line to the alpine zone of succulents and grasses, most of which had turned brown from the drought and freezing nights. We entered a cirque surrounded by mountains on three sides, a lake positioned at the far end.

"Check them for stability first," Nina said, climbing up onto a field of rocks ranging in size from water coolers to Volkswagens. "Scree fields are not the place to break a leg."

She said the small creatures barking at us were pikas, a relative of rabbits, who somehow lived here year-round. Bighorn sheep and mountain goats came through the area in the summer and were target prey for her camera traps. A few fissures of snow clung on the north faces of the mountain but otherwise, early fall made it look like a craggy alien outpost, dominated by rocks standing inviolate against time.

We made it to Upper Grizzly Lake, a small body of water any East Coaster would call a pond, but it made up for its lack of size with beauty, a clear pool reflecting the mountain peaks and sky. We found the other two cameras in short order. One was sheltered amongst shoreline boulders and the other jammed in a concealed pocket near a small cairn of rocks. They had collected eighty and seventy-two photos, a source of excitement for Nina. She tossed the camera traps in her backpack and hopped over to the rock where I was sitting, pulling out two apples from her bag.

"Is that an old mine?" I asked, pointing to a small dark brown shed supported by two weakly-gusseted timber columns on the far side of the ridge. A sulfur yellow-tinged alluvial fan spread down the mountain face below the structure.

"Weird, I never noticed that," she said, biting her lower lip in thought. "Let's go check it out, then we'll get up on the ridge."

"Is there a trail?"

"It's all rock up here, no trails. I'm thinking we go left of that chute and cut over. From the mine, we'll tough it out towards the saddle and see if we're dealing with a knife-edge up there."

"No problem. I've totally acclimated to the altitude in the last three hours."

We hydrated and headed out towards the mine. The slope increased abruptly, becoming a staircase made by a drunken Titan. The large talus abruptly changed to finer gravel, which gave the appearance of an easier traverse, but the rocks were at their limiting angle of repose, sliding out from under me with each step. I fell into the mountain a few times which Nina noticed and slowed down.

"This is getting a little tricky," Nina said. "I really needed this though, being physically challenged and getting away." I stopped to catch my breath and she continued. "I feel like an old junkie sometimes, the neurochemical or whatever threshold to feeling alive has been increased so I'm literally climbing a mountain now."

"The flywheel in my brain takes a while to get started now too," I said between gasps.

"Maybe I'm a lecherous old man, needing more and more extreme stuff to get off. It's always a man that is debauched, though, right?"

I laughed in agreement, wondering what her more porous verbal filter meant. We continued a largely sideways trek across the mixed rock until we reached the mine. Its small metal roof had entirely rusted away except for the standing seam ribs, the remaining wood joints and studs were stained a rusty brown. While the external structure had mostly deteriorated, the large inset header and timber columns at the entrance to the mine remained intact.

"It's amazing this thing is still standing, given the environments," I said, trying to look into the mine shaft. Nina stood on a sturdy-looking piece of structure and pointed the flashlight of her phone into the abyss. The shaft narrowed, probably having suffered collapses over the century-plus since it was last in use. A Three Musketeers wrapper with typography from before our time sat around five feet in, snagged against a rock.

Nina pulled out her camera and took a few shots, then backed up and used rocks to steady her tripod for some external views. She lamented that the mine's machinery had been taken or rusted away but it remained a cool site. We agreed on it being some prospector's summer home in the Rockies, going after silver and coming up empty-handed.

The wind picked up as we headed further up the face towards the ridge, the late afternoon sun now below the brim of our hats. Large talus returned on the ascent, their angular faces more stable than the loose rock but requiring full-body engagement. The thin air produced a sweet lightheadedness and I kept reminding myself to keep at least three points in contact: two feet and an arm or two arms and one foot, and not look down. As we approached the top, the sun disappeared as a set of dark grey cumulonimbus clouds moved in from the West, like the Royal Navy Grand Fleet steaming over the horizon.

"Shit, we need to move. Let's just peak over the ridge," Nina said.

It wasn't a knife-edge but didn't offer much firm footing. Downdrafts arrived from above and the exposure suddenly felt acute, a misstep would produce a fall of several hundred feet. I thrust a leg into a crack in the granite and peered over the edge. To the east, great coniferous forests descended to the plains, that ancient inland sea. After grabbing a few pictures, we started heading down the mountain, butt sliding on the loose sections and moving quickly on the stable areas, the additional kinetic loading absorbed by the knees. I struggled to keep up with Nina who accelerated as the rain started coming down, stopping to wait for me a few times and making a joke about my height being a liability in an electrical storm.

The temperature fell precipitously as the drops became a downpour. The rain turned to blueberry-sized hail which shot peened our bodies as we sped up to a brisk jog leaving the cirque. Trees offered protection from lightning and once we entered them Nina came to a complete stop, holding out her arms. I gave her a firm hug, the two of us soaking wet and slippery. We kissed before I realized what was happening.

"Well, it always rains when you decide to camp," she said, power walking towards the car. "Don't worry about the cold, the elevation's lower on my parents' land."

I pictured my kidneys filtering the incoming fluid and slowly filling up my bladder, the two high-ABV beers being converted into urine. Once I converged on the faint sense of the ability to pee, the knowledge that my bladder inexorably accumulated liquid entrenched itself in my mind, becoming an unbearable itch. Drinking several large gulps of water to offset the dehydrating effects of the beer and mitigate the next morning's mild hangover didn't help.

Consuming two beers with a late dinner seemed fully deserved given the strenuousness of the hiking. We arrived at a pioneer town in a high elevation basin west of the front range around five o'clock and stopped at the lone combined gas station and convenience store. I grabbed a six-pack of IPAs and we agreed on a dinner of macaroni and cheese accented with Sriracha sauce, a straightforward and filling dish for her camp stove, then added a large bag of jalapeno tortilla chips and wonderfully MSG-enhanced queso as a side dish. Her parents owned a large tract of ranch land north of the town. We bounced on a rutted road on the eastern edge of their property to the campsite, Nina implicitly not prepared for a family encounter this late in the day. She made quick work setting up the tent, though I contributed by pounding stakes into the hardpack soil with a large rock.

I counted on the depressant nature of the alcohol to offset any anxiety I had about sleeping next to a member of the opposite sex in what amounted to a backpacking two-person tent, despite the beer's erosion in sleep quality. Thankfully, we each had separate sleeping pads and down sleeping bags, which she interestingly had a large size of both on hand. The physical separation helped with vibration disturbances but even if she didn't hear any unzipping, the inrush of cold air would be ruinous. I decided that even without hearing heavier breathing, a sampling period of ten minutes without a change in her sleeping position would imply slumber.

The banter and storytelling went well through dinner with genuine ease. The cold air forced us into the tent and under our respective sleeping bags, where we played rummy on the mat between us. We had a few instances of glancing physical contact since the kiss without immediate recoil but I sensed a level of restraint. The logical next step would have been to offer her a highly touted back massage and advance based on her cues. Something held me back: the fatigue of the hike or the feeling of being in her world now, camping on her parents' land. Perhaps this was normal given our age, starting with a platonic sleepover to build trust and comfort. Back in college, any overnight spent in close proximity with the opposite gender carried an expectation for sex but that was half of a lifetime ago.

All quiet on the left flank for ten minutes meant she must be asleep. I slid my legs out of the sleeping bag, unzipped the flap, put on the hiking boots sitting outside, unzipped the rainfly, and exited the tent. The cold air cut immediately through my undershirt and boxer shorts. I should have brought my cell phone for a light; I could see only general outlines of bushes without my contacts. My main goal was to pee on something adequately dispersive to avoid a sound while having the terrain gently slope away. We hadn't seen any houses on the drive-in but I squinted for lights on the horizon to be safe.

I had to acknowledge the dull ache in my nether region which had started earlier in the evening, the product of an awakened carnal imagination. It made sense to address this, purge my system, and be clear-headed to meet her family the next day. I started rather mechanically before giving up a moment later. Getting caught would mean being exposed as a completely debauched human being lacking all restraint, requiring a mastery of humor to deflect.

My whole body shook from the cold when I started peeing. I had to clench to stop the stream after I heard a rustling in the distance, worried it was Nina or one of her relatives. The noise stopped as well for a time, then returned as a set of small footfalls through the brush. I thought I made out the outline of the oversized ears of a mule deer. When I got back to the tent, the deer and bitter cold had displaced the other scripts loaded into my short-term memory, and I slid into the warm goose down casket.

*   *   *

I woke up in a sweat after an indeterminate period of semi-conscious rotation through a series of uncomfortable pressure points. The morning sun shone through the tent fabric, mixing with our breath to create a sticky oven. An Oprah reading list book with two butterflies on the front cover was folded open on Nina's empty sleeping bag. I finally got my contacts in without using a mirror and avoided the inclusion of gritty foreign objects into the lenses, a major victory.

"I don't know about you but I could use some coffee," Nina said, yawning and stretching her arms out in the collapsible camping chair. "How'd you sleep?"

"Remind me to never be homeless. I wouldn't last a day," I rotated my core back and forth, trying to work out a knot in my lower back. "Wow, it's gorgeous out here."

The dew on the silver sagebrush – a distinctly Western shrub, one seen after crossing the front mountain range even in cold high-altitude basins like this – glistened in the sun. Trees formed a distinct line at the base of the terrain to our east, filling in the mountain slopes until giving way to exposed rock near the peaks. Seeing three habitats in a single frame made the land more coherent and smaller, a quaint world like drawings of Middle Earth on the inside cover of a Tolkien novel, as opposed to the rolling deciduous blanket of central Appalachia.

Nina turned the laptop towards me and flipped through the shots captured on the camera trap. She had already set a family of bighorn sheep drinking from Upper Grizzly Lake to be her background. We cycled through pictures of deer, marmot, and ground fowl. The night shots were blurrier but one featured a coyote carrying something in its mouth into the forest. A teenager with thick-rimmed neon reflective sunglasses mooned the camera followed by his friends. She talked about setting the traps up in other mountain areas I didn't recognize and debated turning on video collection.

"Let's secure the tent and go grab some coffee and breakfast," Nina said, putting on her backpack and getting into the car. "Most of them will be up by this hour."

"Just need to brush my teeth," I said, not remembering if I brushed them the night before. I needed something to marshal my esteem and offset my three-day stubbled beard. I pulled the toiletry bag out of the cloth sack and started brushing without water, figuring that she wanted to leave soon.

While driving back on the dirt road, Nina talked about growing up on the ranch. She rode horses, went through a pre-teen archery obsession, and had plenty of venue options for high school parties. Her parents owned around 250 acres, and the extended family about double that, since the late 1800s, a significant but not dynastical amount of property. The founders of their Scotts Irish clan migrated from western Kentucky as prospectors seeking cheap land, leaving behind bad debts and feuds. The small town in the center of the valley foundered after a brief silver boom, the area being too cold for productive agriculture, too marginal for timber, and not winning the ski town lottery.

We headed down a private drive until a set of structures appeared. The road ended at a large hangar of some sort with an enormous rollup door. The sheet metal structure dwarfed the other buildings. White smoke rose out of the chimney from a nearby powder blue double-wide trailer. Three other trailers of varying structural integrity sat further back from the central area. They were a mix of vinyl siding, yellow corrugated fiberglass, and at one time painted aluminum.

"Anything special I should know?" I asked, suddenly realizing Nina had provided no Cliff Notes to her family, exposing me to any number of landmines. I could surmise political leanings fairly easily and adapt to the room. On the other hand, it already seemed like the family structure branched out rhizomatically, a proliferation of loosely connected cousins and step-children, parents, and uncles just waiting for me to falsely assign paternity.

"Not really, they're all crazy, don't worry about it," Nina said while walking towards the central trailer. "Well maybe compliment them on the barn, er warehouse. They built it about three years back."

The smell of bacon leapt up on me like a guard dog when we opened the front door. I stayed in the tiled entry area while she gave her mother a hug at the stove and kneeled down for a back pat hug from her father who was seated at the kitchen table. The low ceilings and floral wallpaper made the trailer cozy, aided by natural light coming in through the kitchen window. The living room extended off the merged kitchen and dining space and contained a tweed upholstered sofa and recliner facing the TV. A large serving plate depicting a colonial-era battle perched on the living room wall above the couch. Black and white family photos made up the rest of the decorations.

Nina's mother, who I assumed to be biological but this was indeterminate through appearance, turned down the heat on the pan and filled up two county fair logo mugs with coffee, polling us for cream and sugar while reloading the coffee machine with more grinds and water. She was older than I expected and had the universal grandmother look: dated squircle-shaped glasses, short grey hair, and a full-coverage pastel patterned dress that successfully masked her underlying form. She introduced herself as Margaret and her husband as Ron. I liked her from the start.

"Take a seat and start working on this bacon before the rest of the tribe eats it." Ron slid the plate of bacon slices stacked up in four walls like Lincoln logs on a paper towel to the center of the table. He appeared considerably less mobile than his spouse and sat in the corner of the kitchen with a wide passageway out. An oxygen machine stood against the wall with wound up and stowed tubing.

Margaret asked where we had camped and Nina gave her the details. They talked about the current rancher renting their land, a newcomer to the valley raising Highlands cattle which Ron described as "shaggy-dog-looking things." The women did most of the talking as I worked on the coffee and pork slices which were quickly joined by eggs and generously buttered toast. I obliquely studied Ron from across the table, now that he had finished eating and was resting his hands on a stomach shelf that extended beyond his ribcage. He sported a trucker hat with an outline of a backhoe that read "Tillis Construction Co." which he combined with light brown and plaid workwear. His white sneakers were impressively clean and looked about two sizes too large.

"What line of work are you in Martin?" Margaret asked, finally sitting down at the table after we'd all essentially finished. "Nina still thinks she's in high school, likes to keep us in the dark."

"Teaching," I said, giving the most credible answer I could and keeping it vague as to whether I meant public, private, or charter school. "High school math."

"Union job?" Ron asked.

Having some exposure to this back in Pennsylvania, I sensed a certain contempt from Ron towards monopolistic public sector unions as being responsible for draining municipal budgets and driving higher taxes for small business owners – a class I assumed he was a current or former member of. Jobs were guaranteed for life after tenure barring felonious action and, while the salary was comparatively meager in the metro area, it was envied up here. Alternatively, he could be a man who could put aside his political economy views in favor of secure employment for his daughter's opposite-sex *friend*.

"No, I've mainly taught overseas so far," I said. "The hangar out there is gorgeous, is it new?"

"The boys finished it two summers ago," Margaret said. "Ron can give you the details on the construction, maybe even a tour later?"

"Built to last 100 years," Ron said, stretching out the word *years* for emphasis. He was a man who evaluated structures on their durability over decades and took pride in knowing the building should outlive everyone alive today.

I couldn't remember if Margaret ate quickly or just a small portion, but she promptly loaded the plates into the dishwasher, stuffed the bacon into plastic containers, and refilled our coffee. She peppered her daughter with questions – living arrangements, photography exhibits – as if Nina hadn't been home in a while. She conspicuously skipped over any inquiries about her daughter's romantic life, which I sensed would have ordinarily been first in the queue. Ron rose from his chair and moved slowly across the trailer like he was fighting a headwind until he reached the cast iron wood stove in the living room. I offered to hand him pieces of chopped wood which he accepted. He insulted the fast-burning aspen branches and extolled the thicker maple logs which I found after a few tries.

"Who the hell is this?" a woman asked as she came through the front door. Nina got up from the table and the two embraced.

"Shut the damn door," Ron said and I swept alongside the wall behind the two to close it. I sat back down next to him on the couch.

Nina introduced the newcomer as her younger sister Lexi. Despite being two years Nina's junior, she looked more weathered with dyed blonde hair and a high concentration of reddish age spots, likely from accumulated UV exposure. They shared a nervous energy but Lexi seemed more feral and less predictable.

"What are your intentions with my sister?" Lexi asked, putting her hands on her hips.

"I'm just an extra for her photography, to give a sense of scale," I said, standing up to meet her.

"Smells like bacon in here. You must have passed the first test," she said, filling up a cup of coffee in the kitchen and grabbing a few slices of the cured meat from the fridge.

"Where are the little ones?" Margaret asked.

Lexi opened the front door and scanned back and forth up the hill. "Come on you little bastards, get over here. Now! Now!"

I looked over at Nina who stared at the door in a meme-worthy expression of an older sister's composed concern. Her parents went back to their business, Ron flipping through a tabloid-size local newspaper and Margaret washing dishes. The door swung back open and two munchkins ran in like a hometown football team into their stadium, leaping up on their grandfather on the couch, who futilely tried to keep them off the cushions. They quickly bounced off and into a group hug with their kneeling grandmother. I judged the boy and girl to each be around three years old, though my age detector had a high margin of error.

"Hi there, I like your stuffed animal. What's his name? Or her name?" I asked the little girl who held a plush primate of some sort, trying to make its gender open-ended but still a person instead of a thing. The girl stopped and stared at me without speaking, as if she was just now noticing my presence.

"Avery, show Martin your monkey," Lexi said, walking over to her. Her brother dashed into the back bedroom area and Avery followed his lead, dropping the monkey face-first on the floor. Lexi shook her head. "Kids."

The little terrorists came out of the hallway carrying a large plastic bin at shoulder level like it was the Ark of the Covenant, then tipped it over in the middle of the living room, spilling out a host of injection molded toys. Nina cleared an area and sat crossed legged next to them, helping them sort through the pile. She kissed Ryder, the boy, on the forehead as he tried to extract plastic people from an impractically wide-body airplane.

A rugged, bearded man who I assumed was the children's father stepped into the trailer. Despite having only thrown a single punch in my life during a hit-and-run affair, I subconsciously evaluated the probability of success in a fight against each new male I met. Not much analysis was needed in this instance; my only defense would be pure flight or some manner of sly improvisation with a household item.

"Jake and Brandon, meet my friend Martin," Nina said after Brandon appeared behind Jake, who looked like another outdoorsman archetype but was less bulky and had fewer gray hairs in his beard. "Older brothers."

"Nina, you're going to overdose him with the Tillis clan," Jake said.

"Why don't you boys go for a ride, show him around then come back for lunch?" Margaret suggested.

The two agreed. Nina insisted on staying with the kids and playing the cool aunt. The three of us walked out to the hangar and I filled in the gaps of silence by talking about the mine and camera traps, two subjects that received only tepid responses. The rollup door lifted to reveal a small fleet of recreational and construction vehicles. Two Bobcat compact loaders sat along the north wall, one with most of its fairings removed for some manner of repair. A large yellow backhoe loader occupied the central area with a bucket on the front and a scooping device on the back, a dilated version of the plastic toy on the floor of the trailer. The back wheels went up to my shoulders. Several unhitched snowplows were lined up on the south side of the garage.

"I bet these can move some serious material. Are they yours?" I asked.

"Family business. Excavation and some masonry," Jake said, walking us around to the back. "We use the garage here for maintenance and some smaller jobs. The big equipment is on the lot near town."

I couldn't conceive of these being used for any simple projects, unless they considered adding a retention pond or digging out a foundation for another structure an afternoon affair. At first, I thought we'd pull out a loader, maybe have the kids ride in the bucket and dump them out. We continued to the rear of the hangar and entered the small engine area with a stack of dirt bikes and two camouflaged four-wheel ATVs.

"You ever ride a quad?" Brandon asked as he checked tires and fuel levels.

"A slow one a long time ago." This was strictly true but there had been two people in the seat. Jake pulled out one of the dirt bikes. A quad seemed infinitely more stable than anything with only two wheels, especially on uneven terrain. We pushed the two ATVs and the bike out of the hangar, then stopped to fuel up in the driveway.

"You'll like the 250 cc more, less touchy on the gas. Gonna have to walk the choke down as it heats up though," Jake said and pointed to an adjustable lever on the side of the engine. I moved it to the upper position which I expected to produce the higher ratio fuel-air mixture needed to startup, but didn't want to ask for confirmation.

Brandon walked out of the hangar carrying two rifles, one had a wooden stock and the other had a black body with white streaks, like an inverted slab of marble. He mounted them to the rack on the front of my ATV, which I previously assumed was for cross country skis. Even though I trusted the safeties were engaged, riding off-road with lethal weapons on the hood of my vehicle seemed distracting if not dangerous. But this showed my firearm ignorance: if given the choice, it was best to keep the weapons in your visual field.

Jake led the way through the sagebrush trail up the hill past the other three trailers, the two brothers waving to a brood of children that were swarming around the homes. The top of the ridge opened up to a view of the valley, the state highway, and a faint fence line, the only real signs of human activity. Jake yelled back something about a cousin and he gunned the throttle, leaving us in a plume of engine exhaust.

The amount of habitable land per person in the world is about two acres or one city block. This was easy to forget as we sped through the open basin towards a stand of trees, the cool late morning air offset by the sun rising over the eastern mountain range. Being in an environment surrounded by so much open country tempered my ego, the humbling presence of the indifferent granite peaks, time scales measured in eons rather than years. But maybe the remote landscape preserved a pioneering spirit and a will to survive in the Tillis family, leading to a less restrained attitude towards procreation, as evidenced by the large family units back at the homestead.

I had fallen back a few hundred yards to drive cautiously around the ruts and rocks, fearing a punctured tire more than anything. Jake and Brandon got off the vehicles at the edge of the trees, Jake pulling out a pair of binoculars and scanning the area.

"We're on Pearson's land now," Jake said.

"You hunt here?" I asked.

"He's been letting us hunt in the deer woods forever. Has about three hundred acres backing up to the National Forest," Brandon said, pulling the rifles out from the holder. "We plow his driveway in the winter."

I assumed the shooting would be recreational, since I thought hunting season started in November, graciously allowing the biggest deer and elk bucks to mate before becoming a trophy. My firearm experience was limited to a pump-action BB gun which could propel a small copper ball through an aluminum can at twenty yards. The two brothers went through a host of motions with the weapons, mounting a sight and opening and closing the chamber several times, all done in silence with suitable solemnity.

"Are you guys dating?" Jake asked as the three of us walked deeper into the woods.

"Just friends," I answered.

"I'm guessing you're not a musician, or an artist, right?" Brandon asked.

"How'd you know?"

"Lack of body modifications," Brandon replied. "And those aren't skinny jeans."

I looked down at my classic blue denim jeans, purchased about a decade ago before the inclusion of elastic fibers became the trend. "Got me."

We continued walking through the woods, further and further from civilization. As traditional masculine figures, I knew they needed to remind me of their violent capabilities, even though the sister they were "protecting" was now in her mid-thirties and ostensibly tougher than me. We reached a meadow between the trees and both men laid down on the ground in a prone position. I knelt further behind them, giving them a wide berth like for an amateur golfer on the tee. I finally saw a black sheet metal outline of a deer in profile on the far edge of the clearing, with hanging red spoon targets at the kill shot locations: head, high shoulder, and heart.

"What do they call those forty years the Hebrews were lost in the Bible?" Jake asked as he set up for the shot. "Wilderness years. I think Nina is getting out of those."

"She's finding herself?"

"Hell, it took a while for me too, that's the Tillis way," Jake said, striking the heart target and making it spin like a fast-forwarded gymnast on the parallel bars. "Being around the kids today will be good for her."

"Did you all grow up together?" I asked after Jake handed me the gun along with a few pointers for its use, like leaving a distance between the eye socket and the sight to avoid being punched by the recoil.

"We were raised with our mom. She and Lexi are our half-sisters," Jake said. "They both grew up on the ranch, we moved back here about fifteen years ago."

"Dad needed help with the business and we thought it would be better to all be together," Brandon added.

I eventually hit the deer, putting a bullet through its front kneecap, a horribly painful injury for an actual deer but earning me a modicum of respect from the two brothers. I tried the other rifle, a larger .375 caliber for elk hunting which felt like a cannon, then went back to the lighter pump-action Remington. We talked shop about marksmanship and hunting for the next twenty minutes, and both seemed to respect my general interest and confession as a hypocritical omnivore. Each of them seemed optimized for hunting with their thicker frames, insulation, and an ability to hold still for hours at a time.

After shooting, we hiked around the property to, I gathered, be tracking different types of game, overturning and reviewing various piles of excrement from hairy coyote droppings to marble-sized piles of elk scat. They credited their firearm knowledge to joining the Marines after high school, two years apart. I sensed that hunting emerged from a sublimated form of aggression, an escape from domestic and business routines, before realizing I was the outlier, the one abstracted away from life and death. After I used up or vetoed all my easy conversation starters, like an anxious first date, the silence felt welcomed when we hiked back to the ATVs. I largely kept up with the two of them on the ride back towards the homestead, a slower, victorious pace.

* * *

When we got back, Nina appeared to be in the middle of a game of red rover with the children, who opposed each other in two parallel lines, some fidgeting with excitement and needing her restraint. I felt like a Goth descending on Rome, accompanied by the engine roar and dust clouds as we swung around to the hangar door. Nina waved and Lexi smoked a cigarette on the sidelines, pacing back and forth and looking at her phone.

"You survived!" Nina exclaimed as we walked back to her parent's trailer.

"He's not a bad shot, even started calculating the wind and gravity effects by the end," Jake said, picking up one of the kids in his arms.

A bell started ringing and everyone turned and faced the trailer. Ron was whipping a burlap rope back and forth like a crazed orchestra conductor, striking a brass bell mounted next to the front door with percussive fervor. I assumed everyone would start marshaling into a militia or running into an underground bunker.

"Lunchtime," Nina said. "Just follow my lead."

We were the last ones in the scrum to enter the trailer which was well beyond its capacity. Margaret started grace after we joined hands. After letting the youngsters jump the line, I mirrored Nina's selection of two nicely charred hot dogs paired with ruffled and plain potato chips, folding the thin paper plate into a large taco for transport. We stayed in the trailer after the kids emptied out in a stream of crumbs.

I sat down next to Ron who was watching college football intently. We talked about the inability to transfer running the option from the collegiate to the professional level, both of us assigning culpability to the speed of linebacker and secondary units in the NFL. I always enjoyed watching football and admired the grace and strategy employed in a team's division of labor for the corporeal chess match. My viewing tapered severely after college since I was living overseas and my access to American football was mostly restricted to the Super Bowl or BCS championship. Recent scandals of permanent brain damage had dropped its popularity and threatened to have it become a cultural dichotomy next to NASCAR, MMA, or driving a domestically manufactured pickup truck. The Roman patrician class sneered at the gladiatorial games loved by the masses as a base and barbaric activity, a similar righteousness seemed to be emerging in our time. Ron and I watched in silence as the Mountain West team attempted last-minute gadget plays for massive losses of yardage. I got up to grab us each a refill of Coke when Nina burst through the front door.

"Shit," she said after her phone beeped in what sounded like an Amber Alert. "Forest fire along the pass, they are closing down the highway. Zero percent contained."

"How are we going to get back?" I asked, trying to form a mental image of the map.

"Head south or north to get on either interstate, but it will add two or three hours," she said.

"Camp here tonight, or sleep on the pullout," Margaret offered. "Then drive back early in the morning."

"We need to be back tomorrow morning," Nina said. We both had appointments the next day at Transcendent Health which, with the northern detour, was about a five-hour drive. She looked flustered when saying her good-byes, mentioning the time required to drive back to the campsite, repack, and get on the road. Margaret asked for my phone number and I gave it, not questioning if this was for an emergency scenario or inclusion in her address book. I gave Ron a firm handshake and remarked on the impressive machinery in the hangar, then left with another four hotdogs wrapped in aluminum foil.

A dark beige column of smoke appeared from a notch in the mountains as we drove north, the fire's plume looking like a wayward power plant. The lack of population density and rugged terrain meant the firefighters would likely let it burn and hope that precipitation would slow its advance. I thought about the bighorn sheep family caught on the camera trap, startled by the flames and heading back above the tree line, or more tragically the ground-dwelling and less mobile animals woken up by heat. Whether because I was inured to human violence thanks to video games and movies or because of their general innocence, I found the suffering of animals more heartbreaking than their human equivalents. Jessica suggested my limited empathetic bandwidth implied Asperger's last year after another fight about my lack of being present. The diagnosis was neither convincingly confirmed nor denied in later self-administered online tests. During events like this, I comforted myself with historical framing. Surely other cataclysms dwarfed this provincial threat to life, indeed entire epochs were ones of destruction and widespread suffering. The recent climatic changes accelerated their arrival and volatility but the events were not new.

"Your family is great. They've got a nice spread of land out here," I said. Nina became serious and less voluble after the forest fire changed our plans, letting the car stereo fill the auditory space.

"Everything is easier when it's sunny out," she said. "Being trapped in a drafty trailer during overcast freezing days is a much different experience. They like you. They respect guys that don't try to show off."

"The kids love you. Do you miss not being with the rest of the clan?"

"Maybe I need to park a trailer up on the hill. Or, a tiny house, that sounds better," Nina said.

"Tempted to move back?"

"I couldn't wait to get out after high school. I saw that world as always teetering on the edge: business debt, family dissolution and creation with new girlfriends and boyfriends, not to mention the weather," she said. "My half-brothers came back from the Marines when I started tenth grade. Lexi shifted into an aggressive stage of teenage rebellion around that time too. Everyone just kind of drifted in a semi-alcoholic state."

"Is that when you got into photography?"

"Yeah, maybe. Ron got this Pontiac 6000 that barely ran from a friend as payment for a job, practically rusted out. I'd drive it alone into the mountains, just park there and listen to music. It didn't have a tape or CD player, so I rigged up a Walkman with an FM tuner. Would bring a sketchbook along, developing photos was way too expensive back then."

"It's cool that you had an escape valve, a place of refuge. Back where I grew up, there aren't these large tracts of lands and the idea of getting away from civilization wasn't in the collective consciousness. Instead, we loitered in bowling alleys trying to figure out how we could get malt liquor 40s," I said. In reality, I was always non-essential in the party scene, invited only through several linkages down the social chain. I spent a preponderance of evenings beating turn-based strategy computer games on a Deity difficulty or reading dusty James Michener historical fiction sagas from my father's library.

"Back in high school you were either a cowboy, a cheerleader, a goth, or maybe a nerd – and those were rare. Our class wasn't big enough to have a dedicated group of artistic theatre types so we tagged along with other cliques," Nina said. "Found my tribe in college a little more, though most have assimilated into domestic life or live in a van now."

"Besides wishing people happy birthday on social media, I've effectively exiled myself from my former high school and college circles. My ex and I bounced around the developing world doing humanitarian work and teaching after college, so I missed out on the formative dingy apartment, roommate, urban dating period of my twenties."

"But you got the iconic photo standing above Machu Picchu or meditating in front of a gnarled tree at Angkor Wat, right?"

"Missed out on that but I have a hunch of what they look like," I said.

"Speaking of cameras, I wanted to redeploy the traps on a spur trail near the Divide, but the fire killed that option," Nina said. "Any trails off the highway coming up?"

I checked the map app on my phone as we slid in and out of cellular data, coming up with a promising trail along a creek. Our northern return route skirted the high peaks in favor of a casual descent back into the eastern high desert. The mountains became more feminine as we drove northeast, undulating mounds with clumps of growth in the valleys and north faces. Even though it was less rugged, the land emanated a wildness, a history of great herds and hunts, a movement of semi-nomadic peoples instead of semi-nomadic hipsters. The Harmony Creek Trail started at the end of a dirt road two miles south of the highway.

"I'm giving it twenty-four hours before I get a voicemail from Margaret saying how nice of a guy you are," Nina said, setting forth on the trail. The way she called her parents by their first names sounded intentionally irreverent, a way to knock them down from their parental pedestal.

"Just tell them I'm testing out an experimental drug for mental health, scuff off some of the luster," I said, trying to keep up with the additional weight of her backpack which was loaded with four camera traps.

"Are you really a teacher?"

"I taught overseas, but no, I'm not certified in the state," I said, fighting back an urge to apologize. "I need some additional credits and have to pass an exam." I knew about the test and assumed that while some of the education courses I had accumulated overseas would transfer, there would be a sizable deficiency.

"I was wondering about your flexible weekday schedule. How do you pay the bills again?"

"Some savings and driving for Kinetix. Besides my $100 a day sushi habit, the bills are pretty low," I said, waiting for a laugh. "But honestly, I'm looking to get back to work next year," I said this with conviction to create a self-imposed deadline, my first vocalized promise about the future since moving back.

"I can see you teaching high school; math or science, right?"

I shrugged. We followed the creek up a cascade section, the area becoming more wooded in the narrowing valley. Nina went down to a squatting position, maybe trying to think like a deer or bear approaching the stream, asked for one of the camera traps, then mounted it to a pine tree overlooking the water and the trail. We followed a feeder creek up higher and placed two more traps, one in the woods and the other facing a meadow.

"Have you noticed any changes in your sleep patterns or dreams?" I asked, feeling a quick onset of fatigue, noticing a pain in my quadriceps that historically develops from persistent sleep deprivation, the body cannibalizing itself through protein metabolism.

"Not really. I've always been an easy sleeper; my brain naturally wants to shut off from reality."

"I am getting into these two-day cycles, which I was always subject to but now it seems amplified," I said. "The first day bleeds vibrantly, almost ecstatic in a fugue-like way. I'm interested in everything. I finally fall asleep well past midnight and get up around dawn, then drag along the next day in a neurochemical hangover, collapse in bed at nine or ten, and then the cycle repeats." The day was tipping hard towards the nadir state.

"I sleep nine or ten hours and wake up exhausted, it's only through physical activity that I get to some semblance of functionality," Nina said. I thought about the choke on the ATV, lowering it as the engine heated up.

"My dreams have become more vivid, or maybe I'm just remembering them or waking up in the middle or something. But this feels different, like my brain is a plucky intern digging through the old company records."

"What are you dreaming about?"

"Oh, random stuff, like catching trains. Maybe this will make me believe in psychoanalysis." In truth, a few of the dreams shifted in content from the usual PBS to Showtime, an awakening of the id's megafauna, like sexual liaisons with high school crushes taken to completion, peakier experiences.

"I'm telling you this stuff is activating areas in your brain. Have you told the doctors about it?" Nina asked.

"Haven't mentioned the dream part of it yet but maybe I should."

"I can't believe they put me in the control group. Either that or my neurons are all dried up," Nina said while scouting around for where to place the last trap. "It's like my brain is buried underground in some arctic soil, and I'm stuck in the permafrost, held fixed by the ice."

"And my brain feels like the surface of the Moon, temperatures swinging wildly in sun and shadow, no atmospheric protection."

"I feel like I've been imposing more intense external conditions on myself for the last ten years, trying to thaw out. The truth is that I'm okay being dampened out, I don't need level ten rapture. I want some stability, just not in a frozen state."

"Maybe our chemistry just needs a subtle shift, the way that a two-degree change in the axial tilt of the Earth every 20,000 years can create a mile thick glacier over Cleveland." I spent a few hours the previous week absorbed in ice ages.

"That's the promise of Transcendent for me. I just need to siphon off some of your peak energy and then give you back some ballast, deal?" Nina asked. She found the right tree for the final camera trap, a stately cloud white aspen. "Wait, let's geotag this photo so we can find the traps later."

"I thought you turned off GPS so they couldn't track us?"

"Eh, I gave up on that. Smile." She pulled me close and held the phone out for a selfie. I started with a closed-mouth grin, my best objectively photogenic pose but evidence of restraint compared to her toothy smile. I replayed a dad joke about Texas in my head to initiate a quiet laugh and a more spontaneous grin. My mouth and lips were objectively large, cartoonish even, easily able to bite and hold a tennis ball plus manage any double-stacked burger the world of fast-casual dining could muster. We made out after the photo, a lengthy open-mouthed session that only stopped when the incoming cool air reminded us of the time.

"Want to drive us back?" Nina asked, throwing me the keys. I adjusted the mirrors and seats like a rental car before turning over the engine. "Thanks for coming along, I always dread the return trips. Not that I don't want to leave, which I always do, but it makes me confront my own reality on the drive back."

"What do you mean?"

"Even though they're all crazy, they have kids and family nearby. There is some meaning in having those relationships."

"The justice system within families is less harsh, maybe you get probation instead of outright exile," I said.

"Doesn't matter if you're a loser."

"Do you want to have kids?" I asked.

"I always said no, my genetic material is well dispersed already. But now I kinda do actually, even though kids are gross. How about you?" Nina asked, rotating her body to lay on her side in the passenger seat and look over at me.

"I wanted to," I said and checked the mapping software on the phone which showed a brief ride on the interstate then another hour on a country highway. I could see she was getting tired, pulling her legs to her chest and stuffing a jacket behind her head. "There is something I need to tell you."

"Married?" she asked with a yawn. "Kids?"

"Apparently my sperm has the ambition of a mini-fridge, low motility. My ex and I tried for a year, got tested and took different medications, figured out it was me. It's hard to come back after something like that, not a miscarriage but a breach of contract." After hitting snooze on the biological clock for a decade, Jessica dreamed of conceiving a child even if out of wedlock the last year we were together, backstopped by the financial security of her parents. Nina was now only the second non-medical person that knew about my infertility.

"Eh, the world is overpopulated, adoption is better anyways," she said, stretching and returning to a fetal position, finding my lack of virility boring. "Is that why you broke up?"

"She went back to the States over the holidays and I stayed overseas, didn't have much to go back to and I saved money on plane fares. After some long phone calls, it was official. Maybe it was the holiday mirth that made her end it: children, fireplaces, and eggnog, or something."

"I'm sorry."

Nina closed her eyes, not examining the subject as I expected. This could have been out of a respect for my privacy, genuine disinterest, or simple post camping fatigue. The ridge on her upper lip brought me back to our embrace among the trees. The displacement theory of romantic attachment made intuitive sense to me, mental processes would continue like zombies until pushed out and replaced.

*   *   *

"How are things in Almaty?" Jessica asked. "Is Nissa still naughty?"

"They got her spayed over the holidays so we'll see. Seems to be barking less." Our neighbors, a friendly younger couple named Tanya and Alexei, adopted the mutt after it showed up in the common area of the apartment block. Jessica helped Tanya make flyers to find the lost pup's owner and the two quickly became friends. Tanya worked as a freelance graphic designer and Jessica volunteered to help her out on projects late into the evenings.

"Give her a hug for me."

"Will do."

"Are you doing okay?"

"Yeah, I mean, sure," I said. We had exchanged a few messages to find a compatible time to talk over the phone, something I both anticipated and dreaded. "A bunch of us went to the Medeu Skating Rink a few days ago."

"Ah, cool, can't believe we never went there," she said. Tourist publications boasted that the outdoor facility was the largest high elevation skating rink in the world. It still carried Christmas decorations, the Russian Orthodox holiday coming two weeks after December 25th, a further reminder of my holiday spent alone.

"I'm not coming back."

"As in ever?"

"I've canceled my flight. I'm sorry."

"Is this about what happened before you left?" I asked.

"No, not really," she muttered with congestion. I pictured the tears forming. Physical intimacy had fully halted after we stopped trying to conceive the previous spring. A six-pack and expletive-laden punk rock had always done the trick, but her stomach now violently rejected alcohol at the second drink. My petulant frustration had come out while she packed her bags to travel back for the holidays, leading both of us to pledge an abiding disinterest in each other. Two milligrams of melatonin didn't salvage me any rest before her 6 am departure.

"I can't end up like my parents," Jessica said.

"What do you mean? They're great."

"My dad sleeps in the guest room every night."

"He's quirky, you know that," I said. My nocturnal neuroticism led us to abut two twin beds for vibration isolation, a condition easily concealed from guests with a large comforter.

"My mom confessed that they haven't kissed in over a year. He's on another fucking planet in his study."

"They should go to therapy."

"Martin, I'm not getting what I need from us."

"What do you need?"

"Something meaningful...," she trailed off and breathed heavy, blowing her nose. "Oh Martin, I need a break."

We never talked again, exchanging icy emails about the practicalities of our split over the next two months until we reached a state of complete radio silence. I mentally prepared the coroner's report of our breakup – different love languages, the divergence of shared interests, and the old standby of communication breakdown. The *chapter* analogy felt especially satisfying when re-telling the events to myself and, I thought, would work well in future conversations.

*　　　*　　　*

I bit my lip to stay awake on the drive back and noticed that Nina's lower jaw had opened slightly against her coat, causing a small dark pool of saliva to form on the periwinkle fabric. Her ability to sleep while being driven by a relative stranger at high speed made me happy and made me want, almost desperately, to reach across to touch her. I opened the music app on my phone and selected a chill playlist, reducing the volume to a whisper.

After a few tracks, I switched to *Dark Side of the Moon,* an album imprinted into my long-term memory twenty years before during high school. My musical preferences were skewed by the cultural mirroring of my crush Amanda, a soccer player insouciant of her beauty who wore a hemp necklace, bell bottoms, and consumed large amounts of cannabis. Despite the phone's tinny speakers, the instrumental sections seemed perfectly designed for driving across a country road in the dark. I played *Us and Them* three times, sautéing myself with its plaintive saxophone solos and Gilmore's smoother vocals.

The shoulder season weekend return traffic was heavy but kept flowing, fellow travelers moving with a contentment very different than the escaping frenzy of drivers at the start of a weekend. The darkness cast each car into greater relief, the calming bilateral symmetry of the taillights with illuminated license plates for mouths and the drivers' uncanny way of turning their heads to meet my gaze when passing. The train of cars felt like the march of red blood cells down a capillary to deliver oxygen to the tissue. It was a steady movement compared to the stark desperation I found during my midnight drives ferrying passengers to and from the airport. The car was the perfect modern machine for moving an individual through space: the sense of agency with movement, complete anonymity, the security of a protective exoskeleton, and all the technology of the last 120 years abstracted to a simple user interface while still allowing a human being of average intellect to disassemble, repair, and customize it with their bare hands. I had to agree with Victor in the relentless ascent of the virtual, the car's victory over space would be replaced by digital content's victory over people's time and attention, culminating in neurological instead of material vehicles. I turned off the music, increased my following distance, and stayed in the slow lane, savoring the drive.

"You must be Martin." Sergey greeted me upon opening the door after the first knock, thankfully repeating his name which I had forgotten. "Victor said you might stop by."

I leaned my backpack, which was lightly loaded with the heat transfer book and a sketch pad, against the living room sofa. Victor's legs extended out on the recliner which had been pushed from the corner to near the center of the room.

"Could be the maiden voyage of our difference engine today, chassis is complete," Victor said. "Reservoir insert drawing is back on the workbench, ready for the lathe."

I asked if I could get him some food or something to drink but he waved me off with a sideways palm. "Give Sergey a hand with the underwater vehicle back there."

I helped Sergey mount the O-rings inside their channels and attach the two elongated clamshell pieces onto the frame with countersunk screws. The rear propeller remained unprotected without a shield. I looked around for the weldment that was promised earlier.

"We'll sneak into the university pool for an initial sea trial," Sergey said. "The team will be upgrading the sensor package so we can spare the final closeouts."

"Are you going to leave the propeller exposed like this?" I asked. "We built some of the angled supports for a protective ring."

"Good point, I'll have Miriam finish it," Sergey responded.

After carrying the bullet-shaped submarine to the back of his car, we both sat on the sofa and the two older men talked shop about the project, punctuating their speech with Russian-sounding words that I assumed were curses or insults. Sergey mentioned to me that he worked as an emeritus professor, choosing to help graduate student projects and engaging subject matter experts, like Victor.

"Damned flu shot yesterday afternoon, my immune system thinks it's under siege," Victor said, straining to get himself up from the chair before heading down the hallway. "You keep talking, I'm going to rest for a bit."

"Is he okay?" I asked Sergey.

"He'll want some private time. I know Victor. I think the two of us are his main social connections, besides maybe the garbage man," Sergey said, checking the hallway. "He speaks well of you, says you two have been working on a water machine?"

"Yeah, it's a little bit like the other devices he's built but more hydraulic and less chaotic. Simpler. Have you seen the others?"

"I know his brother designed and built some Rube Goldberg-type pieces but that was forever ago," Sergey said. "It's a really sad story. Tragedy swallows some families whole. A lot of people disappeared back then. I initially submitted Victor's green card application out of pity, having only met him once or twice. Lucky for me it turns out the man is mechanically brilliant."

It didn't make sense that Sergey didn't know that Victor built the now valuable artistic works, but that must have been intentional. I assembled our hydraulic machine with him, explaining each element and its basis in the network, acknowledging its simplicity but highlighting the artistic flair of including black lights and a hypnotic periodicity. Victor had completed the primary structure, mounting the pump, the main reservoir, the power strip, and the timers. The electrical wiring had been condensed down to a single twelve-volt socket and toggle switch on the rear of the base. It still needed covers on the platform to conceal the internal organs which were less elegant than the waterwheel mechanisms.

"There is a grace here," Sergey said as we both sat down on the kitchen table drinking flavored seltzer. "The forcing function will dampen out over depth, should be fun to watch."

"Did you ever see Lukyanov's water integrator?"

"One of those early analog computers?" Sergey thought for a moment and pulled on his predominately white beard. He looked like a grandfather character from *Fiddler on the Roof*, having a compact frame and cherubic face, but his blue eyes jittered with youthful intensity. "No, but I think I know the principle, modulating flows from different stocks into central columns. There's a monetary system one, I think. Is that what you're building next?"

"That was Victor's inspiration but this is what we came up with."

"Your machine has simplicity, as a physicist I can appreciate that," Sergey said. "It simulates one-dimensional diffusive phenomena. A little faster to build than an accelerator."

"Didn't Victor build parts for that project?"

"That's how he came over, my initial research area was particle physics and we built a compact collider called a fixed-field alternating gradient accelerator. You learn through collisions, over short periods you can produce extreme conditions and tease things out," Sergey answered. "But I shifted into applied physics about ten years ago and now dabble in computer science. The last forty years of particle physics have been limited to polishing the standard model with massive computer simulations or huge colliders. Everyone hopes the next anomaly will tease out a new branch of physics but I've lost the faith. Particle work doesn't hold my attention anymore, all of the everyday interactions of matter and energy are essentially known. I've moved into complex systems."

"I keep thinking our difference engine needs some reflective element, some recursion to add complexity."

"A machine becomes meaningful through its connections or attachments to other machines. The Large Hadron Collider is the world's largest machine, but, as an island, it's academic, it needs a connection to human beings, actual applications. You could add some self-feedback loops to your hydraulic engine but it may degenerate and become a repeated response. Maybe think of your engine like a module, a function, you can tie it into other machines, like say the weather with a photosensor or something."

"Make it reactive and productive with the environment, not just self-reflective."

"Right. Moving away from pure science into applied computation, I've started thinking of everything as a form of machine, accepting inputs, changing its state, outputting values, and so on. It started when I re-read Schrodinger's book on life. It came out in the 1940s before DNA was discovered, but he foresaw the need for cells to encode information in some type of aperiodic crystal. Life is a process that continues long after it should have stopped. The real perpetual motion machine, it is an uphill push against settling into the lowest free energy state. I had regressed into tenured laziness, died in a way. Particle physics felt like deep mining, digging some long dark shaft to find a grail. The equations were still elegant but now felt sterile, like a perfectly clean empty city." Sergey said, finishing his drink.

"Biology is still too analog and statistical, maybe it succumbs to mature engineering in fifty years but I have twenty years left give or take. Computation gives the same potential bottoms up emergence and beauty as life does, but without the mess. We wrote adaptive learning avionics software for the underwater craft, simulating its navigation, searching for the best control loops by training the code on different scenarios. The algorithm adapted in days versus nature's nearly random walk taking millions of years. Trying to evolve a dolphin I guess."

"Is this artificial intelligence?"

"It's more intelligent than a person at a very specific task. Don't ask it to get you a drink though. You want another?" Sergey got up and opened the refrigerator, pulling out two seltzers. The fridge looked more stocked than previously, perhaps he was spending more time over here. "As we keep developing these provincial intelligences, more and more of the world is downloaded, increasing the data available. We'll soon see general intelligence develop, pass the Turing test, its performance indistinguishable from a human for more complex situations."

"You mean conscious machines?"

"I suppose, but I don't get hung up on that word. I don't see the hard problem of consciousness as being that hard, the whole self-awareness thing. It will either just emerge from the complexity or evolve into a specialized module. Do you hear people still talking about the immortality of the soul? I expect in 100 years we'll consider consciousness the same way we think about the soul, a nice historical concept but not essential to our understanding." Sergey said. "Not that I'm an expert in these fields. It won't happen in my lifetime, maybe by the end of yours."

"Does the idea of conscious machines out there scare you?" I asked, having listened to a few podcasts on the subject from technologists and philosophers.

"More sophisticated intelligences will arise. I don't see humans as worthy of having an eternal claim as the dominant being. One underlying thread in the advancement of human knowledge is the continual demotion of our species. The Earth is no longer at the center of the universe, we are not in God's image, we aren't the only tool makers or animals using language, there is no intelligent design, and so on. I think the Buddhists were onto something about the absence of the self, we're just a collection of programs with packets and islands of knowledge, albeit pretty smart in their aggregate. Now it's popular to see our consciousness as something unique, but it's another constructed transcendence like the others."

"But as a machine, it works? Connects to other machines, has inputs and outputs?"

"It's quite functional and persuasive to itself," Sergey said.

"Where does that leave you, as a person?" I asked, noticing the wedding ring on Sergey's left hand.

"Operating with the illusion of autonomy is still useful to get through the day. I like the idea of hacking my internal programming every few years. For me, it's primarily intellectual pursuits, but for a different neurochemical profile, it could be something artistic, like the grace of dancing, or embracing universal love, as tacky as that sounds. What about you?"

"I default into getting lost in activities like long-form historical podcasts and daydreaming in the shower. I haven't thought about internal programming in experimental terms," I said, trying to recall how I spent time the previous five months before meeting Victor, Nina, and joining the Transcendent trial, the acreage of time spent grazing around the same pasture. "Working with Victor over the last few months has woken me up."

"Victor's work at the university exhausted him towards the end, he was ready for retirement. I dropped in on him here about two years ago, and he leaped at the opportunity to help with our projects, to start building again. Finding pleasure in one of your talents is a wonderful thing. Sometimes this house feels like one of our vacuum chambers, isolated from the outside world to keep things simple."

"Why do you think he let me in?"

"He finds most people boring. Maybe you remind him of Leo or his younger self. You should ask him. I love working with students but my greatest pleasure is spending time with my six-year-old granddaughter. I can see the processes developing in her mind, but I don't try to analyze anything, just let the two of us play. I hope Victor has found that joy," Sergey said and looked down at his watch. "We need to check on him."

We both walked down the hallway and opened the door to Victor's dark bedroom. Sergey stepped inside and came back out a few seconds later. "Sleeping. We need to take turns stopping in on him each day."

"He's sick?" I asked.

"He's not well. He blames the flu shot but that should have cleared up days ago. It could be a change in medication, he mentioned something about a new blood pressure medicine this morning," Sergey said, putting on his coat. "Let's let him rest. I'll come back this evening."

"I'll take tomorrow," I said and we exchanged numbers.

"My wife cooked some lasagna which I brought over, help yourself," Sergey offered on the way out. Unable to find a microwave, I heated up a small rectangle of the tomato and cheese strata in a cast iron pan, and worked on the assembly of the hydraulic engine, tightening the connections and making drawings for the external housings. I pulled up the calendar on my phone, one empty of events beyond the Transcendent appointments and pre-loaded national holidays, and added a recurring reminder to visit an eccentric elderly man I had only recently met, a new constraint in the desert of my commitments.

I thought about Sergey as I turned the acrylic round stock into an hourglass shape on the lathe to act as the seasonal insert in the first tank. He adopted an intellectual nomadism late in life, moving from territory to territory, seeking new ways to connect machines to each other. Having tenure could have made his life comfortable. A productive desire fueled their work, Sergey seeking algorithmic intelligences and Victor trying to capture grace through craftsmanship. By fortune or personality, one expanded outward in social life while the other pulled inward. Victor hadn't designed any of the chaotic machines but he'd built them and must have enjoyed creating potential instabilities in each system. I placed a note on the table praising the lasagna when I left.

I changed the music from Enchanted Forest to Castaway Beach and hoped the wave action would carry me into Stage 1 sleep. Lying on my back maximized comfort but promoted a stubborn expansive mind. Shifting to a side position encouraged an earthly focus and I pictured myself taking cover in a shallow wartime foxhole. The sculpted pillow tried to reduce awareness of the headset, a starfish spilling over my skull, the arms extending down and hosting a set of reasonably low-profile sensors.

I admitted to having florid dreams a few days before and Dr. Patel quickly insisted on conducting a sleep study, monitoring my brain activity through the stages of slumber. She emphasized the criticality of cortical purity, that no sleep medication or other sedatives were allowed. I agreed but expected to have a fitful night's sleep since I was at the extreme restless end on the pendulum of vitality.

I resolved to get up, urinate, and attempt some manner of reset, maybe by reading the labels of the bathroom cleaning supplies. I closed the door behind me without snapping the latch and looked out to the lobby, keeping the wireless headset in place to avoid setting off any alarm while knowing that later processing of the data would show my movement. A college-aged girl propped her feet up on the desk and scrolled through her phone, likely an intern stuck with the night shift, serving an emergency rather than a medical or security role.

Transcendent expanded two weeks ago, moving into the second floor of the office building, presumably opening up new space for exam rooms and staff. I went up the stairs, finding solid wood doors with brass cipher locks and dark breakrooms. I could pony up some good excuses to the cleaning crew if necessary. I finally succeeded in pushing one door open, triggering a set of overhead lights hooked up to a motion detector. It looked to be offices of some sort, an open floor plan with long white tables and ergonomic chairs. No name tags. I snaked through the workstations, past the stress balls and plastic tubs of pub mix until I saw a photo of two South Asian toddlers playing in a sandbox in an otherwise immaculate workspace. Dr. Patel kneeled next to them. The top drawer held office supplies and a few bound conference notebooks on neurology and data science. The second drawer had a stack of hardcover laboratory notebooks. The uppermost one was about half full and had yesterday's date in the signed footer. The other two notebooks showed dates from the past two years.

I thought about creating some kind of covert entrance for the next night so that Nina and I could slip in like cat burglars and decipher the notebooks, though I knew it would never work. There was far too much security and it would be hard for the two of us to negotiate an ingress through a second-floor window. Not to mention the fact that none of the windows seemed to open, which even eliminated the option of dropping the notebook and calling Nina to come grab it. I had to do a fast download. I was already going to arouse suspicion so whatever I did needed to be quick and in an area of reduced surveillance. As an overnight guest, I could offer an excuse of opting for the more luxurious second-floor bathroom and if necessary, admit to pursuing my secret crush on Dr. Patel by checking out her office. Putting my phone in airplane mode, I held open her most recent notebook on the bathroom counter with one hand while the other took photos of each page.

*　　　*　　　*

I sent Nina a teaser text message boasting of some enhanced data collection. I skimmed a few of the pictures in the morning after the sleep study while heading back to the apartment to attempt a nap. Six frozen pizzas filled up the freezer, two for me and four for Victor which I planned to bring over. Sergey recommended lunchtime visits with a meal.

I brought pasta on the first visit, planning to cook a pound and fill up containers with leftovers, but mistakenly got the whole wheat variety, the grainy tubes proving impervious to sauce and every other attempt at flavor enhancement. After that failure, Victor's taste buds regressed to those of a teenager, wanting supreme pizza and ice-cold Coke, though his appetite remained weak and he ate only a slice or two per sitting. I prepared food and we talked at the kitchen table, the conversation skewed towards scientific and historical events or sketching out concepts for new machines. He took on more of a consulting role in the machine shop as I worked on more turned reservoir inserts and a few parts for Sergey. Our exchanges, without the social scaffolding of a television screen, usually lasted two or three hours and we parted ways in the late afternoon. I often returned home with a homework assignment.

He had suffered a precipitous decline from our first meeting months ago, but aging went that way sometimes. He deflected questions about his health, ascribing his recent difficulties to old age, changing the subject to machines or Russian reminiscences. His mental acuity remained, but his movement through space slowed and became more deliberate, planning out pit stops for each route and keeping a tight orbit around the bathroom. We talked about walking to the neighborhood park to watch basketball but were interrupted by a long overdue Alberta Clipper which dropped directly south last week, riding the eastern flank of the Rockies, delivering a half-foot of snow.

I never medically cared for another human, having been spared that major life experience as an only child in a nuclear family. My insulation was aided by the sudden nature of my father's death and the intercontinental distance between me and my mother during her terminal period. Bringing over frozen pizza and doing simple chores was easy, the next stages of the aging process would be dramatically harder. I could see myself helping Victor to get dressed, assisting with personal hygiene, and facilitating trips to the bathroom. This could be my stoic self-imposed hardship, an inverted inheritance. Instead of running from responsibility, I would embrace it. At some point, his pride would fight the most embarrassing assistance and perhaps he'd hire a home health care aide, contingent on his financial state, something even more cryptic than his current guarded medical condition.

*   *   *

I lugged the vintage compressor up the basement steps, stopping to take two breaks along the way. The unit was built heavy with titanic margins of safety, a welded steel frame supporting the motor, piston, and a ten-gallon horizontal tank across the bottom. It was one of the random tools grazing on the dusty basement floor, next to an old lawnmower, a circular grinder, a sump pump, and what looked to be a set of pneumatic paint sprayers. The dated equipment suggested buying them used at a discount store or being accumulated after breakups with handy boyfriends.

Nina and I met up after our Transcendent appointments then headed back to her place to sun ourselves on the front porch. Her prewar era bungalow presided over a spacious yard with clumps of drought-tolerant grasses and perennials. The house had two bedrooms and a single bathroom at ground level with an unfinished basement, a crawl space attic, and a faded windowless shed at the back of the yard against the alley. It was a modest but enviable dwelling that given its lot size could easily be scraped to build a triplex townhouse as the bow wave of gentrification came through.

"Ever blow out sprinkler lines?" Nina asked and I waited for her to elaborate. "It's a big racket, people charging $80 now."

"I'll knock it down to $75 with a friends and family discount."

"You know how to impress a woman."

"Actually, I hate plumbing, everything leaks. You just try to limit the damage," I said. While never being a homeowner, every apartment I had ever lived in had experienced some sort of plumbing ordeal, from leaking sewage lines caused by an upstairs toilet knocked off its wax ring, to sudden water heater leakage, to root intrusions into century-old clay pipes, and so on.

"A friend gave me an old compressor last spring, let's give it a shot after lunch," Nina said and left to drop off some framed pieces at a gallery in the city.

Taking a customer to the airport would be a good way to kill time until she returned, and it would help get my balance sheet closer to the breakeven point for the month. Instead, a few amateur online videos later, I was dragging the compressor up the stairs and dashing to the hardware store to get pneumatic push fittings and a discount air hose.

Our intimacy level had simmered at a low heat for the past few weeks, small air bubbles collecting in the bottom of the pot of water occasionally rising to the top. It was clear we were taking the slow route and building up trust, avoiding being outflanked by alcohol or waves of oxytocin. Decoding her romantic preferences remained a challenge but it seemed plausible that a spontaneous *Act of Service* like the pressurized purging of her sprinkler pipes would be well received. After a few unsuccessful attempts, I finally drained the backflow prevention plumbing coming from the house and used the compressor to blow out the system while listening to a podcast on Neolithic agriculture.

*   *   *

Nina pulled out her laptop as we ate a food truck lunch of spicy rice noodles with egg and fried meat out of brown paper trays. We copied the twenty dual-page photos of Dr. Patel's medical notebook from my phone to her laptop and expanded them on the screen.

"At least it's a woman's handwriting. How did you get these again?" Nina asked.

"Overnight sleep study and a distracted intern working security," I said. "I kept the headgear attached and took a long bathroom break, I guess they forgot to lock the staff offices."

"This could be a gold mine, but deciphering it will be tough," she said while flipping through the images. "In a double-blind experiment, there will be no references to individual names. Although maybe you're the only one with the sleep study."

One page had a large table with headers labeled *polygenic class A* through *D* and *study groups I, II, and III*. Each cell within the table listed metrics: *PFC-E(t), Self-Well(t), META(t)*. Dr. Patel rough-sketched a third axis of the table coming out of the page, making it a three-dimensional dataset, but without any axis label.

"Looks like some sort of design of experiments, trying to span over a range of genetic profiles. Maybe looking for drug effectiveness?" I asked.

"They are definitely tracking genetics. I bet the doctors are only tasked with gathering a diverse population to feed the algorithm, let the machine learning stuff find the correlations."

"What about *PFC-E(t)*? Probably a function of time in some way."

"No idea. Maybe prefrontal cortex engagement with those fMRI scans? Or perceived functional control or something. Has to be medical, one of the things they keep testing each week, hence the change over time."

"*Self-well* must be those exams we keep getting on our phones," I said.

"Yeah, or something they download from us each visit."

"*META*?"

"Metadata maybe?" Nina offered. "Geolocations, search histories, that sort of thing, what allows Xmundio to know more about you than yourself." She studied the writing, panning across the screen. "But it's in all caps, could be an acronym. She seems like a person that would be consistent with capitalization."

We moved on to the next images of the notebook which looked to be less structured medical experiments than a sketch pad. The pages were covered with arrows of abbreviated symbols joining and looping back on each other, perhaps suggesting neurochemical release and uptake, vague tables of presumed character traits, and many items starting with the letter X followed by three numbers: X450, X107, X884.

"I bet those X's are programs funded by Xmundio, part of their overall human wellness initiative thing. We could be in X343, that one is mentioned a lot," Nina said.

"Scroll back, I think I saw X343 on the bottom of some pages. X for Xmundio?" The cube of seven kept leaping out of the ether.

"Everything is sexier as an X. Yup there it is again next to the signature panel. We must be part of X343 and she's signing off this page for that program. Not every sheet has that though which seems careless. She's supporting multiple X numbers, hell this could be her doodle pad for all of them."

We searched through the disjointed sketches, looking for telltale language and finding mentions of *default mode*, a potential reference to the default mode network which becomes activated during daydreams and is commonly tied to the sense of self, the always running kernel of the mind's operating system. Psychedelics can disintegrate the network and lead to a perceived loss of ego, per a recent podcast on the therapeutic value of the drugs I had listened to. I thought back to Leo's notebook with sketches of machines, well-defined electromechanical systems with intentionally added chaotic elements. This seemed like the inverse, a probing for order amongst the miasma of multiple variables, which could only be approximated through statistics. Instead of designing a machine, it was an archeology, feeding their wealthy patron and big data analytic engines our artifacts.

"Have you noticed any changes to your ego over the last few weeks?" Nina asked. "Less stressed about day-to-day personal troubles?"

"I'm not sure, maybe a bit," I said.

"It's getting cooler, we'll come back to this," Nina said while getting up and stretching out in the sun. "Come help me get the bikes from the shed."

She noticed the compressor on the side of the house while we moved the two bikes from the shed to her car, and gave me an emphatic hug, lifting her feet off the ground to load up my dorsal lat muscles. I instinctively tried to smell her hair without her noticing but she released too soon. We loaded up the car quickly, the compressor's return to the basement could wait, but the autumn sun would not.

The bike and pedestrian trail did a drunken meander along a late nineteenth-century canal. Several towns pitched in to make a well-maintained path of crusher fines along the edge of the water utility land. The banks of the canal were a jungle compared to the otherwise brown landscape, with clusters of yellowing cottonwoods and patches of green grass. The weekday afternoon meant less traffic, retired couples walking labradoodles, and new mothers' groups with high-end strollers.

"Today an up or down day?" Nina asked while she remounted the front tires on the bikes. She let me borrow an extra hot pink hybrid while she rode a smaller frame mountain bike.

"Trending up, but I could use some endorphins." I picked up the pace to ride alongside her, feeling tightness in my knees. My success with the compressor had raised my spirits immensely; I had been validated through labor, had completed a necessary task, and been recognized for it. Perhaps I should become a skilled tradesman, underappreciated but reasonably compensated, like an electrician, a trade guided by a coherent logic, abstracted from physical toil yet still out in the real world. "Yesterday felt a little foggy."

"Let's work out those hard water mineral deposits," she said, speeding up and shifting into high gear while standing up on the bike, her quads pumping to sway the frame from side to side. We stopped for a water break where I parked and pretended to explore a footbridge to catch my breath. "She had three study groups, what does that mean: test, control, and something else?"

"Some sort of gradient test, higher dosage for one group?" I offered.

"Can I see your new set of pills?"

I pulled them out of the front pocket of my backpack. Nina took one out for inspection, lightly scratching it with her fingernail like a miner inspecting fool's gold.

"Can we swap for a week?" she asked.

"The pills?"

"Yeah, I know they've got me in the control group, or maybe the lowest tier."

"That would compromise the experiment."

"This place is so fucking ethically compromised already, don't you think they're collecting all of our information and just feeding it into some massive algorithm?" Nina said, the first time I heard her use an expletive out of frustration instead of for emphasis.

"They'll catch it in the blood test," I said, mostly believing that to be true. I didn't want to start taking placebos or get thrown out of the study. Going to their office every other morning had become a routine way to start the day. And I needed the money.

"We'll split the pills now, then tell them they're destroyed, put through the wash or something. You'll get another week's supply, easy."

The app had an emergency feature allowing the user to message the pharmacy for issues and this seemed plausible, especially for a single week's worth of pills. I pulled up the form and tapped around on the screen, looking for a pre-canned request. As a youth tennis player, I got praise for the fluidity of my groundstrokes, the ability to snap an inside-out forehand winner from an open stance with just the right amount of topspin and speed. After initial gains, my game stalled out at the high school level. I was chronically hampered by a reluctance to move forward while hitting shots, I didn't watch the ball into the strings and didn't dictate the point. I was too comfortable to sit back and wait. I tapped out a message about the washing machine turning the pills into a white paste and then gave Nina four of them before we started biking again.

Sunlight bled through the gaps between the curtains, its intensity implying it was mid instead of early morning. The room was comfortably messy with pants and shirts draped over standing mirrors and strung across open dresser drawers. Most of the battalion of pillows were scattered on the floor and not in a pillow wall formation Nina had apparently marshaled for other bed inhabitants to keep physical distance. I grabbed one of her undershirts from the floor for a makeshift eye mask and laid back down on my side using one of the thicker pillows.

A heaviness fell over my body, and I tried to sink into the bed for another hour of sleep. I bit off a quarter of an edible varietal of cannabinoids designed to produce relaxation an hour or two after midnight, which helped my mind surrender but was still swimming around in the bloodstream in the morning. I carefully rotated my neck towards the opposite wall until seeing a ringlet of hair against the white duvet, then returned to a fetal position fighting to not reawaken memories of the previous night.

"That ride wore me out. You getting tired?" Nina had asked. We'd both finished nursing beers at the bar near her place where we had gone after coming back from the bike ride and having noodle leftovers.

"Yeah, I'm fading," I said, watching the new band setting up on stage.

"I've learned that the longer they spend tuning their instruments, the worse they sound."

I laughed and agreed. "You come here much?"

"Used to, it was even grungier back in the day. My ex played here a lot," she said. "Lives in Louisiana now."

The dive bar was patronized by small groups of locals, post-college friends shooting darts, and dudes in Carhartt with thick calluses. I checked some kind of leader board behind the bar, seeing rows of patron names and tallies, while waiting for my credit card to process. I guessed either stock car racing standings or the number of phone numbers collected at the bar.

"The scoreboard is for the locals. The bar chooses an MVP of the night: best songs, best rounds, best jokes," Nina said as she came back from the bathroom. "Happens at midnight I think."

"You want to stick it out for another thirty minutes?"

"Nah, it's late, not sure they even do it on music night. It's more of a bullshitter contest."

We walked back under the streetlights, concluding that the suspiciously wide street must have at one time been a trolley route connecting the outer bungalow district to the town center. Each lighted window became a subject for an invented story: the second job and second shifters, the night schoolers, and spectral figures saving money on red-eye flights. I waxed poetic about the joy of a tree lawn and wider sidewalks that allowed a couple to have a dignified shoulder-to-shoulder stroll. Some of the post-war streets nearby had a lazy merged sidewalk, curb, and drain channel with the concrete only two feet wide, shrunken down in the age of the automobile just like windows in the age of electric lighting. As Nina and I walked, we used the curbs as balance beams for field sobriety tests and the alleys became an Attenborough narrated urban safari for rats, rabbits, racoons, and coyotes.

"Do you fall for the musician type?" I asked as we sat at her kitchen table.

"Maybe, though I never became a groupie. I always went for the poor, angsty ones. Struggling seems sexy and noble when you can sing about it," Nina said with a smile. "Water or tea?"

"I'll take some chamomile if you've got it."

"The sexiness wears off when they spend all your savings on studio time or black-market pain killers. I hope I've escaped my bad boy phase mostly intact," Nina said, sipping herbal tea in a teal-colored glazed ceramic mug, a baby boomer line she collected from trips to Goodwill with surgical precision. "Have you dated anyone besides Jessica?"

"I've gone on some dates, but nothing serious," I said, essentially answering the body count question without answering the question. I went on two dates with a civil engineer early in the summer but her face suddenly snapped into a strong resemblance of a college male friend, something that couldn't be unseen. "Though I think seriousness was either a cause or symptom of my and Jessica's breakup."

"What do you mean?"

"You get locked into these roles. You're no longer laying out in a field and looking up at the stars, instead, you're getting anal about separating the colors from the whites and retreating into yourselves."

"Or making up a reason and leaving for a weekend camping trip by yourself and your camera," Nina said and gave me a supportive smile. "It was more than the kids stuff, huh?"

"We coasted on our memories from the early days for too long, transitioned into being friends but harboring the resentment of that absent passion. And we were too stubborn to fix it, I guess," I admitted. "I think she had a revelation that time was running out for her and she needed to make a dramatic change."

"I'm sorry. Relationships are complicated."

"I think I needed a fail-fast approach earlier, try a bunch of stuff and see what works."

"That's why we're a good match, I've got a surplus of that," Nina said and opened my hand to inspect my right palm. "Ah see, it's so obvious. Your love line is long but has a strong intersection with your fate line here."

"You're the real drug from this study," I said, using my other hand to support her neck as we kissed, then we stood up and I guided us into the bedroom.

I anticipated a traitorous abandonment of the body, that wreck of flesh increasingly reliant on some enigmatic consuming *chemistry*. Whether we were aided by a lingering buzz or just stumbled into an alchemy of the senses, we found each other.

*   *   *

The smell of coffee and the sound of the shower running filled the air when I woke back up. I sat up in bed and stretched, the fatigue somewhat abated. Nina's phone vibrated against the nightstand with an alert. I tapped the front of the screen which previewed two emails, the first from Transcendent:

Ms. Tillis, We acknowledge and appreciate your continued participation with Transcendent Health, however, we are unable to provide you with more information...

The second was from Bristol Consulting:

Ms. Tillis, As an independent consulting group for cutting-edge medical research, we work to ensure that all of our contractors uphold the highest standards of conduct...

The phone prompted a facial recognition test which I failed, then requested a PIN. I put my jeans on and went into the kitchen, filled a mug with black coffee from the glass carafe, and warmed myself in the sunlight coming through from the living room window. Nina turned the thermostat down to fifty-five during the night.

"Can you load up my IV drip with coffee?" Nina said as she walked out of the bathroom using towels as a turban and miniskirt, and headed into the bedroom.

I found some creamer in the fridge and poured her a cup, then started doing the dirty dishes in the sink, an activity that I always found relaxing. I loved seeing the surfactant action of the dishwashing fluid pull off the oils and encrusted layers, knowing their continuous effort was underway without any required work, providing time for mental wandering. I thought about the emails. Nina must have been asking about her status in the study but the other one made no sense.

"I'm so excited to take one of these." She took a pill from the set I gave her. "Have you heard back from them yet?"

"Ready for pickup this morning," I said, finishing up the utensils.

"I can't believe it's already eleven-thirty," Nina said while sipping coffee on the sofa and checking her phone. "I'll clean that stuff up."

"Just realized I need to take off." I remembered that it was my day for lunch at Victor's. I usually came by before noon and lingered through the early afternoon.

"Airport ride?"

"No, I'm helping out a friend who is sort of stuck at home."

"Martin Rasmus, I thought I had you pretty much all to myself."

"It's this older guy, he's sort of a retired eccentric. You'd like him," I said, wondering how much I told Victor about Nina. At most, I recalled mentioning her in passing, expressing my confusion about our relationship status before quickly returning to more familiar topics.

"I grok weirdo, speak it like a native-born. I guess we should leave now huh?"

"Okay, just ask before taking any photos or anything."

"I love this space, very open, must be the original floors. This okay?" Nina asked as she went around raising the Venetian blinds and wadding up the window coverings into a ball balanced on top of the curtain rod. She worked the windows free and raised them a few inches. "It's gorgeous out, but let me know if you get cold."

"Uh oh, Martin, let's not point out that the walls are empty," Victor said with a chuckle. He snapped to life when Nina arrived, acting more awake than he had been in days.

"No offense but the walls would benefit from a very light gray color, almost white. Martin is a good painter," Nina said, touching a flaking area of the dark beige plaster. "I like minimalism, but these are really blank. Cool rug though."

A reddish carpet with a kaleidoscopic pattern hung from the far wall. A small silver framed black and white photo of a couple dangled at the upper left corner.

"Relatives?"

"My parents, must be early 1960s."

"I can see the resemblance; you've got a bit of both. Where do they live now?" Nina asked as she looked closely at the photo.

"In a few feet of Russian soil. How old do you think I am?"

Nina laughed and I took drink orders to pair with the frozen supreme pizza. She broached personal subjects with ease, quickly gathering information I only gleaned or sniped. They talked about his family and his emigration to the States. I caught excerpts about harrowing school experiences while pouring tortilla chips into a bowl at the kitchen table.

"Martin wouldn't send a student to the blackboard to take a derivative," Victor said buoyantly. "You should show her our hydraulic difference engine."

I took Nina back to the workshop and pulled out the device, explaining the original intent of building a water computer but starting out with this discrete diffusion network. The machine struck me as comically simple as I talked about the role of diameter and height difference in filling and draining the tanks.

"The platform still needs to be closed out to cover up the plumbing and electronics down there," I said.

"It's cool. People always connect with water. I'll take videos of it to post on my channel," Nina said. "What are these big drills?"

"End mills, you can cut on the tip or the side," I said and picked one up from the milling machine platform. "For precision metal cutting."

Nina took the fluted tool and felt its sharp edges. "Photographs are so flat. We already have enough screens. I should have taken shop classes; this is actual material." She kissed me lightly on the cheek.

"You should see some of Victor's machines," I said before we went back to the front room where Victor was reading his newspaper. "Is it okay if Nina and I check out some of your older stuff?"

Victor waited to respond, doing some type of mental calculation. "They are boxed up in the basement, but we can go down."

Victor unboxed the chaotic waterwheel and placed it on the workbench, showcasing it with a desk lamp before turning off the ceiling lights. The orange and red rings danced back and forth leaving retinal afterimages. Victor swept the concrete floor with a push broom while we watched captivated.

"This is great, why do you keep it sealed up in a box?" Nina asked once Victor turned the overhead lights back on.

"It's from another era. I'm more interested in creation than exhibition," Victor said, placing its cardboard box back on the table. "I'm glad you like it."

"Can I take a picture before you put it away?"

"Are you going to post it on the Internet?" Victor asked, looking at me.

"No, I won't share it. I have a memory like an Etch a Sketch so I need this."

Victor went back to cleaning while Nina took photos and a short video of the device, marveling at the elegance of the gear train and asking why the wheel changed direction. I pulled up a video of the Lorenz waterwheel on my phone, showing how it can rotate in one direction consistently until a subtle change pushes it into chaotic behavior. Exact trajectories cannot be predicted but rather future positions lived in probabilistic neighborhoods, like an electron's position around the atomic nucleus.

Nina's phone rang as the three of us headed upstairs and she stepped outside to take the call. I fixed me and Victor glasses of soda with ice and we sat back down at the kitchen table.

"Are you two dating?" Victor asked.

"I think so."

He chuckled. "Very spirited, that can be a good thing. Most people are happier with a partner in the long run."

I nodded in agreement, thinking about the need to define our relationship. Without the gravity of children, partnerships could turn experimental and malleable, even polyamorous. "What about you?"

"I stopped feeling that pressure a while ago. Maybe if I planned to live another twenty years, but I've reached the end of my service life."

The timer on the oven sounded and I pulled out the pizza, cutting it on top of its flattened box and setting slices on three paper plates. I expected Nina to pick off the meat and allow me to create super supreme slices.

"Damn batteries are dead," Victor said while opening up the cover on his CD player.

"I can get you the same music on your phone. Or how about some podcasts, do you listen to those?" I asked.

"Another monthly fee?"

"No, most of them are free. They've got ones on philosophy, history, science stuff. One has like ninety episodes on the Russian Revolution. Let me see your phone."

Victor handed it over and it unlocked without any password. It was an older model but should still have enough memory to handle some episodes. A wave of fear swept over me when the web browser started loading a page. A person's browsing history, especially one without the skill to use privacy settings, could be disastrous. I allowed the website to load and it pulled up a quote for two tickets on the Western Sky Narrow Gauge railroad. It was a historic train ride that left town and meandered into the mountains, spending a night in a former mining hamlet before heading back. I switched to the podcast app and subscribed to a few, then showed Victor how to find the icon on the home screen and listen to episodes.

Nina bounced back into the kitchen and took a sip from my soda while I brought the plates of food to the table. We ate efficiently as she stepped through her bucket list of hikes and joked about a current high-maintenance print advertising client. She pressed Victor to tell us more about growing up in Russia, but he deflected and said it was time for his afternoon nap. I closed the windows while she cycled through photos of the waterwheel.

I stopped in front of a powder-blue freshly painted building and double-checked the address on my phone. The message from Transcendent said to report here, a nondescript office in the industrial area south of the state highway at nine o'clock instead of the regular location, exactly one hour after taking the medication. I circled the area a few times before parking next to a pickup truck with its front bumper removed, a jarring sight like seeing a face without a lower jaw. The town must have zoned several blocks for commercial development, producing a set of high vacancy Executive Business Plazas and unused parking structures. The few areas of activity were an HVAC repair business, two auto garages, and a group on a smoke break outside of a catering company. A one-way glass door said Mountain Medical Imaging.

I took a seat against the wall in the narrow lobby. Stacked moving boxes sat in the reception area, sturdy white copy paper ones with orange numbered tags. The light blue and green pastel color pattern on the walls suggested that it had either been a children's dental office or an aquarium store.

"Martin, right?" a woman strode into the lobby and reached out to shake my hand. She stood a few inches over me with an unmistakably Scandinavian look: long straight blonde hair, light eyebrows, and broad swimmer's shoulders. "Please come back, sorry for the wait. I'm Anna."

"Is this where I'll report for the Transcendent study from now on?"

"Transcendent?" Anna paused typing. "Oh right, sorry. I work with that team as a specialist. It looks like we'll be doing a SPECT test today."

"SPECT?"

"Single Photon Emission Computed Tomography. We'll inject a radiotracer that selectively binds to a neurotransmitter, in this case serotonin, and visualize its movement in the brain."

"They ordered this test?"

"Yes. Since you're in a study, they don't give me many details. Sometimes they want to strike a baseline before the next phase."

"Do you do many of these for Transcendent?" I asked.

"I can't talk specifics for any one client, but I can tell you that business is very good. We just moved here to get more space," she said and went over to the refrigerator, took out a small vial, and drew up a clear liquid into a syringe. The sleep study must have raised a concern about my neurological state. Or else this marked the start of a new stage in the trial and they needed to check my chemical health before venturing further.

I laid down on the table after she injected the radioisotope. The machine had two sensor heads the size of thick reams of paper which rotated back and forth overhead, collecting nuclear emissions from my skull. Anna reminded me to stay still in the head cradle. I excelled at this, attributing looking five years younger than my actual age to keeping a consistent flat affect and avoiding large skin deformations or cyclic strains from laughing.

"I want you to think about a positive experience from when you were a child and without speaking, please replay that in your head," Anna prompted. This was very similar to a request at Transcendent so I retrieved the memory of getting a poodle mix puppy at the age of six for Christmas. She then prompted me to retrieve a negative experience, without requiring it to be from childhood. In the abstract this was easy but I tried to find something acute, one that would elicit a groundswell of emotion. I made the easy return to a memory of that same dog, now thirteen and being taken to the veterinary hospital, giving me a soft stare before I left the room to let the vet administer the lethal dose. My mother assured me it was the right thing to do on the phone that afternoon, she was a nurse after all and knew the importance of a dignified death. I questioned the signal strength of each memory, wondering if the instrument would see these emerge from the background. We continued through other prompts that seemed to mirror the ones from Transcendent.

"I'll see you back here at five o'clock. Please avoid any caffeine or other stimulants or depressants," Anna said. As I left the office, I walked past a crew of technicians assembling a tank-sized piece of medical equipment in the room next door.

*   *   *

I parked behind a black glossy imported sedan then grabbed the bag of frozen cheese and potato perogies, butter, and onions from the front seat. A woman was standing in the living room when I opened the unlocked front door.

"Martin, find out who this lady is," Victor said, his hands folded against his chest like he was trying to keep them warm.

"Hello Martin, I'm Andrea Eastman. Are you a family member?"

"No, a friend. What's going on?"

"More people wanting to take photos," Victor said.

"I'm a journalist and would love to do a story on his brother's machines," she said. She looked more like a corporate lawyer than a journalist with salon smooth hair and a bleached white smile.

"Who do you work for?" I asked.

"I'm freelance, magazines and newspapers mostly," she said. "You've seen that streaming documentary on the Samoan sculptor?"

"No, missed that. Do you have press credentials? Are those still a thing?" I asked while unloading groceries on the kitchen counter.

"Here's my article on environmental art in the Canadian Rockies," she held up her phone, showing a byline with a pen and ink sketch that looked like her. The newspaper was the *LA Metropolitan*, a daily rescued from bankruptcy three years before by Kory Gorman. The paper leaned progressive but kept curiously silent on technology monopolies and data privacy.

"What's for lunch?" Victor asked.

"Fried onions with a side of perogies," I answered.

"I apologize for interrupting. Would it be possible to just take a few photos of one of the devices, then maybe I'll come back later for an interview?" Andrea asked. "With you both present of course."

I looked over at Victor who rolled his eyes. "Martin, go get the hydraulic difference engine."

Andrea positioned a camera on a miniature tripod facing an elevated platform in the center of the kitchen table. I placed the water machine down next to it. "What is this stage thing?" I asked.

"Programmable rotation table, allows the camera to take precise images every degree so we can generate a three-dimensional image of the object," Andrea said while inspecting the acrylic tanks and reservoir in the base. "Is this one of Leo Ivantusky's machines?"

"This one works. Martin will add some water."

"Are there any of Leo's devices here? I believe you're his brother?" Andrea asked with confusion. She opened her phone and scrolled quickly.

"Our time is done, young lady, I'm not interested in an interview or any pictures," Victor said and opened the door.

Andrea put the equipment back in the duffle bag and left. Victor shrugged on his way to the bathroom, bemused by the guest. I diced onions for lunch.

*   *   *

The photo showed Kory Gorman cutting a red ribbon in front of the new abstract expressionism exhibit at the LA Museum of Contemporary Art. He had loaned the museum several of his pieces, including an apparently very valuable but goofy work with two large red and black rectangles. Gorman had become a patron of the arts over the last decade: creating new fellowships for young urban artists, funding museum wings, and loaning out works from his private collection.

In a *60 Minutes* interview, Gorman discussed his transformation from a 100-hour workweek tech billionaire to an enlightened humanist. He described how his own life had unwittingly followed the narrator of Proust's *In Search of Lost Time*, a novel he consumed a few pages of each day during morning coffee. He started out seeking celebrity through material wealth only to become disillusioned. He then jumped into the convulsions of romantic love, his money giving him easy access to beauty, which he found pleasurable but ultimately unsatisfying. He landed on artistic creation and appreciation as having the potential for finding real meaning, to cut through the mind's default programming to re-engage with the impossibility of life. He acknowledged his futile attempts at art and reframed his role as a well-financed enabler, one who would help others find new planes of creative expression, which like any new artistic movement needed its own vocabulary and a fresh set of tools.

I accidentally pulled up the phone's privacy settings while trying to attach Bluetooth headphones to listen to the latest BBC Sounds installment on the Crusades. The Transcendent Health app allowed sharing of all personal data, including location and photos, something I distinctly remember Nina disabling in the cemetery. The defaults must have been reset during a software update. I slid the toggle buttons back to the left. An ad about male vitality-enhancing micronutrients halted Gorman's interview and made me shut the laptop cover.

Nina was coming back to town the next night after going spelunking with friends at remote limestone caves to the south. Our daily text messages mixed sarcasm with photos of cave bacon. I needed to clean my apartment, cut the clutter by returning library books and sweep up the red pepper flakes that had somehow migrated across all the horizontal surfaces. A strange instability had grown over me over the last few days, which could have been a symptom of the new round of medication, or just ordinary sleep deprivation. I caught myself eating an entire bag of tortilla chips at the kitchen counter and cycling through the first thirty seconds of each song on my playlists, not enjoying just consuming synaptic junk food. A general uneasiness also arrived. Turning down an aisle of the grocery store felt like entering the women's bathroom by accident, pressing an elevator button required the same triple checking as the sleep-deprived selection of the overhead light instead of the help button on a flight.

An evening shower drew out a realization that the reporter had arrived two days after Nina's visit, one in which she took pictures and a video on her phone that was surely uploaded to the Xmundio cloud. That would have confirmed that the machines were at Victor's residence, something likely verified through GPS geolocation. Of course, the interviewer worked with the newspaper owned by Gorman. Leo would be another trophy for Gorman, the discovery of cryptic machines made by a Cold War-era missing genius. Not only would it make great copy, but Gorman could play the hero and help restore some of the pieces. Anyone watching the interview could see that he was still stuck in Proust's stage one of maturation, a nerdy kid desperate for recognition. I was now an easy target, having given my name to the reporter and blithely sharing phone data for who knows how long. The previews of Nina's emails I had seen from the morning after the night at her place zoomed back into my mental foreground, the unusual direct email denial from Transcendent and another one from an odd consulting group. The water started getting colder, pushing me out of the shower and straight into bed.

"I didn't know you could get a tan in a cave," I said as Nina got out of her car at the playground parking lot.

"The last night we stayed at my friend Louie's ranch next to some BLM land. Spent a day in the sun removing invasive bullfrogs from the streams," Nina said, catching the basketball and dribbling as we walked towards the court. "It's gorgeous down there, sort of like here seventy years ago maybe. The prairie dogs have plague though."

"Get some good photos?"

"Yeah, I think so. The lighting in the caves is tough, but it's another world, and there's a purity to it. You should come next time," Nina said and did a layup. "I'm wiped out."

We took turns shooting, then transitioned to a game of horse. I set up for a classic behind the backboard shot while Nina checked her phone.

"Have you been in other Transcendent studies?" I asked.

She kept looking at the screen for a second. "Why do you ask?"

"Just wondered, I recall you saying something about other clinical trials."

"I've done a few out of the hospital, some psych ones," Nina said after catching a firm bounce pass.

"I saw an email preview on your phone mentioning your continued involvement with Transcendent."

"You've been spying on my phone?"

"I heard a ding and thought it was an alarm – it was instinct," I said, realizing that looking at someone's phone was currently the most egregious violation of their privacy. "You've worked with them before?"

Nina paused and we caught eyes. "I've done two trials with Transcendent before this, but no idea what they are doing now, really."

"The same protocol with the fMRI, headset scans, blood tests?" I asked, surprised at my forwardness.

"Similar but fewer tests. Only went in every fourth day back then."

"Were you in the experimental or control group?"

"Experimental, though they never confirmed afterward, no requirement to disclose for privately funded research," Nina said and passed the ball back to me without shooting. "But something changed, I started getting up early to take photos and updated my webpage which I hadn't touched in years."

"And they brought you back for a second round?"

"They contacted me four months later saying I showed *outcomes of interest*, so of course, I jumped at the chance. By that point, the first round started to wear off," she said and we both walked over to the park bench. "The first trial could have been a screening, the second one felt much more clinical, more tests and the phone app thing."

Being selected for three consecutive rounds didn't make sense but maybe she represented a target genotype. The study was now unblinded with repeat participants and being in the control group for a third round seemed even more bizarre.

"Why would they stick you in the control group now?"

"Long-term study?"

A subject of long-term study but included with the current trial participants was reckless. "Are you working as a consultant with Bristol Consulting?" I asked, recalling the other email.

"We don't have a fall here, it's just a fast turn to mud and browns," Nina said, pushing a clump of black-spotted cottonwood leaves with her foot.

"Are you a confederate?"

"It's not like that. I needed to get back in the study."

"What are they even paying you to do?"

"I'm a facilitator. But honestly, they don't tell me shit and it's like $100 a week," Nina said hurriedly and pulled out her phone. "Here look at my bank statement."

"How many other marks do you have, two, five, twenty?" I asked.

"Martin, you're blowing this way out of proportion. They are going to fire me anyway. Look at this email," Nina said, sliding against me to show the message.

I couldn't focus on the text on the screen, looking through it instead of at it while feeling a wave of nausea nucleating in my stomach. A gust of wind blew leaves back onto the court, spinning them in a small vortex for a while until the momentum dissipated. Nina pushed the locks of her hair back from her face and then we got up to finish the game. I stagnated at H-O-R-S on her, then lost after badly missing several bank shots at the end. I expressed excitement that the airport ride prices were trending up and we exchanged a wooden goodbye hug.

Charging through space at a nautical mile a minute felt exhilarating as I drove away. I had resisted the immediate nihilistic urge to break up with Nina but still felt a sense of release, a confirmation of the impossibility of our relationship. I regained permission to become like Victor, broodingly brilliant living in splendid isolation.

I got back to the apartment from Victor's around mid-afternoon after cooking the two of us bratwurst and sauerkraut on toasted buns with mustard. You could chew on the umami in the air and we both enjoyed the meal in near silence. I brought in the morning newspaper from the porch and we slowly browsed it, lingering on the classifieds and agreeing that the prices of used vehicles were highly inflated. I left earlier than usual saying I had an airport ride gig but instead headed back directly to my apartment.

I set a twenty-five minute alarm, an excusable amount of time for an underemployed grown man to nap on a perfect fall day. I felt simultaneously tired and restless. It all made sense now. From the very beginning, it was a setup. Nina and I were placed together in the exam room, our meeting surely arranged given that I never interacted with any other participants. She flirted immediately, borrowing my phone to protect me from prying companies when in reality she had removed all the privacy protections. She followed that with a restrained teasing affection, all the while implying I wasn't her type, keeping me hooked on the line. Giving her some of my pills unlocked the next level of intimacy. She knew that the most effective stratagem for attachment is to give pleasure centers occasional rewards. The most likely scenario had her being contracted through a consulting company to keep legal distance from Transcendent, serving in some type of surveillance role, and scoring some pills from me to continue her treatment. She may have even developed feelings over time. Romantic comedies installed in me a belief that superficially asymmetric relationships could evolve into genuine affection, enabled by the alluring woman's malleable attraction to her invariably ugly but funny male co-star.

I opened one of the dating apps on my phone. Having turned off notifications, I had missed ten Likes, which were now digitally arranged like a stack of cards with only the top one visible. The initial excitement collapsed after I cycled through the queue. Several were from college-aged foreigners giving peace signs, posing on horseback, and partying on yachts, clearly bots, while another was a polyamorous couple, the guy giving off a woodsman *bear* vibe and the girl layered with tattoos and piercings. I went back to the general pool, mindlessly swiping through large swaths of humanity. The algorithms had clearly placed me in the misfit category, suggesting women performing fellatio on cigars and profiles made up exclusively of headshots with puppy dog ears and glitter filters. I suspected that Nina had a profile on one of the apps which would pop up in an act of ironic cruelty eventually, maybe our joint picture with deft cropping or an outright digital black marker over my face.

Our text messages halted after the basketball court confrontation. Outside of texting while drunk, the chances of our breaking a stalemate now seemed negligible. Ghosting her now must be some sort of revenge against Jessica, some negative way of proving my agency and returning to personal freedom on my terms, while keeping a degree of ambiguity to avoid guilt.

Adjustable dumbbells stared back at me from in front of the television, unmoved since I purchased them last week at a garage sale. I decided that I would earn each shower I took with perspiration, build up my core body strength with weight training as the days got shorter and the sidewalks became covered with ice. I needed to focus on interior work anyway, develop my physical and mental machinery, the Luxor temple of the body and the Rome of the mind. Leo and Victor's machines made sense, they were works of art but carved out of physical laws, demonstrating a truth independent of intersubjective validation. Sure, I needed to establish financial stability with some manner of employment, but then I could direct excess time towards cultivating an artistic hobby like the Russians, picking an art form removed from my identity as a single, middle-aged, cisgender, straight, white man, a category which according to the list of the twenty best works of fiction of the year, was not only completely tired but also boring. I needed something universal, some undeniable essential truth.

The morning sun compacted the overnight snow, revealing the dirt-infused ice substrate. Spring in Almaty brought increased precipitation but warmer temperatures, mud overtaking snow and creating a messy vestibule to pass through before entering the glory of late spring. The herds of sheep in the outlying farms exhibited an increased restlessness, individuals venturing out of the barn into the still barren snowy fields in greater numbers.

The road conditions made Amir a few minutes late to pick me up. He and the van shared an indeterminate age and a high level of reliability. The cab squatted over the front wheels and managed four rows of seats behind the driver. Amir drove me from my city apartment to the exurban school each weekday, a solo journey for the three months since Jessica had left. His mobile number on the side of the van helped collect a few other passenger pickups each day along the route. His weak English and my butchered Kazakh made for comfortably quiet early morning and after-work trips.

The van fishtailed around a tight uphill curve, but Amir gently accelerated and corrected the oversteer to keep us out of the ditch. I gave a nonverbal compliment and thumbs up then returned to staring out the window. Each morning trip during sixth grade, I wished the school bus would get into an accident, an event that would obliterate loitering by our lockers and homeroom periods. The bus's sheer tonnage and low speed unfortunately made us invulnerable, more than capable of withstanding sideswipes. These daydreams beat staring into the cigarette burn-scarred forest green vinyl seat. Amir made up time on the straight segments and reduced traffic areas as the landscape transitioned into looser development and farms.

"Mr. Rasmus, can I join you, sir?" Alan Sultanov asked, already starting his descent onto the break area bench.

"Sure, please do," I said and gathered up my lunch, two plastic containers with pretzels and a peanut butter and jelly sandwich. The inexpensive vegan meal could handle long periods without refrigeration. Kazakh food felt biblical, a nomadic cuisine tied to the land. I tried some of the horse meat and mutton but tended to patronize Western pizza shops and buy canned food from a grocery store in Almaty.

"I'm sorry to hear about your friend, Jessica," Alan said between gulps of lumpy brown stew. "She won't be coming back?"

"No, I don't think so."

"The paintings on the schools are fantastic. Some are unfinished, did she leave any sketches of the completed works?"

"Not sure, I'll see what I can find," I said, thinking about her cluttered stack of drawings back at the apartment. Her fellowship as an artist in residence was the proximate cause for our placement in the Central Asian country. The predominately Muslim nation favored geometric art over Western iconography though not militantly as evidenced by the tolerated Soviet-era murals and sculptures. Navigating this cultural complexity in the rugged sunlit country excited her, while getting slightly faster data rates in the second world instead of the third convinced me. She worked with a dozen local schools, designing murals of vibrant angular patterns that merged into mountain peaks and soaring golden eagles. The schoolchildren screeched with delight filling in the colors.

"How are you doing with the students?" Alan asked after wiping the corners of his mouth. His genteel look contrasted with the other local men: tightly crossed legs when seated, King's English, and non-leathery skin. He functioned as some manner of school superintendent and enjoyed stopping by unannounced. One of the teachers tipped me off, so I was somewhat prepared for his arrival.

"Their English is far ahead of my Kazakh, or Russian," I answered.

"Easy to learn from a young American," Alan responded, leaning back to sip his tea. A breeze through an open window in the break room carried in a smell of manure and hair. Teaching English was my official responsibility, though many students lingered after school which became a free-form session of math puzzles and kickball. Alan and I chatted about the state of education in the country. I expressed concern with digital literacy, but he maintained a detached optimism, thinking in centuries rather than years.

"I need to travel back to the States, clear out a storage locker," I said after Alan started collecting his things to leave.

"Storage locker?"

"It's like an expensive garage. Stuff from my mother's apartment," I said ineffectively, not producing a change in his confused expression. "The rates go up dramatically at the end of the month."

"I see. Is this a one-way trip?"

"Yes, I've notified the program that the winter quarter will be my last," I said, then looked to recover with a scholastically-minded topspin return. "The kids will do great in the national exam next week."

"I am sure they will. It's not easy being away from home, I know that," Alan said and shook my hand. I followed him to his car, discussing more of the details of my departure which he took with unsurprising grace.

I needed to spend my last two weeks in the country dancing around contractual obligations. Jessica's residency paid for the apartment. Though I knew she notified them of the termination, they only recently realized her freeloading ex was still holed up in the room. My own notice of job termination came four months after the commitment deadline, but I planned to claim the life event of Jessica's departure and keep a pro-rated amount of the teaching stipend.

The storage locker in Pennsylvania was a real thing, though not the urgent situation I made it out to be. It housed a set of side chairs, an antique dresser, and a cedar box full of worthless baseball cards. Each monthly fee reminded me of unfinished business. I spent two months mentally vacant while paying for a storage locker.

"Will you be going to California, or New York?" Makpal asked, looking up from her math workbook. I showed the students maps of the U.S., but they seemed only to recognize the existence of coastal states.

"Pennsylvania, but I think I'll be moving," I said.

"You should move somewhere very different."

I nodded and smiled thinking how their country had once been populated by nomads. Makpal went back to her geometry puzzle about drilling a hole through a sphere and finding the residual volume. A quiet girl in her mid-teens, she often stayed after class to work on problems and showed a real gift for math. Judging by her clothes, her family kept to tradition and I expected her to be suffocated with domestic responsibility within five years.

"You'll be teaching, right? In an academy like this?" she asked.

"I'm not sure," I looked out over the farms and the scrub beyond. "I'm going to get a car. I need to drive again."

"That will be lovely," Makpal said. We talked about the math problem. A cynical solution was easy, but the more complete general proof required an insight to change it from two variables to one. She unlocked the answer and jogged off to hang out with a cluster of girlfriends watching a pickup soccer game. I had dreaded telling her the news but now it was over. I decided I would notify the rest of the students the next day. Many likely suspected something given that I had mentally checked out since the new year.

Amir made better time on the drive back to the apartment. A different version of me could spend another year here, try to make a life. A popular pastime in Almaty Internet cafés had young women chatting with international suitors. I could post up there, woo them by talking in English about pickup trucks and football. It wasn't the worst idea.

The landlocked nation, once a breeding ground of fearsome mounted warriors from the steppe, had transitioned into a seemingly comfortable petroleum-supported economy. The people no longer appeared driven to *make history* but ready to accept it. I thought about the storage locker, about unloading it into some modern-day version of a Conestoga wagon and traveling west. Despite being a nomad for almost fifteen years, the past dozen felt the same. The tree rings of life collapsed into a single band, each indistinguishable from the other.

I dropped off a woman from Georgia who was visiting her grandchildren, assuring her that her light coat was thick enough given that the NOAA 8-14 day forecast projected a return of unseasonably warm days, and slowly pulled away from the suburban castle. I lingered in the car, debating between grabbing another ride, getting four items for four dollars from a fast-food value menu, or heading back to my apartment to make a peanut butter and jelly sandwich. The phone rang through the hands-free console interrupting the public radio news program I was listening to. It was Sergey, who usually texted, the short messages a technological aberration for a man his age but the mode of communication I preferred.

"Martin, I have unfortunate news," Sergey said and paused. "Victor was admitted to the hospital this morning."

"What for?"

"He has late-stage stomach cancer. I fear we are heading into the final period," he said. "He mentioned you on the drive over this morning. I'm sure he'd appreciate a visit. Room 423. I'll be here for a little longer."

He was at the hospital across from my apartment, the same building whose ER I frequented as a spectator. I thought about bringing him something, concluding that flowers were not his style and food was clearly problematic for a GI disease. I drove to his house first, checked that the front door was locked, and picked up the newspaper off the porch. A new fire in the mountains grabbed the headline, this one joining the existing blaze to consume the acreage of a small New England state and forcing two in the morning door-to-door evacuations. I stopped by my apartment, grabbed my sketchbook and an energy bar with an androgynous cyclist on the wrapper.

Victor was propped up in bed, looking thin beneath the hospital gown, a glazed-over look on his face. He didn't notice my arrival in the doorway. Sergey arranged the items in the room, placing a black and white family photo on the window sill.

"Glad you came. He was terribly sick this morning in the ambulance," he said quietly while walking over. "Just received some pain medicine but he'll recognize you."

"Hey, brought over your newspaper."

"Now I know why the British fought in two opium wars," Victor smiled. "You thought it would be lung cancer, right?"

"No, I was expecting a Russian mafia hit," I joked, producing a strained laugh. "The science and technology section looks interesting."

I tried to hand him the clumsy broadsheet newspaper but he brushed it away. I began summarizing the different stories aloud and looked for a reaction to dive in further. An interferometer in a two-and-a-half mile long vacuum tube measured gravitational waves from the merging of two black holes. The event produced an extreme amount of energy causing the mattress-like surface of space-time to bounce, though it was only detectable using the most precise sensors ever built which overcame the protection of vast distances. It was a spiraling collision of two enormous indifferent states of matter seven billion light-years away, the orders of magnitude of all the quantities completely unfathomable in human terms. The article seemed to capture his attention judging by eye contact.

Sergey pulled up a chair and the two reminisced about building their accelerator, chasing down vacuum leaks and solving alignment problems. Both shared the necessary neuroticism for experimentation. The control paddle for Victor's bed had buttons for the overall height and angle of the back and leg sections but the mattress looked thin. At over thirty years younger, I woke up early with a severe backache every morning, needing some level of daily activity to stave off pain, so the thought of being kept horizontally for days was terrifying even with a heavy dose of medication. Or perhaps his pain threshold was higher than mine. Victor's levels of acute and existential agony must be in another universe, light years away and spiraling toward oblivion, barely sensible ripples in space-time.

"Take the house key," Victor said. "Finish the difference engine. Turn down the heat to fifty degrees."

"I'll still need your advice," I said, taking the key from Sergey.

"Adjust the tool speed with the pulleys," Victor said, waiting for the information to register. "Go faster with aluminum."

"I've started a new hydraulic machine," I said, filling in the silence with a lie. "Conceptual only."

"Show me the sketches," Victor responded.

"I didn't bring my notebook, but I will next time. I'm counting on you to set me straight." Sergey put on his coat when an attendant entered the room and I followed him out to the hallway. We walked away from the nurse's station to an unused seating area.

"He doesn't have a will, last or living," Sergey said. "I've finally convinced him one is necessary. My lawyer will be coming here tomorrow to review and help everyone sign it."

"Will you be the executor?"

"Yes. You will be the delegate medical durable power of attorney."

"What does that do?"

"In case I'm unavailable, you have the legal authority to make medical decisions when Victor loses that capacity. These are common arrangements but they're important to establish before things turn."

"What does the doctor say?"

"Unclear how long he has but it looks grim. Stomach cancers sometimes get very advanced before they're caught. Once you get old, you'll realize that the GI tract is quite the diva," Sergey said. "I'm glad the two of you got to work together before this, he's a character. You'll be in the will, by the way, once we get it written."

I knew better than to ask for specifics. Sergey pulled out a small notepad with a handwritten to-do list. He took point for the legal and medical matters while I would handle mail, bills, and personal errands. I diligently took notes and mentally hashed out how I might accomplish each item on my list. Sergey acted like several years of unpaid taxes had already passed and Victor's house was about to go on sheriff sale. Perhaps discovering the lack of a will created a paranoia of other missing obligations. We shook hands and he shuffled down the hall towards the exit, reading his checklist along the way.

A reality courtroom TV dispute over the return of a security deposit due to a canine-soiled carpet filled the room when I came back, Victor futilely pressing all the buttons on the remote control. After breaking the down volume button free from its encrusted shell, we walked through a punch list of items to get from the house: CD player with headphones, a compact photo album from the sock drawer, checkbook, and a two-pound bag of peanut butter M&Ms. He reluctantly agreed to substitute nicotine gum for cigarettes.

"Is there anyone you'd like me to call?" I asked.

"No. Sergey will tell some college friends, the wine and cheese crowd. Roman and Irina will find out without any help."

"Let me know. I'll write my number down." I tore off a strip of paper from a lunch menu and wrote down my cell number with my name in all caps, then pinned it to the corkboard. "How are you feeling?"

"Better than this morning, the drugs severed my brain from my body. As a former Orthodox Catholic, I should embrace the soul's release from the vulgar material world. But this will be temporary."

I offered Victor a drink from a Styrofoam cup and he refused, pointing to a case of soda in the corner. "It's like an airplane here, the soda they give you is immediately flat, or else they just get the cheap shit." He took one sip from the can and then pushed it away, a single splash of sweet carbonic acid against the back of his throat was enough. He sunk back into the pillow and looked at the ceiling.

"Bogdan kept snoring through my morning routine, he got back from the bar after midnight. I had *The Possessed* by Dostoevsky on some bootleg tapes and looked forward to driving to the three lighthouses by myself. I left the tape player in the car overnight, and the cold killed the batteries. This must have been around 1990, when things were accelerating. I picked up some wiring and tools at the local hardware shop, the electrical on these lighthouses was shit back then, they used solid aluminum wire and the temperature swings wreaked havoc on them."

"I can still picture this old guy at the store. Had a wild white beard, and he desperately wanted to come along and kept playing up his experience in the Great Patriotic War. I let him join me, which was against protocol but so was letting your drunk partner sleep in. The maintenance on the first two lighthouses was easy: we redid the wiring, changed out the bulbs, sealed up some of the buildings against water, standard stuff. The third one took a while to get to, it was on a thin strip of tundra sticking into the ocean. Everything was broken to some extent. The rotating reflector motor bearings growled at us once we got it going, so they had to come off to be fixed. The whole thing was a pig. Salt spray and oxygen had eaten everything away."

Victor continued. "He kept insisting on doing the heavy lifting, carrying the tools from the truck and refusing to use mechanical advantage as we pulled apart the drive. He sang old Soviet Navy songs when he worked, these patriotic hymns about saying goodbye to your family and protecting the Motherland, a true believer, I guess. It was getting late, though the sun never actually sets there in June, just rides along the horizon. We divided up the tasks and then he starts dragging, dropping screws, walking slowly – all this after telling me he maintained the entire Northern Fleet ten years before."

"Sneaking some vodka on the side?" I asked.

"No, he was intentionally going slow, stretching out the job. Working on these lighthouses brought him back to his days of servicing the ships and he didn't want to go back to his one-bedroom apartment surrounded by loud families."

"He wished he had gone down with the ship," I said.

"Exactly." Victor took another sip of cola. "We worked past midnight in the dim light, taking breaks to listen to his war stories. The fog rolled in from the ocean during our drive back at around one in the morning, making the trip take forever."

"At one point I had to slam on the brakes to avoid hitting a caribou carcass. It was an older animal separated out by the wolves. He wanted to stop to take a look and we both got out. The wolves go after the organs first, the high energy density parts, but we must have scared them off. You could see everything, the diffusion of tissues into a shapeless mass, the plaques and puss and fat. It's not the rainbow of distinct organs illustrated in books. I almost threw up. He stood there for a while even after I went back in the truck," Victor said, trailing off.

"Did you ever see him again?" I asked.

"No. We exchanged phone numbers when I dropped him back at his apartment. But I never went back to the Kola Peninsula, everything was different the next year."

We both sat in silence for a few minutes. "You'll like this new hydraulic machine I've started sketching, we'll brainstorm it over the peanut butter M&Ms," I said. "You want me to load up some more of those philosophy podcasts?"

"The mind gets tired of learning. Plus, I think the phone is dead."

Victor closed his eyes. I moved the open can of soda away from the edge of his tray, folded up the newspaper, and plugged in his cell phone.

*   *   *

I picked up three orders of Chinese food to drop off around town, one to a house of college-age gamers in headsets starting a tournament, and the other two to small businesses which were my real cash cow given the size of the order. The rideshare app had recently branched out into food delivery, which I found to be an easy in-town option. I could gate each of my own meals with this financial carrot, just like the self-imposed perspiration requirement before each shower.

The lo mein was still reasonably warm by the time it was dumped on a plate at Victor's house. He probably owned the place outright, he seemed like the old-world type that would be allergic to debt. I knew that he had caches of hard currency spread around as well, which were unlikely to be entirely enumerated during the writing of the will. Victor was too cagey for that. I couldn't help thinking about how my rightful – whatever that meant – inheritance would expire over the next two years at the current rate and another absurd windfall could float me into an early semi-retirement.

The backroom looked just as I expected, the centerpiece milling machine holding out its platform of freshly sharpened end mills and fly cutters like a butler holding a tray of hors d'oeurvres. Our hydraulic difference engine sat on the workbench. It still needed the platform covers to be machined and installed. I realized I'd been procrastinating the completion of the machine for the last few weeks, working on other side projects for Victor. Putting off its finishing allowed it to keep lingering in the future. Its final state would be finite and banal, ready to be stuffed into a basement for long-term storage. I picked it up, surprised at its weight without water, and put it back. It felt like a betrayal to take it back to my apartment. This would skip its full black light demonstration, the two of us comparing the results to a spreadsheet model and then drinking a vodka tonic for a job well done.

I looked around for the Ivantusky brothers' notebook without success and then returned to the kitchen. The cooler temperature brought out the salt and MSG of the lo mein further improving the taste. My own notebook sat open to a blank page and I started making triangular patterns along the edge. I had about two hours to come up with a concept to share with Victor.

There were still meters of the precision silicone tubing Victor had bought for the water computer left on the shelf, so I started down that path before giving up ten minutes in. It needed to be something elegant, like the drinking bird which dips its beak into a cup with apparent perpetual motion. Internet videos explained how an exquisite heat engine cycle of evaporation and condensation was converted to mechanical motion, a brilliant interplay of forces that sobered my ambitions and made me think I should try something more pedestrian, like a toilet bowl, a simple chain of floats and valves. I sketched out a circulating capillary structure, maybe the transpiration of a tree or the two-phase transport of heat pipes. These devices efficiently move heat in a sealed microclimate with liquid and vapor phases, apparently having widespread use in the zero-gravity environment of outer space, something Leo would appreciate. The sketch morphed into a pump with a branching network of tubes, quickly aping a two-chambered heart with a plunger pushing on a large ventricle and moving fluid through a set of elastic ducts and one-way valves.

This diaphragm pump system was not particularly novel, but maybe some dye could be added to monitor convective transports across the network. The forcing function, the pumping action, needed to be chaotic or irreversible, ideally both, to make it meaningful to the observer. The evaporating liquid from the drinking bird made its beak dip up and down. Eventually, all the water will evaporate and leave the bird standing upright. All real heat engines were irreversible, there was no perpetual motion, there was always some friction in the system creating generalized disorder. The new circulation network could be powered by feeding the machine boiling water or liquid nitrogen, energy sources with much shorter half-lives than the nuclear decay of Victor's RTGs. Adding a chaotic element would be harder, maybe the timing of the compression stroke could introduce some randomness.

The illusion of reversibility dominates youth – there is always the next summer, the next girlfriend, another shot at the target. In the end, irreversibility always wins out, the arrow of time marches forward, and the diffusive processes triumph. The organs of a dead caribou turn into a homogeneous mass. Victor must have understood this on an intellectual level but now he was living through it. I grabbed the compact photo album and portable CD player and headed out. I quickly flipped through the photos, mostly black and white shots of people standing together. One showed two pre-teen boys, one wild and gap-toothed who pulled the other in close for the shot. Leo must be the serious one with the fully buttoned shirt and sharp parted hair.

"Martin, good to see you again." Aldous waylaid me before I left the porch. Roman and Irina got out of the black full-size SUV which was parked in the driveway. I thought back to my trip on the way here, wondering if I saw Oscar's blue car in the rearview mirror. "Is Victor in?"

"No, he's out."

"That's odd, his car is in the driveway. You're here alone?"

"Yeah, just taking care of a few things for him," I said and shifted the grocery bags of personal items away from the three.

"Oh, he's out of town?" Aldous questioned.

"A situation has come up; he was taken to ..." I stopped myself, realizing I had gone too far. "He'll be away for a bit."

"Look, Martin, I know Victor is your friend, I would be suspicious of us as well. He is being served for unlawful possession. We'll find him in a day or so with or without your help," Aldous said, sweeping locks of dirty-blonde hair back from his eyes. "If this gets into criminal territory, you'll want to be on the right side."

"Sounds like a family dispute to me."

"You don't even know our uncle," Roman said as he joined shoulders with their lawyer. "Has he told you why he left Russia?"

"The economy tanked?"

"Ask him about Max Ivanov or Gregory Kuznetsov."

"Okay." There was no chance I would remember the names.

"On paper, he worked for an oil company doing security, but in reality, he helped eliminate rivals for an upstart oligarch. Maybe he didn't pull the trigger but he was part of their crew," Roman said. "Of course, every old man is likable, just take that old Italian mobster from the movies, what's his name?"

"Vito Corleone, playing with his grandkids in the garden," Aldous answered.

"Victor was in the mafia?" I asked.

"By association. The regional government exposed a huge ring of corruption that included Victor's patron. I'm talking about money laundering, extortion, drugs, prostitution. I could go on. A number of them went to jail. A new set of elections eased the pressure on the investigation, that's when he fled to the U.S.," Roman said.

"Was your father involved?" I asked.

Irina had now joined the circle and spoke up. "Not with the criminal side. He lost his job and became desperate. Victor found him work at new gas company developing oil fields out east. Father sat us all down at the kitchen table to explain why he had to leave. He always wanted to solve problems, figure things out. He was excited about something, having discovered major inefficiencies in their process. We never heard from him again."

"And Victor was responsible?" I asked.

"He knew it was an inside job, there is no other way," Aldous said affirmatively.

"He then stole his brother's genius, pretending to be anonymous but hoarding these inventions for himself," Roman said. "Our mother let him go, but we won't."

I expressed general sympathy and checked the time on my phone. I needed to get to the hospital. Aldous gave me his business card as I passed through the group.

An older man with slicked-back grey hair and bushy eyebrows pulled documents out of a leather briefcase, his suit and shoes formal in a way reserved for attorneys and aspiring immigrants. Angelo Grasso rose to shake hands when I approached Victor's bed and then unfolded a chair for me to sit on at the bedside. Afternoon sunlight came through the window, which felt incongruent with the gravity of the meeting.

"Did you bring the CD player?" Victor asked.

I nodded and started setting it up on the nightstand, showing him the CD cases of Chopin and Beethoven. I used the house key to initiate a tear in the peanut butter M&M bag and I then gave a heavy pour to his outstretched hand. He handed me a few that spilled on the bed sheet but I discreetly tossed them, having a phobia of all exposed surfaces in the hospital hosting microbes eager to continue their journey along the fecal-oral highway.

"Here is the advance medical directive," Angelo handed the single-page form to Victor for review. "Sergey is the primary agent and Martin is the secondary. This will only take effect when a physician or other qualified professional determines you are unable to make or express decisions. You can add additional instructions above where you sign."

"No feeding tubes, do not resuscitate," Victor said and Sergey wrote them on the lines below. We all signed the form, including two elderly visitors Angelo recruited from down the hall to serve as witnesses. I assumed that being the secondary agent would be for backup purposes only, Sergey projected responsibility and would take the lead.

"We're going to talk through the will, would you mind staying for another ten minutes?" Angelo asked the visitors, who said they were in no hurry to leave. I was surprised by the brevity of the document, which looked to be only around six pages. Once again, Sergey would be the executor and I would be the backup, another, I hoped, remote prospect. No spouses, no children, and no pets trimmed the document length down.

"As discussed, the house will be bequeathed to Heidi Chapman of Lawrence, Kansas. After payment of all debts and bills, monetary assets will be divided evenly between the United Way and the Brenner Scholarship. Your vehicle will be donated to Goodwill. Finally, all possessions inside the house will be bequeathed to Martin Rasmus, with an allowance for Sergey Antonov to collect any personal items."

"Like parts for the university projects," Victor said.

"Exactly. This will permit him to do that. Does everything else sound in order?" Angelo asked and Victor nodded. "The remaining sections are standard last testament language but let's read through them."

This meant I would become the owner of all the machines and boxes in the basement, the milling machine, and the stocks of raw material, far beyond what I could stuff into my one-bedroom apartment. I wanted to ask about his niece and nephew but it was clear that the will was finalized and the only thing left to do was collect signatures. Victor signed followed by the two witnesses who then left the room. Angelo snapped up his briefcase after handing Sergey the documents and gave us each a handshake on the way out.

"Don't be afraid to throw things out," Victor said, folding up a copy of the will and putting it on the side table.

"We'll need you to give us the tour," I said, implying his upcoming release.

"Personal items are irrelevant, like dead leaves." Victor looked out the window, a recent cold snap had finished off the remaining leaves from the trees. "Collect into a pile and start a bonfire, return the chemicals back to simpler forms."

"Would you want to do that, erase it all?" I said, struggling with the idea of a legacy of cinders and diffusing gases. "People now take pictures and then toss, digitally save the objects for later."

"That's why you got the stuff, you have some idealism left. I never thought about my own legacy, but now that I'm surrounded by family, I have nothing to worry about," Victor slyly smiled and then started coughing. I grabbed a handful of tissues and passed them over to him. The coughs rattled in his chest and sounded productive but I couldn't bear to look at the tissues and blindly threw them in the garbage.

A nurse came in to check on his readings and take away the Styrofoam cup of soda and chocolate pudding with only a spoonful eaten. Sergey patted his friend on the back and gathered up his things. I helped Victor put on headphones and started a Chopin CD. The simple familiar buttons made more sense to him than tapping on a screen. He was too exhausted to discuss any new designs. I followed Sergey's lead and headed out.

"Who is Heidi Chapman?" I asked Sergey as we walked down the hallway.

"Victor's ex-wife. He never mentioned her?" Sergey asked and I raised my eyebrows. "They were only married for about two years, shortly after he came over. Ran very hot and cold, she was about twenty years younger I think."

"Does she know she's getting the house?"

"I doubt it, but knowing her it will be a good thing. She's a single mom with a few kids. None are Victor's," Sergey said.

"Have you talked to his doctor?"

"Yes, before you came. It's not looking good; the cancer has metastasized into his liver. His food and water intake have dropped significantly. He'll be transferred out of intensive care soon."

"This happened so suddenly."

"Better it is quick. Bring drawings of that new design, he'll enjoy discussing that if he has the strength," Sergey said as we left the hospital.

*   *   *

As I waited in the hospital lobby, I scrolled through news articles on the midterm elections, then opened the Xmundio app. I pulled up Nina's profile. The app had a feature that showed how long ago each user was active. I found myself checking this each night and morning, seeing that she had been active until midnight and again before seven in the morning. This indicated an anxiety, a constant checking in to count likes or doom scrolling.

Her recent posts were photographs of sand dunes, granite monoliths, an empty barbershop shot in black and white, and thunderstorm supercells moving across sagebrush valleys. The last one was dated two weeks ago, before our break up. I moved further back in time, past the watercolors and Christmas family photos, into a series of couple shots with a large, boxy-framed, bearded man presenting upper arms covered in Eastern symbol tattoos. Posts of the two of them lasted for three months and then stopped, perhaps it had been a fast-burn romance or Nina became self-conscious about personal content distracting from her photography. Their posts ended with a set of group photos taken at an alpine lake, the two floating on some inflated craft. I tapped the screen to like four of her most recent pictures since keeping a well-visited online portfolio was probably essential for an independent artist. My own online personal mythology was a pathetic assembly, a herd of Kazakh goats crossing a dirt road with five likes, and a group photo of teachers at the end of last winter's semester.

Pierre Mercer walked through the double doors, adjusted his glasses, and looked around the hospital lobby. We agreed to meet at nine o'clock in the morning in an attempt to avoid Victor's mental malaise after lunch. After we caught eyes, he shuffled in my direction with an apologetic brisk pace.

I stumbled across Pierre's proposition for another sit-down meeting and felt compelled to reach out to him, not for more negotiations with Roman and Irina but instead to give him access to Victor before he passed which now felt imminent. He was a real admirer of the machines and could help with Victor's legacy. I also felt sorry for him, picturing the man sipping tea and reading Rudyard Kipling. We confirmed the visit last night over text.

"Parking lot was full," Pierre said as he sat down and went through his cluttered briefcase, double-checking that he had brought extra batteries for the voice recorder. "What's in the box?"

"Something Victor and I worked on." I had packaged up the hydraulic difference engine the night before. I started by looking for the chaotic waterwheel, but it had felt wrong to take it without permission and getting a hold of Victor at ten o'clock at night was laughable.

"Is he expecting us?"

"Not exactly," I answered. "He's fading quickly physically but there are periods when his mind is still sharp. Let's hope for a good day."

We took the elevator up to the third floor to the general care unit where Victor was transferred two days before. He acquired a neighbor in the process, a senile man recovering from a stroke who made lewd comments to the nurses but fortunately had the sleep schedule of a basset hound.

"Good morning. I brought you some more peanut butter M&Ms," I said, walking through the door. The last two-pound bag disappeared during the move. Victor insisted on foul play which was honestly credible. "I brought along a friend too, he's a fan of your machines."

"Pierre Mercer, collector. It's an honor to meet you."

"Another lawyer?" Victor asked.

Pierre laughed and reassured him that no signatures or formal depositions were required. I started unboxing the hydraulic engine while Pierre opened his briefcase, asking permission to audio record the conversation due to his terrible penmanship. Victor shrugged in tacit approval. He pointed to the stack of soda cans and I prepared him a drink.

"I've admired you and your brother's works for several decades, these magnificent devices that blend order and chaos. There is very little backstory on you both. Could we start from the beginning, the two of you growing up?" Pierre asked. During the elevator ride I told Pierre that both brothers created the machines, a collaborative work.

Victor began with their childhood in Voronezh, a large Russian city east of Ukraine on its namesake river. Wehrmacht Army Group South pushed to its western shore in 1942 during the fateful drive towards Stalingrad and the oil fields beyond. Their father worked sixteen-hour days in a munitions factory for the war effort. The Nazis broke through in early 1943, destroying the urban center until they were beaten back in fierce fighting. The city was later reconstructed with somewhat restrained Soviet flair. The two brothers were members of a short-lived baby boom after the war and grew up playing games on the rubble.

"One of our mother's friends was an amateur radio operator. I remember tuning to 20 MHz and hearing the steady beeping from Sputnik, this little sphere orbiting overhead," Victor said. "Of course, we had propaganda about the superiority and historical inevitability of communism but that beeping spoke louder than any of that. The idea of an orbiting satellite above the corrupted planet really connected with Leo, who was always more captivated by the ethereal than me. Space is a purer environment, no gravity or air friction, more reliable, predictable."

"We grew apart in our teenage years. Back then the government pointed you down a path and you didn't jump the rails. He grew more studious, absorbed in books and science clubs while I dedicated myself to wrestling, hanging out in the weight room, getting into fights here and there. I won regionals in the seventy-kilogram class in the final year of secondary school, the peak of my athletic career." Victor took a drink from the soda and started coughing. I adjusted the back of his bed to be more vertical and handed him some tissues.

"What made you both interested in creating the machines?" Pierre asked Victor after he returned to respiratory equilibrium.

"Leo got accepted into the space program, building huge antennas using complex linkages he invented. Much of it was classified so the specifics are anyone's guess. Back then money flowed into space work. After vocational school, I worked maintenance for a power company but slowly made a name for myself as a machinist. Our father worked as a clockmaker, I suppose we regressed to our hereditary destiny of tinkering," Victor said. "The end of the Soviet Union threw everything into chaos, sand into the gears of our lives."

"Is that when Leo started designing the machines?"

"Yes, out of boredom. He never thought of them as art. Hell, I doubt he ever stepped inside an art museum."

"What did he want to say with these devices?"

"Everything he designed before that had a purpose with clear intent and some creative element to get to a solution. He lost that so this became a mental sandbox," Victor said, tossing back a handful of M&Ms. "Maybe these machines were unconscious products of the overall change from a centrally planned economy to this creatively chaotic but corrupt capitalist system. He never built any of them, in fact, I'm not sure they were ever meant to be built, just simulated in the mind or maybe a computer."

"Leo never built these?"

"No, I built them after he disappeared. I needed to see them converted to the material world. Some could never work but others actually did," Victor said and took a drink of soda, looking away from Pierre to the space in front of the bed. "With a good user interface, technology becomes indistinguishable from magic. Electricity and software only accelerate this move to abstraction. Sergey has said that the latest artificial intelligence codes are even inscrutable to their authors. Most of our machines are the opposite, no external housings, intentionally complicated just to relish in the movement."

"Everyone thinks that Leo designed and built them, there are even Internet blogs devoted to his work. Why didn't you put your name on them too?" Pierre asked.

"They were his designs, I just midwifed them into existence. His family blamed me for his disappearance, it would be painful for them to see me grabbing the credit."

"Do you blame yourself?" I asked when he paused.

"I did. I set in motion the circumstances of his disappearance, getting him a job with the company. Any sufficiently reflective person can see an event as contingent on their actions to some degree but how do you assign guilt?" Victor said. "I stepped away from the world for the next year, that is when I built most of his machines and submitted them to a traveling art exhibit."

Victor gave more details on his brother's disappearance, which Pierre seemed particularly interested in Lake Baikal, the gas fields, the underworld elements oozing up like the petrochemicals being extracted. The art world knew that Leo Ivantusky had disappeared but none of the Siberian intrigue, which could push them to new heights of obsession, like with drug overdosed musicians or assassinated rappers. The mention of the notebook ignited Pierre's interest, he wanted to see the handwritten sketches of a mind at work. Victor seemed confused by the collector's fascination with the pieces.

"Do you have the notebook here?" Pierre asked.

"I think it's back at the house," I said.

"It's on the southeast upper shelf of the workshop," Victor stated. "The machines are inside boxes in the basement."

"I'd love to see everything. I will feel like Howard Carter peeking in the door of Tut's tomb," Pierre said. "Can I ask why you've kept them hidden?"

"I tried to leave that stuff behind when I came here, bury them in a corner of the basement. I needed to free myself from history and living out here in the West makes that easier, the air is thin and light, people care more about the future. Sergey helped me start over at the university working as a precision machinist." Victor paused while Pierre fiddled with the recorder. "My last gasp of hormones produced an impulsive marriage and a subsequent divorce. I guess that makes me a real American," he said with a smile. "Enough about me, looks like Martin brought over his hydraulic difference engine."

I moved a potted flower off the top of the dresser and set up the device using water from the bathroom sink. The two men inspected the contoured insert in the first reservoir designed to simulate seasonal variation in the height of the first tank. I sped up the timers and feed rates and kicked it off.

"We started out trying to build Lukyanov's water integrator, an analog computer, but punted to something easier," I told Pierre, who inspected the piping network and pumps. "This can calculate frost line depth by proxy. I like the periodicity of it but maybe it needs something non-linear, like permafrost thawing and releasing methane or something."

All three of us watched in silence as the pumps cyclically raised and lowered the level in the first reservoir which diffused liquid into the interior of the linear chain of vessels.

"Connect it to the Godzilla of non-linear action: people," Pierre said after a few minutes.

"The feed rate could be based on the average speed of highway traffic, or something else with a high degree of unpredictability," I said. My own mental bandwidth hovered in a dial-up modem speed this morning, having made the mistake of a late-night three-mile run which must have constructively superimposed with the medication to combat sleep, putting the brain into a low-interest rate economy of ideas, overheated markets resulting in the listening of extensive alternative history podcasts at two-thirty in the morning, then lying in bed with my eyes closed but still awake.

Victor's hospital neighbor awoke, found the remote control, and launched the home shopping network at one hundred decibels. My requests to turn down the volume were met with a blank look. After some exploration, I managed to find the buttons on the back of the TV but stopped lowering the volume when the man groaned in protest.

"Mr. Ivantusky, are these guys giving you a hard time?" a woman with a Caribbean accent in light blue scrubs said as she walked in. "I have four older brothers and I'm not afraid to throw a few elbows."

"Just friends..., Jada," Victor said, pausing to think of her name.

"We're going to give you a fresh gown and a new set of sheets. This will take a little while, you boys are welcome to hang outside."

While Jada muted the TV, ignoring the neighbor's crude comment about her curves, Pierre snapped his briefcase shut and thanked Victor for his time.

"This will be a longer scan than usual, would you like to use the bathroom, Martin?" Vanessa asked. We had grown friendly over the two months she had been administering my scans, keeping me updated on each chapter of her adopted mutt's separation anxiety and lack of bowel control.

"I'm sufficiently dehydrated this morning," I said, which was true given my amber lager-colored urine and low-level headache. The fMRI platform glided into the magnetic chamber. I closed my eyes and prepared for the upcoming prompts. The instructions this time were broader, bouncing between memories, thought experiments, logic puzzles, and body scans. The procedure took about forty-five minutes, twice as long as usual. I wondered if I should offer my services as a dog sitter despite her little nightmare, but her gaze remained fixed on the screen as I walked by.

I was in the middle of a written test when Dr. Patel entered. She crossed her legs as she sat down and let me finish the final questions before speaking. I tried to look at the underside of the lab notebook in her lap to see if it matched the one I found on her desk.

"How have you been feeling over the last two weeks?"

"Fine, not as many intense dreams as before," I said, which was mostly true.

"Have you had any changes in perception, like out-of-body experiences or anything like that?"

"No. Just these waves of fatigue and energy, usually alternating each day."

"You've been saying that for a few weeks now. Does that lead to depressive and manic periods?" she asked, taking notes.

"Maybe a bit, but it's more like shifting between numb and aware states." The aware periods produced a clarity that was exhilarating compared with numb days when I lurched around half asleep. Historically, my psychological hardware made me happy *in* life with simple pleasures, but the mind's software questioned its happiness *with* life. This seemed to still hold true but with heightened day-to-day variations.

"And that has grown since you started the trial?"

"Not much, I'm probably just thinking about it more," I said, trying to end this particular line of inquiry.

"We're stopping your medication. I believe your weekly set of pills ends today."

"Am I still in the study?"

Dr. Patel paused. "You will continue to come in for evaluations. Your compensation will stay the same."

"Why don't you just switch me over to a placebo?" I asked. This likely meant I was in the experimental group and the medication was producing some adverse reactions.

"I'm not able to disclose the decision-making process but I can assure you it is consistent with medical best practices," Dr. Patel said, uncrossing her legs to signal her upcoming departure. "Do you have any more questions?"

"What side effects have you concerned? I really don't feel different."

"I'm not at liberty to say but please know that Transcendent maintains the highest standards of ethical practices."

"Is this because of Nina?" Her exposure as a confederate could have compromised the study, not to mention the photos of Dr. Patel's notebook possibly uploaded to Transcendent or the wider Xmundio ecosystem.

She stood up. "I'm not sure who you are referring to. I apologize if it seems like I am withholding information, but I can assure you our approach is consistent with the agreements you signed at the start of the trial. This is an adjustment and not a rejection, you will still come in every other day for testing."

La Niña weather patterns result in a persistent northern jet stream, the train of cold fronts pulling in warm air from the south, drying out the center of the continent, and generating winds that produced a large pile of cottonwood and ash tree leaves in Victor's front yard. I found an old wicker rake in the shed and put on a set of wireless headphones, settling on an Oxford-style debate on the proposition "Liberal Democracy is in Retreat."

I sat down on the poured concrete retaining wall, which had developed a ten-degree list towards the sidewalk under the weight of the elevated land. Effects from stopping the medication would take a few days to manifest and I expected arrivals of fatigue, headaches, irritability, and low energy. Stopping the pills and returning to a ground state would have happened in a few weeks regardless, reducing my contribution to Xmundio's database but not in any appreciable way.

The speakers on the side of the motion argued that the ideals of liberal humanism, specifically, and the Enlightenment, in general, had lost their currency with the masses through a breakdown of institutional faith thanks in part to postmodern cynicism, identity politics, and general pessimism. A rejuvenation of Enlightenment rationality required a new currency to stay relevant or risk sounding like ragtime or show tunes. One of the panelists made an analogy to the second law of thermodynamics and the descent of a closed system into disorder. There are essentially infinitely more ways to arrange items in a disordered way than an ordered one, making disorder the natural state unless energy – like the Enlightenment ideals – is applied. External power structures, like corporations, still have enough inertia to persist, she argued, but extreme pluralism had turned the landscape of shared values into disordered islands of personal confusion. The second law fought against structures and gradients, just like the heights of water in the reservoirs of the difference engine, unless acted upon by an external force.

My separation from Nina, Victor's decline, and my meaningful exclusion from the Transcendent study returned me to my factory default settings, back to a mental one-bedroom apartment without roommates, back to the lowest energy state, back to the center of the bell curve, the cold calculus of the central limit. They all carried an undercurrent of impossibility anyway, their machinery was suspect like the impossible machines drafted by Leo at the end of the notebook: conceptual, flights of fancy. The wind started to blow the leaves away from the raked rows, scattering them across the yard. I stepped into the bag, compressed the leaves to half their original size, and then hobbled between piles, hand shoveling the diffusing mounds into the bag like a panicked shopper clearing the shelves before a storm.

Pierre pushed his visit to Victor's house back one week after his trip to the annual conference on early colonial antiques held in Harrisburg, Pennsylvania. That didn't stop him from sending perfectly punctuated text messages expressing his excitement and pre-coordinating permission to see the notebook and "the waterwheel and any other machines or devices with a creative or artistic character." I promised to wait for him to unbox everything in the basement.

Victor was transferred to a skilled nursing facility three blocks away from the hospital, a rehabilitation center that seemed identical to a nursing home. Sergey explained that *rehabilitation* was a loose definition that helped families convince their relatives it wasn't a terminal destination. His food and water consumption dropped far below the levels necessary for sustainment and his cognitive decline accelerated. I had just finished bundling up the bags of leaves when Sergey's text message arrived, explaining that the hospice nurse advised me to visit now instead of later. I grabbed the notebook and locked up the house on the way out.

Cindy greeted me when I entered, remembering my name immediately. She was a calm woman around the same age as most of the residents, a strong qualification for a hospice worker. Victor's new roommate Rudolph had a poster-sized photo of a family reunion behind his bed and a bottle of small American flags like those given to veterans. We had yet to hear him speak.

"Victor's resting now, he has been in and out today. When he wakes, he may recognize you," Cindy said. Sergey got up from his chair and walked over.

"How much longer does he have?" I asked.

"You can never say, but based on my experience I would expect him to move on in the next day or two," she said. It made sense to use vague afterlife language given the comforts it provided and the range of religious alignments. "The palliative care appears to be successful. He shouldn't be in much pain."

Cindy left the room to check on the other patients. I opened one of the card table chairs and sat down next to Sergey, who was reading the newspaper. He handed me the national news section which was headlined with a story on a U.S. coalition-led airstrike on terrorist camps in the Caucasus region. Victor was out cold.

"Here are your copies of the documents," Sergey said and handed me the will and the advance medical directive.

"Thank you. Have you heard anything from him since you got here?"

"No. I've been waiting to see some movement for the last hour. The redundancy of the human body generally makes us slide away slowly, but it can sometimes happen fast."

"Like the stock market, changes generally compound gradually over time but big drops are almost always negative," I said. "Makes it easy to remember the bad." I started to feel guilty about comparing Sergey's friend's life to an economic system but I knew Victor would have appreciated the analogy.

"He mentioned you were designing a new machine, something hydraulic again?"

I handed him the notebook and we walked through the sketches of the diaphragm pump circulator. He asked if I ever read *Frankenstein* and I admitted that I hadn't but pledged to put it on the list. Sergey suggested celebrating rather than hiding the plumbing and machinery in the circuit, using old-fashioned brass fittings and an accumulator with an accordion bellows. A variable heat source could expand and contract the circulating liquid, perhaps moving a float in the accumulator to actively change the speed of the pump.

Victor rocked back and forth to move up towards the headboard and his eyes shifted to a half-open position. We said our names but he slumped back down into the blankets.

"Were you planning to go on a train trip with Victor, one of those narrow-gauge ones in the mountains?" I asked, thinking back to the website that came up on his phone.

"I've never heard of that. Did you find tickets at his place?"

"No tickets, just came across something on his phone when I was loading podcasts a few weeks back."

"Huh, he never mentioned that. It must have been for the two of you."

I pictured Victor and I sitting on opposing seats with a table between us, books opened and a freshly cleaned window to watch the slow ascent past autumn snowcapped mountains and aspens full of yellow medallions.

"I'm heading out. We'll text each other later," Sergey said, handing me back the sketches as he put on his coat. "Don't feel obligated to stay late. I've made my peace; you should do the same. We've done what we can."

* * *

A nursing assistant with snowflake-patterned scrubs carried four coffees in a cardboard tray, at least two liters of central nervous system stimulation. I asked if they were all for her and she laughed, explaining it was the start of dark twelves, the six pm to six am night shift. She asked if Victor was my father or uncle and I told her he was a close friend.

A plastic bag with a footlong loaded three meat sub hung from my arm along with a bag of corrugated multigrain chips. On request, they cut the sub in thirds instead of in half, something I had learned to do as a rationing technique. Managing moisture from the excessive mayonnaise, tomatoes, honey mustard, olive oil, vinegar, and assorted vegetables over time would be a challenge but at least it would be an interesting one.

Victor was in the same position as he had been earlier. The nurses told me he had skipped dinner. I went back to my apartment to pick up headphones and showered in an attempt to wake up. The days since I had stopped the medication crept along mechanically. Two cups of coffee produced a short-term boost of energy but any buoyancy capsized by late morning, a likely withdrawal symptom from dopamine detox. I had turned sports news notifications back on my phone, which meant I was now receiving a dozen banners each day about MLB playoffs.

The fresh smell of the sandwich displaced the general odor of urine and that ubiquitous roasted nut smell secreted by the elderly. The first third of the sub only lasted one minute, so tided myself over by extracting the remaining pickles to savor the salt and vinegar. Nightfall darkened the room and I turned on the hallway light instead of the overhead, though I knew neither resident would care.

"Mr. Rasmus, pleasure seeing you again." I knew it was Aldous before I turned around. The two siblings and their lawyer entered the room, filling the space with a meaty, fried aroma.

"He's resting," I said, remaining seated.

"We talked to the hospice nurse on the phone earlier," Irina said. "I can't believe it happened so suddenly."

"Where should I put these?" Aldous asked as he set an admittedly gorgeous bouquet of flowers down on the side table. I nodded in silent approval.

"We also brought over some pirozhki," Roman said, setting an oil-marked paper bag down on Victor's food tray. "Have one."

Roman handed me one of the fried pastries, which looked like some type of Russian calzone with a meat and onion filling. He joined me in eating one while his sister knelt along the bedside, touching her uncle's hand.

"Has he been unresponsive all day?" Irina asked.

"More or less. He shifted earlier but nothing verbal."

"Painkillers are working I hope," Irina said. "Are you staying by his side for support?"

"Yeah."

After wiping his hands with a paper towel Roman went over, knelt, and briefly touched Victor's hand, then stood up next to his sister. I heard a briefcase snap open and Aldous walked into view carrying two manilla envelopes.

"Martin Rasmus and Victor Ivantusky, you have been served to appear in civil court for the theft of Leo Ivantusky's designs and devices," Aldous said, handing me both packages. "Apologies for the timing."

"Sergey told us you will be acquiring all physical property from his house, is that right?" Irina asked.

"If he dies," I said.

"It sounds like Sergey will be the executor. We'll deliver him these court orders," Roman said. "The court date is in three weeks. I expect you'll be using his lawyer unless you want to represent yourself."

"You still want to get revenge on a dying man?"

"We're past revenge. He's suffered enough, and he is still our blood relative, after all. It's about legacy and authenticity, our father deserved better than to disappear in Siberia and then have his masterpieces vanish from the world thanks to his manipulative brother," Roman said.

"You know that Victor built all of these machines, right? They are more his than Leo's."

"We'll see you in court in three weeks," Roman replied.

Roman and the lawyer left the room, but Irina stopped on her way out to take a pirozhki from the bag. "These don't get better with time. The last one is for the two of you. Maybe the smell will bring him back. Thanks for being here with him, everyone deserves that." She handed me a business card. "This legal stuff has a way of turning people into robots. Call me if you want to talk."

Her title on the sparse business card was *medical device compliance consultant* and listed a phone number. I flipped through the legal documents for a few minutes, then put them down to listen to a podcast on the moral philosophy of John Rawls.

*   *   *

Given my experience with improvised sleeping arrangements in international terminals during twelve-hour layovers, I expected that a pair of chairs facing each other along a wall would make a tolerable bed. Instead, the chair's sharp edges proved spinally devastating, giving me a level of stiffness in one hour which usually took five to develop. I placed the back of my hand on the beige tile floor to gauge its temperature and pictured building up a platform of blankets but quickly dismissed this as looking pathetic.

The room was dark but for the ambient glow from the hallway and the changing digital display on the heart rate monitor. There was no sound of snoring from either of the two patients, due to their diminished weight and favorably tilted airways. The only noise was the occasional oil canning of the baseboard heating panels. My phone said ten minutes past midnight, about an hour since I turned off the lights.

I had never kept a bedside vigil before, only processing the expiration of life afterwards at an intellectual level. The utility of my being in the room overnight got more and more remote with the lack of any activity from Victor, but I took it on as some sort of a personal challenge, a self-imposed hardship. This narrative worked for a few minutes until I realized my own need to make it personal, constructing an internal heroic story instead of meditating on the fragility of life and friendship. There was still a chance he'd wake up and issue some final directive or at least know he wasn't alone – there had to be.

I turned on the desk lamp and opened Leo and Victor's notebook, paging through the designs. Defocusing on the individual gears and pulleys, I tried to see the systems as black boxes of inputs and outputs, electricity creating mechanical work ultimately ending with heat dissipation, the cheapest form of energy. Seeing them this way, each one eventually just became an artistic heater with greater or lesser movement on the stage.

Most of the material world has come under human understanding and modest control through the predictive power of science, but cancer remains a powerful example of the randomness and utter stupidity of death. Well-adjusted adults no longer sacrifice animals to the gods for bountiful harvests, they use genetically engineered corn, precise irrigation techniques, and nitrogen replenishment. I understood heart disease, an inherently mechanical process where plaques accumulated through a mixture of genetic and lifestyle decisions. It was a condition that could be monitored through LDL and HDL levels and treated pharmaceutically or surgically. Cancer worked on the level of software, an insidious turning of the body against itself, triggered through genetic mutation.

I started to sketch out cancer's key elements, its replication and avoidance of cell death, the way tumors invade nearby tissues. It was a simpler and more subversive machine than any crude collection of gears and pumps dreamed up by me or the Ivantusky brothers – life's obsession with reproduction turned inward. The cruel randomness of its victims also made it perversely just, the blind valkyrie often ignoring the virtues of good personal health habits of the wealthy. Rawls would appreciate the lottery of the disease – any one of us could fall prey – which demanded a system to care for the least fortunate.

*   *   *

"Have you finished the Henderson book?" I asked.

"Almost done, the book club got me started on a new one about this Iranian immigrant family," she answered. The quarter-to-half second latency on the international call between Kazakhstan and the U.S. made each statement weightier, though my mother always left time to listen.

"Did Sandra get your tablet working?" I asked. Sandra led the book club and also went to First Presbyterian. Her tech-savvy daughter lived at home and served as a digital translator for the club.

"Yes, I listen to the audio versions now, the words are too small." Audiobooks were a lifesaver for an older bibliophile, especially one like her who averaged two hardboiled detective novels a week. "How is Jessica?"

"She's good." It was the only practical answer. The camping trip we'd taken the past weekend hadn't reset our relationship like it usually did as we fought about the appropriate distance from the passenger wheels to the road's shoulder and who forgot the headlamps. "I think she's getting worn out of international living."

"Maybe it's time to move home."

"Yeah, we've talked about moving, somewhere in the middle like Harrisburg." I offered up the affordable mid-size city between the metro areas where our parents lived during floor sprawling daydream sessions, though neither of us took it very seriously. Going back felt like a surrender and better left to fate, like Jessica's parents swooping in with an offer we couldn't refuse.

"That would be nice. I'll be moving too."

"Wait, really?"

"Linda found an assisted living area in West Mifflin. Many people there have MS," she said. The multiple sclerosis diagnosis came four years before after a string of imbalance incidents, events like difficulty getting on and off escalators and walking with heeled shoes. The infusions seemed to initially help, but the loss of coordination had accelerated when I visited last year. This meant she could no longer drive and handrails in hallways and the bathroom had to be installed, which her cousin Linda coordinated. Like other sufferers, getting the disease late in life produced faster nerve degeneration in both motor control and cognitive functions.

"I'm glad you'll be in a supportive environment, though I bet you'll have trouble finding any competition for canasta," I said. Her agreeability made it easy to picture her surrendering her independence, with no stubborn pride requiring an intervention. "I wish I was there to help. Was it something that happened?"

"I hurt my hip a little bit. Nothing big. Tell me about where it is you're at now."

"It's pretty, we're on the outskirts of town, with a great view of the mountains from the roof. The people are a little cold, but the kids are great." I gave her a rundown of my work and living situations. We talked about books and the most recent member of my old high school tennis team to get married until I had to get ready for school and her for bed.

The attempted monthly calls over the next seven months suffered from dead cell phone batteries and silent ringers, often requiring protracted front desk intervention at the assisted living facility with limited success. The few conversations we did have were shorter with simple questions that could be answered with yes or no responses. Like damage to the outer layers of a coaxial cable, the breakdown of myelin on her nerve cells created transmission losses and distortions, the disease creeping into new tissues each month. Dysmotility quickly advanced across her body from the legs to her esophagus.

Getting a phone call through became even more heroic after the move from assisted living to a nursing home. Thankfully Linda interceded and began sending email updates every two weeks, short status messages about her change to a liquid diet and enjoying special victims unit TV homicide show marathons. I checked international flights after Linda and the pastor indicated she had stopped eating and refused a feeding tube. The price for a single stop in Frankfurt or Paris was murderous, the alternative being a three-connection flight at the start of the winter storm season.

A part of me knew a call from Linda was coming that night. Jessica and I were on opposing edges of the bed after yet another fight. My advice for frying vegetables sparked an extended clash about my lack of respect and her hypersensitivity. Desperate to recover from a lack of sleep the previous night, I enabled the phone's Do Not Disturb until mid-morning. The phone showed three missed calls from Linda when I got up, and a voicemail with the news.

I rationalized that any verbal communication with my mother at that stage would have been essentially one way. Likewise, the Herculean effort needed to make the trip back for the funeral felt like an unpragmatic and purely symbolic act. Jessica offered support and an ember of intimacy between us returned until we quickly settled back into our well-worn patterns.

* * *

The three stars of Orion's belt approached the southwest horizon, the hunter more visible than usual with a new moon. All early societies realized the inherently religious nature of the heavens, the consistency of their movements implying a similar determinism on Earth. Despite being an omnivorous nerd, space didn't hold any particular fascination for me growing up. I stopped walking and scanned the cloudless sky, searching for constellation patterns through the light pollution, returning to the seven main stars of the hunter. I digitally stumbled into the Orion nebula, a diffuse fire-hurling dragon tucked into Orion's sword, on the free online encyclopedia a few weeks back, getting lost in the photos of the turbulent stellar nursery churning out new worlds. Trying to comprehend the vast scale of the cosmos now struck a convincing ontological argument for some type of deism, one made obvious by the sheer greatness of the universe. I had skipped through life with a blasé atheism for the last two decades, procrastinating its implications while on pensive nights occasionally repeating the prayers I had recited in childhood before bed, even though all the people in the thanksgiving section of the prayer had died.

The twenty-four-hour convenience store was four blocks away, located across from the hospital to supply caffeine and snacks to its employees working all three shifts. The rows of cigarettes behind the counter caught my eye on the way in, the seductive absurdity of smoking on the walk back to a terminally ill cancer patient's bedside. I could buy twenty to smoke one and toss the others, then offset it by a three-mile jog in the morning. I placed the cup of Colombian brew coffee on the counter and waited for the pair of college-aged women in front of me to finish buying malt liquor. The southeast Asian attendant had two rows of photos of his kids, the majority of the shots were of brown bodies swimming in grey water, wild happiness on their faces. I went back to grab two small red stirring straws for a replacement oral fetish and left with only the coffee.

"You're Martin, right?" a nurse asked after she buzzed me into the lobby. "You're needed up in 321."

I took the stairs, the coffee spurting out of the plastic top on the way up. Two nurses were in the room and all the lights were on. The older one came and met me in the doorway.

"His blood pressure and heart rate dropped suddenly which triggered our alarms. Breathing is shallow and inconsistent," she said and looked down at his file. "We called Mr. Antonov but have not gotten through yet. It looks like you are his delegate. The advance medical directive states non-resuscitation so we are monitoring but not intervening at this point."

"Is that the standard practice?" I asked.

"Yes, when we have the medical directive. We will address pain if needed but in this case, it's not."

"Is he close?"

"Yes. I'll be at the nurse's station in the hallway, please come get me if you need anything."

I texted and then called Sergey, leaving a voicemail. I thought about opening the brothers' notebook, reading off some of the design features in case they could cut through Victor's mental fog, but put it down. I gripped the coffee to warm up my hands and reached out, cupping his fingers into mine, and sat in silence.

I inspected the three-day-old beard on the gaunt folds on Victor's neck, the thin leathery skin pulled away from the underlying tissue. I kept trying to produce an emotional response in myself, a tingling cold chill or teary eyes, thinking about his life and drawing parallels to my own, probing avenues of pathos without success. Our relationship existed in the world of forms and thought, groping for some essential truth through machines, perhaps drawn together because we shared the condition of being genetic dead ends who were detached from our families. I never knew about his ex-wife or his pending criminal prosecution back in Russia. I knew nothing about his deepest fears or joys because I never asked. He never offered, either. We had been content to dwell in our shared interest in engineering and historical analysis.

It struck me that Victor was a degenerate case who tried to find order in chaos, pumping against the second law of meaninglessness by manipulating the physical world. He found refuge by crafting simple machines with elements of disorder and by becoming a nearly closed system in his dark house with only a few inputs and outputs. The return loops of his life, the key reflective processes for any intelligent machine, remained local to Sergey and me. Victor wasn't the answer for my future, but he was a friend.

The late morning sun had preheated the car and I lingered in its warmth before turning off the ignition in front of the apartment. I left after the doctor certified Victor's death and arrangements were made for the funeral home to pick up his body. The mixture of caffeine and sleep deprivation produced an addled impatience and exhaustion in me, each car noise an act of violence. I laid on the sofa and played "The Wreck of the Edmund Fitzgerald" on the stereo, a song I had not listened to in decades but had somehow summoned from the deep. The tears blew in like the song's fateful November storm and wrecked me on the rocks of time and loss.

The eastern sun reflected off painted white brick walls and created a warm microclimate on the sidewalk patio during the otherwise chilly Sunday morning. Sergey and I grabbed a seat after each getting a café americano. He pulled out a laptop and started typing quickly.

"I'd like to submit the obituary by tonight," Sergey said. "Let's choose a photo."

We flipped through the pictures he pulled from his collection and the ones I retrieved from the house, both of us agreeing that one from his university days made the most sense given that is how people in the town were most likely to remember him. The photo showed a smiling younger man with his raised arm around some kind of vacuum chamber, a stainless steel vessel with ports poking out that looked straight out of a Jules Verne novel. He assembled a list of publications and projects at the university in which Victor played a key role and we tossed around ideas for how to incorporate the salient periods of his life into a simple narrative.

"This is becoming more like a biography in a scientific journal than an obituary, just a list of accomplishments," Sergey said after he read aloud a list of Victor's achievements.

"We have to include something about the machines."

"The ones his brother designed?" Sergey asked. I gave him the full backstory, which was greeted with some initial skepticism until I described the detailed engineering drawings from the notebook. "Makes you wonder what other lives he lived."

"Do you believe Victor was responsible for his brother's disappearance?" I asked

"I worked with Leo on some projects a few times back in Russia. He told me that his brother was a gifted craftsman. Leo described him as his shadow, less academic and a bit of a troublemaker but brilliant." Sergey picked up the black and white photo of the two brothers in an embrace. "There were a lot of irregularities back then, we invented misinformation after all. No, I don't believe he played a role."

"I know he blamed himself. I think the machines were an attempt at redemption."

"I got something in the mail from his family, a court summons?"

"They are filing suit to return all the machines and notebook, claiming Leo as the sole creator," I said.

"Talk to Angelo about this, everything in the house is yours now. The will is very clear."

"What would Victor want us to do with them?" I asked.

"He kept them hidden for decades. There was a reason he opened up to you. Sure, you're smart and likable but I'd never seen him so excited as when he talked about you both working on the water computer."

"We never got to that one."

"I'm not sure that was ever the goal. Do what you think is right, fight it in court or try to reach a settlement," Sergey said and we returned to hashing out which nuggets of information were important to include in the obituary: his work with the school, his skill as an artisan, his sense of history.

Most of Victor's information was now forever lost or isolated flotsam in the ocean of digital, analog, and human memories. Maybe Sergey was right: human brains were Turing complete systems at a minimum, capable of implementing any algorithm, further aided by the distributed processing and storage abilities of culture. Given enough time, all fundamental scientific knowledge was possible, perhaps inevitable. There was still impossible data, events forever lost in time.

Victor Ivantusky passed away peacefully on November 2nd in the company of his close friends. Victor was born in 1950 in Voronezh, Russia in the former Soviet Union, and moved to the United States in 1995, drawn by the optimism of the American West. He was universally renowned for his craftsmanship in both his professional and personal life, which included working with his brother Leo Ivantusky on a set of intricate machines which captivated the art world after the Cold War. His intellectual curiosity grew throughout his life, and he lent his creative talents to both students and research projects selflessly. A private ceremony will be held. Memorial contributions may be made to the United Way referencing his name.

Only the roads and a few orphaned parking lots from the old nuclear processing plant remained on the land, the last traces of a large complex that manufactured plutonium pits, the spherical cores of nuclear weapons. After a series of mishaps and lawsuits, the plant was closed and the buildings were demolished. In a stroke of genius, it was labeled a Superfund site by the EPA, initiating cleanup efforts and eventually leading to its designation as a National Wildlife Refuge, an oasis for migratory birds and elk wintering grounds within the creeping suburbia of the metro area. It opened to the public three years previously after the EPA certified the radiation levels in the air and soil samples, although visitation remained a curiously fraught decision for the environmentally woke residents of nearby cities.

I parked at the trailhead at the southern end of the refuge and rotated my seat back to near horizontal. My brain fog seemed to be improving over the last few days but an overall fatigue and occasionally sore lymph nodes persisted, which could either be attributed to poor sleep, an incipient cold, or medicinal withdrawal. My appointments at Transcendent had become shorter, more like checkups than interrogations.

Nina responded to my text message invitation for a hike with a thumbs-up emoji and a four-letter response: *word*. Her brevity could be because she was busy or annoyed with me and I didn't press her. I set an alarm for twenty minutes and turned down the public radio station on a low enough volume for it to be a sufficiently boring distraction, like an Ambien-esque college thermodynamics class. I felt like an asleep dog hearing a turn signal and springing to attention when I heard gravel crunching outside the car.

"Are you trying to irradiate me?" Nina said while I blinked to rewet my contact lenses and searched frantically for the seat lever. I blindly finger-combed my hair and got out of the car.

"The government says we're perfectly safe," I said and grabbed my backpack. "How are you doing?"

"Same old. How about you, are you still in the study?"

"They pulled the medication after some sort of SPECT test," I said. "You?"

"They kicked me out," she said and put a fleece over her pink t-shirt of a band named Minor Lack. "Maybe they knew about the photos. Who knows? Why are we here?"

"We're on a mission of sorts, a funded one too." We started down the trail, keeping our interpersonal distance at a safe level.

"Do we get per diem for lunch later?" she asked. All of her responses seemed a bit too easy; I expected more tension given our last exchange.

"We're looking for a memorial site for Victor, he died last week." Victor's will set aside $10,000 for funeral arrangements, which more than covered the cost of cremation and a memorial gathering of friends. The celebration of life amounted to a meal at an Italian chain restaurant with fifteen co-workers and plenty of wine. Sergey assigned me the task of spending the remaining $7,000.

"Sorry to hear he passed away, that was really fast," she said.

"Stomach cancer," I said. "Didn't seem to be in pain."

"That's good, better to be cut off than fade away. We're all fading, just a question of the rate I guess," Nina said. "Interesting guy, I wish I got to know him more."

"You broke through his shell, he mentioned you a few times." We transitioned from shortgrass to an area with more rabbitbrush and yucca. "I finally got through to the park administrator for this place. They'll accept a memorial donation, after some sort of architectural approval."

"There is always the bench thing, people seem to like that."

"It needs to last, maybe an inch thick stainless steel superalloy, a tank. Nothing flimsy." I pictured something milled out of a large metal forging.

"Everyone does the bench."

We continued on the trail which followed a dry creek bed along a shallow canyon. Two older hikers with trekking poles walked along the canyon ridge, likely European tourists given their matching high-performance gear and lean physiques. Other than them, there was no one on the trails, not even packs of mountain bikers who wintered at lower elevations this time of year. We took a switchback path to get up on the ridge, the view opening up in front of us.

"This is the place," Nina said and stood on a flat area in front of two stunted western juniper trees. "Good view. Blended vegetation is more aesthetically pleasing than uniform grassland."

"How about a bench here facing west?"

"West, yes, bench, no. I'm thinking of two oversize Adirondack chairs, turned slightly inwards to face each other, large enough to fit two people in each if needed. Less neck strain – old folks don't like to turn their heads – backing up cars or otherwise."

"Big chairs are more comfortable, give more personal space." I pictured two people watching a sunset together. "These would make sense, he wasn't a touchy-feely kind of a guy, but he liked to talk."

I sat down, rotated to maximize my exposure to the warming sun, and pulled out two honeycrisp apples, handing one to Nina. We ate in silence sitting crossed-legged.

"Thanks for meeting me out here. I feel good about this spot," I said and picked up a juniper berry, cutting it in half with my thumbnail. "Each leg of the chair will be anchored to a concrete pylon. Would it be weird to mix his ashes into the concrete mix?"

"You're asking a weirdo. It's odd but in a good way. He really meant a lot to you, huh?"

"I guess. I'm not an expert at this mourning thing," I said, thinking about how it was often easier to be sentimental with a concept than a real person. "I've been thinking more about legacy lately."

"Share his stuff with more people, it's worth it," she said casually.

"How's work going?" I asked.

"Busy. Fall always produces a mad rush to get trips in." She pulled out her phone and tapped through black and white desert photos and a terraced set of polygons arranged like a topographical map. She stopped on a picture of the abandoned mine we had hiked to together.

"I'm sorry for ghosting you," I said and pushed the nail of my middle finger against my thumb, the same technique I employed when getting hypodermic injections.

"Let's blame the Transcendent bastards."

"It's easy for me to fall back into the safety of negative freedoms, freedom from stuff."

"I'm good at cutting people off too, assuming the worst," she said, tossing her hair to one side, then running her fingers along the part. She self-groomed during periods of introspection. "I'm too eager to find stability. I wanted Transcendent to fix me but I need to build it myself, one boring brick at a time. Not that I'll stop buying lottery tickets."

"Let's buy some and then watch the tragic stories of those who win to console ourselves when we lose," I joked, producing a close-lipped smile. We both looked out over the rolling hills onto the float glass flat suburbs. "Were you really a confederate?"

"Such a weird term. They called it a facilitator. Transcendent didn't hire me of course. A shell company called Bristol Consulting sent me a private message on the Xmundio app thing. They must have learned about my participation in the two previous studies." Nina snapped stalks of the dried grass at her feet. "The assignment was to follow the participants, report back on their living situations."

"The privacy settings thing?" I asked in a neutral tone.

"I changed them up for the app." She threw a handful of blades and tassels beyond her feet, then looked me in the eyes. "I'm ashamed I did it, wanted to score points with Bristol, get a bottle of the pills or something. You're the only one I actually hung out with, swear to God."

"Were you ever going to tell me?"

"I came close but didn't want to screw things up between us, kept telling myself the study would end in a few weeks anyway."

"Do the pills really do anything?"

"I thought so for a long time, that I needed to be cured," Nina said. "Now I'm not so sure. This kind of stuff is what I needed, meeting you, re-engaging with the world, veering outside of the tire tracks of my past."

She leaned to her side and we held each other for a shoulder-pressing embrace, then she pulled back and gave a distant smile.

Just looking at her curls produced a hardwired pleasant sensation in my mind, something that felt sweet but now a chasm away. Our relationship had undergone a phase change, shifted into something more mature.

I had dreaded confronting Nina on her role in the study, preparing mental excuses for outright avoidance or deftly juggling jokes. That would be a variation of the same secure strategy used with Jessica, retreating rather than resolving until indulging in a single destructive impulse like ghosting. We had lost something but could still grow together.

The wind picked up, sending a shiver down my spine. Nina torqued her torso back and forth to stretch and we both got up. She mounted a 300mm lens to her camera and stepped off the trail to look at a raptor's nest down in the canyon. There were worse places to be entombed in concrete. It was here that the shallow inland sea uplifted to resurrect the ancestral Rockies into the current range, exposing spines of red and brown sandstone and providing a sweeping backdrop for tracking summer thunderstorms and bluebird mornings after a snowstorm. Victor would appreciate the lingering half-lives of weapons created for a war that was never fought and the interplay of geologic and anthropologic time scales. I used the heel of my shoe to mark out spots for the chairs and took a photo.

Pierre extended the legs of his tripod, pointing the camera towards the kitchen table. He insisted that we not stack boxes on top of each other but rather lay them out in a single file, like a child on Christmas morning spreading out their gifts. I volunteered to bring boxes up from the basement, as their extraction and negotiation up the kickplate-less stairs would be too much for him.

We unboxed the first article which turned out to be loosely arranged soldering tools and electrical wiring. No hints of higher-order assembly. Angel hair pasta-shaped wood fibers topped the next box and digging in it revealed a carved mouse, a large glass bowl, and an assembly of gears.

"That's the drunken mouse!" Pierre exclaimed and urged caution around the parts. "It must have sat in this box for decades."

Pierre pulled off the tablecloth and cleaned the kitchen table with wet and dry paper towels. I spread the parts across the surface – gears, pulleys, a support frame, fasteners, a brass bell, a motor, and the base platform. The oil and grease must have crept along the surfaces and hardened into some sort of resin.

"He disassembled the entire machine for storage," Pierre said with a long exhale. "Let's look at the notebook."

We found the pages describing the device which included sketches of the gear train, the bobbing rodent, and some detailed part drawings in Victor's section. We shifted the pieces to create an exploded view on the table in an attempt to reconstruct it, but the correct assembly remained unclear.

"Is this a chaotic machine?" I asked.

"Reports from the Warsaw exhibit said the mouse lurched along the rim of the bowl in an unsteady fashion and bent over to take sips. The rotation of this timing ring appears loosely coupled to the rest of the machine, that could do it." Pierre answered, scribbling down notes. "No videos from back then, only photos."

"These may help," I said, pulling out a set of small parts that were tucked into a corner of the box.

"Careful flexing that, it's completely cracked," Pierre said. I kept the embrittled small belt in its circular shape. After he took several pictures, we slid the items to one end of the table and I started on the next box. It contained a machine that appeared more pneumatic and had a set of tubes and chambers. We flipped through the notebook but couldn't find its corresponding drawing. The horizontal surfaces of the living room and kitchen quickly became cluttered with machine parts and subassemblies as we worked our way through all the basement and workshop boxes.

"What's your tally?" I asked after putting a set of wood lathe blanks and turning tools back in their container.

"Two completed assemblies, the waterwheel and the flying geese. Three disassembled machines, all of which are present in the notebook. Three more partial assemblies that appear to correspond with notebook designs, plus two that do not," Pierre said and looked up from his notepad, his nostrils stopping the downward slide of his reading glasses. "It's remarkable."

"Can they be rebuilt?"

"Using these original parts, probably not. I'm sure we'll need to replace some bearings and gears. It doesn't make sense why some were completely disassembled; he could have easily found a large enough box for storage."

"Maybe he wanted each machine to be unique."

"I'd be honored to attempt the reconstruction," Pierre said, flipping through the notebook.

I went back to the workshop while he continued cataloging the parts. I now owned all of the aluminum extrusions, the silicone tubing, a workbench, a wood lathe, and the 800-pound "lightweight" imported milling machine, and I needed to figure out how to fit it all into a four hundred square foot apartment. Victor's ex-wife Heidi would be moving in soon with a caravan of her children and have no use for a full arsenal of light industrial equipment.

"They are early," Pierre said after we heard three sharp knocks on the front door. The visit had been coordinated through an exchange of text messages with Irina, with the goal of having a cordial meeting before the court date in two weeks. I began to regret not bringing Sergey or his lawyer when the three walked in.

"Very sorry for your loss," Aldous said and shook our hands. "He was one of a kind, no doubt."

I made eye contact with Irina who sat down on the sofa while Roman surveyed the machine parts on the kitchen table. Pierre closed the notebook and started moving chairs out to the living room, forming an arc facing the couch and recliner.

"What the hell happened? Did you tear these apart?" Roman accused us. He picked up a small spur gear and turned it in his hand, dropping it back on the table. "These damn things may never work again!"

"You said the machines would be ready to review," Aldous said while turning back box flaps and peering inside.

Roman walked over to the window while Pierre explained how they had been disassembled by Victor with the parts likely, but not necessarily, in the boxes. Irina suggested over text messages that her brother had reached the limit of his patience and was anxious to get the case before a judge. She convinced them to sit down for a final discussion before resigning to the legal solution. Aldous prompted us to take seats.

"It should be clear that our position has only strengthened since Victor's death. The artwork should be returned to the family," Aldous said, pulling out a small stack of papers with yellow sticky arrows for signatures. "But we didn't come here to bluster and make demands. We are offering a very equitable agreement."

"You will receive $150,000 in exchange for the full set of machines, a massively generous sum for boutique items that are, apparently, largely disassembled," Irina said. Aldous seconded the insanity of their generosity.

"Will these be donated to museums or kept with private collectors?" Pierre asked.

"The contract has no terms in those regards and my clients require full flexibility to do with the art as they see fit," Aldous responded quickly.

Pierre and I scanned through the pages. All the machines and the notebook would be transferred to Leo's children, along with the rights to any photographs or digital copies in perpetuity. I reflexively ran through some quick math in my head to calculate how much money would be left after taxes and a courtesy fee for Pierre. Nina would understand, all artists existed on some level of largess and the money from this agreement would allow me to focus on my craft – once I found one. Plus, one fifty was their starting offer, what they wanted to pay, like the MSRP from the dealer.

"Will Victor be recognized as a co-creator of the pieces?" I asked.

"We retain all rights for any descriptions of the articles, see the first paragraph on the second page," Aldous said. "When you agree, sign and date the bottom of the last page and initial each one as well."

"These are worth several million dollars," Pierre stated with confusion, finally digesting the low-ball offer. In principle, I agreed with him. The growth of wealth in the top one percent and the growing stigma of ostentatious consumerism resulted in a reservoir of disposable money searching to buy something unique, differentiating items between their rich peers. That being said, the parts were caked with grease and splayed across the kitchen table like organs on a butcher's block.

"No way. Even indulging your fantasy that they are worth one million in their current condition and you multiply that by our ninety percent chance of winning this lawsuit, results in $100,000," Roman said, clearly frustrated that he was still negotiating with us.

I completely failed at doing opposition research on the siblings. I didn't know the depth of their pockets or anything about their personal circumstances. The beauty of the machines must be irrelevant to them, having never shown any interest in how they worked or the content of the notebook. Roman wanted to correct his father's legacy, restore his genius to the world, with a bonus of increasing his standing amongst the jet set. Pierre and I walked back to the workshop where I unconsciously turned the handwheels on the milling machine platform as we talked through our options.

"Is your original client still interested?" I asked. "Maybe we can use their offer as leverage."

"Her foundation can easily pay much more, but they are wary of the lawsuit," Pierre said. "Have you been preparing a defense?"

"Nothing," I admitted.

"They'll end up back in a basement or a freeport gathering dust, never even being turned on," Pierre said and I agreed. I spun the milling machine's handwheel and thought about when Victor and I originally unpacked it, then the joy in taking the final cutting pass of an aluminum part. Irina and Aldous broke out of their huddle when we returned to the living room.

"You need to restore your father's legacy, get him the recognition he deserves," I said while sitting back down opposite the three. "Getting these pieces restored and into a museum accomplishes that better than any private sale would."

"How do you know that isn't our plan already?" Roman asked incredulously.

"Think about twenty years in the future. Now try to think about two hundred, when everyone living is long dead. Showcasing these machines in a protected environment will ensure they – and Leo's genius – will last long into the future," Pierre said.

"You may not believe in a personal afterlife but these works can have one," I added.

"What is your offer?" Irina asked.

"Almost all of the machines are disassembled, some may be nearly impossible to repair. Pierre is the world's foremost expert in their design and overall aesthetic intent. He will carefully reconstruct them, staying faithful to the original materials and methods," I said while looking over to the collector, checking his body language to make sure he stayed committed. "He will serve as their primary – and volunteer – curator at the Museum of Contemporary Art. He already has many contacts there. Ownership will be transferred completely to the museum as a donation. This will only cost you any special materials Pierre requires during the re-assembly, otherwise, it's free."

"Who writes the biography of the artist?" Roman asked.

"Both men will be featured. You and your sister will narrate your father's story and I will write Victor's," I said.

"You don't even know...," Roman cut himself off when Aldous tapped his leg. The three walked out to caucus on the front porch.

"They realize that going to court is a crapshoot, that's why they're here," Pierre said and then thanked me again for the endorsement. He went back to inspecting the parts on the table and flipping through the notebook. While watching Roman gesticulate through the window, a calmness sank into me. I knew that the parallax of memory would mean that during quiet moments on future Sunday nights or midnight walks I may regret this decision of exchanging future financial freedom for public art, but at a deeper level it felt right.

Machines need to roam across the landscape, fertilize other systems, find new territory, not sit in the basement of an investment banker's Tuscan villa. At least this sounded noble, appealing to my same impulsiveness that usually scuttled rather than created. It was the same urge that brought exhilaration with doing a radical act, like the initial taking of Victor's waterwheel, the love of one's fate. Unlike my previous personally rebellious decisions, this would be an opening up to the world and away from myself.

"I'll email an updated contract this afternoon. Digital signatures are required by five o'clock," Aldous said as he stepped in through the door. Irina stood on the porch with a Mona Lisa smile on her face, her brother nowhere in sight.

A compact sedan pulled out of its spot and I hastily did a nine-point turn then precision parallel parked thanks to the rear backup camera. The neighborhood saw a massive influx of hipsters and wealth since the dawn of the new millennium turning a patch of urban blight into a four-letter, directionally-nicknamed district. This meant that parking required intense prowling on every street within six blocks of the industrial bars and restaurants. I headed west to Omega, which the mapping software described as *funky,* with photos showing bartenders colorfully inked like the murals on their warehouse brick walls. I walked the four blocks to the restaurant past the curtainless illuminated slot townhomes and tree lawn gardens.

I accepted Nina's text invitation to join her and her friend Jasmine at the bar and arrived fifteen minutes early. The passenger I had just taken to the airport insisted on making up time, and repeatedly checked his phone for his flight status. Cars have a natural maximum speed, the velocity at which the vehicle begins to protest and produces a feeling of instability, like an amateur skier's chattering skis on icy turns. This was around seventy miles per hour on the used Buick I drove in high school but my current car unfortunately accelerated to eighty-five with aplomb, getting my bossy passenger to the airport ahead of schedule and me to the bar early.

I grabbed a small table on the patio, a minor coup given the foot traffic, and nursed a local draft IPA. The unseasonably warm weather kept the Friday night crowd outside in the open-air beer garden, lit by filament lights hung from weathered steel I-beams. I tried to listen in on a nearby conversation but only gleaned a few acronyms and hyperbolic statements, so I watched their animated body language instead. I had skipped over the stage in life when people move to urban centers and lead lives of sexual fluidity and digital immersion. They carried a spectating interest like watching a raunchy reality TV show, and the thought of repeating this life phase felt utterly exhausting.

Despite my position on the far-right tail of the bar's bell curve for age, it felt good to be surrounded by human activity, a confirmation that I was in the right place. Nina and I had met a few times and were settling into a friendly rhythm of a text message every one or two days. We forwarded one another podcasts of interest and made vague plans to get a drink. It was clear that we had entered the friend zone.

Jasmine showed up first, bouncing in from behind me with a copper cupped cocktail in her hand and congratulating me on getting a table. She had driven in from Santa Fe and looked the part: wild wavy hair and four bracelets on each wrist.

"Nina says you have a good eye for photography," Jasmine said while tying back ropes of dark hair. She was striking in a universal way, an indeterminate ethnicity that subsumed all the others with light brown skin and sharp features.

"That's generous, but I do have advanced tripod skills." I helped Nina and another female friend set up long exposure late-night shots of run down motels and some of the solitary street light near Victor's house. "I also like sharp lines and empty spaces."

"She's not the perky wedding photographer type," Jasmine said with a laugh.

"How's Santa Fe?" I asked.

"Bit of a bubble but it's good. I run a yoga and meditation studio down there, cliche I know," Her attitude alone would be enough to draw in retirees, even before they saw her in synthetic, form-fitting clothes. "I think we're seeing a return to the Greeks, people trying to find the good life."

"How's that?"

"The different schools with their formulas for finding tranquility. Plato with contemplation, Epicurus with close friends, the Stoics with reason and social engagement, that sort of thing. I offer a little more of the Eastern variety with meditation, but each approach is valid," Jasmine said. "I listened to some podcasts on the way up here. It's not about how *should* one live anymore, but how *could* one live."

I texted her Kory Gorman's TED talk video, the biochemical machine learning solution to well-being but didn't mention my involvement with Transcendent. We waved to Nina who was hustling in from the street.

The two friends immediately dove into conversation, catching each other up on friends and family news. Jasmine ordered tortilla chips with cowboy caviar salsa and vegan samosas for the table, which gave me something to do while they talked and I people watched. The menu appeared to be entirely vegetarian but still delivered on flavor. Food had regained its intrinsic religious status from the cosmic cycle of life in the Hindu scriptures to the current righteousness involved with selecting vegan/organic/non-GMO/fair-trade dishes.

We moved closer to the fire pit when a spot opened up to offset the cooling night air. I stared into the natural gas-fed flames which danced along cement logs, a clean chemical combustion with no residue. Victor's cremated remains sat in a faux tropical hardwood box on my dresser, sealed in a plastic bag. Sergey hadn't questioned my taking his ashes and I never mentioned my plan to include them in the concrete footings for the two chairs. It would take several months to get the project approved before they dug the holes through the frost line. I had intentionally placed the box of ashes above my sock drawer as a daily reminder not to let the memorial turn into a public works project that limped slowly to completion.

The patio hummed with the impatient conversations of humble-braggers and flirters: clusters of juvenile males showing off bar feats, couples on single-digit date numbers peeling away beer bottle labels and wondering, and college grads lost in the infinite. I started to see different versions of myself spinning away from the present moment, then collapsing from many worlds to a single one through choice, without the immunity of youth but able to use a few constellations to help navigate – knowing that there was some degree of order.

Nina bounced her foot up and down on the table footrest, producing circular waves in the glasses of water. I set a reminder on my phone to put snowshoes, gloves, and ski pants into the back of my car before going to bed. She had sent me a rejoicing text when fresh powder dropped over the mountains a few days before. The idea of the desiccated, brown, alpine area transformed under a blanket of white crystals appealed to me, and I had decided to get up early to solo snowshoe the next day. I looked over at Nina who struggled to get words out while laughing as the two recounted college misadventures. I expected our friendship would drift apart if either one of us began dating, further reconfigure itself into lower intensity states.

Finding a partner would not be the result of overcoming the impossible romantic Drake equation but instead emerge from immersion in the riotous world. I thought back to the time I got my first eyeglass prescription and saw the world in precise detail, a richness that felt artificial, the vibrancy and resolution of space too real. The same sensation came over me now, but in time rather than space – the density of now.

"You know how to salsa, right?" Nina tapped me on the shoulder, breaking me out of the reverie.

A girl ran through a field of sunflowers, the camera zooming in on a flower to deconstruct its petals into a wireframe repeated unit which merged into the icon for Transcendent Health: an octagonal shape built from curvy triangles. This concluded the three-minute-long outbrief video, vaguely thanking us for our participation in the study.

"Yeah, I know. I'm just the messenger," Dr. Patel said with a sarcastic exhale. "Some forms to sign as well."

"Do any of these explain the study?" I asked, leafing through the pages of legalese.

"Probably not," she said with a jocular tone. Her hair came down in two opposing curtains, a change from the single braid she usually adopted. Her eyes had a softer, post-coital look. "You can ask me questions if you'd like. This is my last contracted study with Transcendent, they are bringing on a new team."

"Was I in the control or experiment group?"

"I'm not sure those categories apply. This wasn't a clinical trial, there is no drug they are trying to bring to market at this time," Dr. Patel said. "Did you see a change?"

"I felt heightened somehow."

"Interesting. You're not the only person who's told me that. I'm still bound by their NDA but I'd like to give you some closure," she said, pausing to think. "You know how when they do investigations after an airplane crash there is never really one cause but instead a collection of them?"

"The study was more than just the pills?"

"The physical world follows scientific laws so as a law-abiding society, we like having a single guilty party or a single hero. It's never that simple," she said and pushed her lips together as if holding something back. "I wish you well, Martin."

We shook hands and I left the office after picking up my last check. I didn't expect any real answers from Transcendent. Dr. Patel's cryptic description could have all been a planned delivery of misinformation, a way to cast doubt in the patients about the experiment. I knew that my scraped personal biodata tumbled around in Xmundio's servers, ingested by algorithms and training new systems. An earlier version of me would see this as a dystopian privacy violation but perhaps the data could speak in a way I never could, help a future Martin against the headwinds of life.

I had stopped speculating about whether the medication had been a placebo. My oscillating sleep patterns and subsequent bouts of despair or bliss would not be solved pharmacologically. The mind was the quintessential chaotic machine, but it needed to be trained rather than fixed, not always granted primacy and consumed with 2 am arcane podcasts but allowed to rest, allowed to not think. I needed better hygiene, not surgery.

Pierre's daily status message arrived. He just installed a new bearing in the drunken mouse's pivoting body. My digital literacy helped in the search for metric gear forms and custom belts when he hit a roadblock. I still owed him the write-up on Victor's life for the museum, but I was waiting for the buds to breach out of my mental compost pile.

I looked out the rear window into the box, hoping the gesture would be noticed and the truck's speed reduced, especially through the crowned intersections. The ratchet strap mechanism vibrated freely in the air, the amplitude growing and shrinking as we stopped and started. It was mesmerizing to watch. I looked around the cab for a compliant object like a rolled-up towel to add tension in the strap or at least dampen the vibration during an upcoming red light, but only found a few receipts and jumper cables in the narrow slot behind the seats. Theresa cracked both windows as if reminding me to keep breathing, the air twirling her cranberry-dyed hair.

Theresa and her son had pulled up behind me in front of Victor's house, both of us getting there a few minutes after 8:00 am. Their pickup truck showed some age but sat high over its wheels through intentional lifting or a fresh suspension.

"It's a full-size box with plenty of tie-downs at the corners. Hell, I've stacked mattresses along the sides and front, cleared out his one-bedroom apartment in a single trip," she boasted. She offered up her truck as we left the neighborhood bar when the book club dispersed earlier in the week. We had both been given the title *youngster* by the retired ladies in the club, though I suspected she had about five years on me.

"Looks great, only a few large items today," I said.

"Baxter, grab the dolly," she ordered her teenage son, who avoided eye contact and sipped an oversize Mountain Dew. Unlike Baxter, Theresa kept her shoulders back and moved powerfully as we both grabbed things out of the cab. She somehow went sleeveless on the brisk morning, the cold air turning her thick upper arms into red and white marbled slabs of meat. "He's not a morning person."

"It's the equipment in the back," I said and gave her a tour.

"Where is the lumber, the two by tens?" she asked while looking at the cast iron base of the milling machine.

"The shed is in the backyard. It's unlocked." I said, remembering she had asked about planks when we talked earlier and that I had never confirmed having them. She spoke quickly in Appalachian English and was easily the most colorful member of the book club. Working as a parcel driver allowed her plenty of time to blaze through audiobooks.

"Baxter, get some boards in the shed," she hollered out to the front. "You're gonna have to get creative, son."

Theresa started disassembling the milling machine while I gathered up smaller tools and put them into plastic bins. Victor's ex-wife Heidi kept calling despite my pleas for her to text instead. She spoke in a hurried, disjointed way, usually while disciplining a child or fighting with the cable repairman. I always ended up with fresh action items. I tried emailing her sketches of the floorplan but she insisted on a verbal description of each room in the house, and we walked through the interior options for each space. She said that the milling machine had to go with the rest of the tools and I acknowledged that motorized equipment probably didn't belong in a kid's bedroom. The Chapman clan were set to land the next weekend and were eager to set up camp.

We reduced each section of the milling machine to around the weight of a human body and strapped them to Theresa's supplied dolly. Baxter fashioned two wooden planks and cement blocks to bridge from the front porch to an unfolded tailgate, having backed the truck over the curb and through the yard to the front steps. I tried taking photos during the process to help me later when I had to reassemble it, but it looked straightforward, requiring only brute force and bolts rather than Pierre's restoration efforts. The workbench anchored the other side of the box, hosting a metal grinder and a compact welder, while the wood lathe and raw materials sat in the center of the truck bed. Theresa ran a web of bungee cords and a ratchet strap from the workbench to a front corner post.

I helped Pierre with the third and, presumably, final pickup of the Ivantusky brother's machines the previous weekend, painstakingly packing up each of the articles after canvasing the basement and upstairs workshop for loose parts. Pierre scheduled a debut on New Year's Day with the museum and invited me, Roman, and Irina to a private soirée with the institution's art director and most generous philanthropic partners. I could tell the deadline both excited and exasperated the collector, judging from his daily text missives.

"Where am I going?" Theresa asked as we left the house. Baxter leaned against the passenger window buried in a screen, gothic font empty energy drinks in his nearby cupholder.

"You'll cross the tracks and head north on Fremont for about six miles," I said while confirming the route on my phone. The road followed the meandering bike trail along the former canal, the tree-lined streets of the old town giving way to strip malls and fields of prairie dogs. I rode a recently purchased used bike through the semi-industrial neighborhood last week, passing by apartment buildings smelling of curry.

"Bax, turn this shit off and put on something good," Theresa said when another dubstep song came on. Empty energy drinks sat in the cup holders. "Pull up my Guns N' Roses playlist."

I had modest success selling Victor's yard equipment and excess furniture through an online marketplace, then searched for other milling machines for sale to gauge the price points and presentation. A user called *High Plains Academy* had several posts asking for equipment: machine shop tools, 3D printers, laser cutters, power supplies. I called the number given on their profile and Eduardo's enthusiasm leapt through the phone when I mentioned the milling machine, an excitement outside the behavioral norms for a sober non-adolescent man. I let the fact it was an inheritance slip out, which snuffed out any plans for a sale rather than a donation.

We turned off Fremont and into the school parking lot. The brick building must have been repurposed from a more mundane structure. The south-facing wall was decorated with patches of Moorish-looking tessellations while the western side hosted a large community garden. A weathered aluminum observatory sat about 100 yards away with fresh dirt at its base. A sign along the rooftop listed the school as an Xmundio New Millennium Project Partner.

"The back is sitting low, I like it!" Eduardo, also undeterred by the cool breeze, trotted out to meet us wearing a t-shirt and vest. I pulled down the tailgate, letting him go through the contents.

"Threw in some 8020 aluminum extrusion and piping," I said.

"Beautiful," Eduardo said and lifted a piece of sheet metal to inspect the smaller items on the truck bed.

"You have a loading dock around here?" Theresa asked while walking along the side of the school.

"It's in the back. I'll meet you there with another hand truck," he said and clapped his hands together, which seemed to be his preferred way to finish a sentence.

"Quite the chipper lad," Theresa said as we backed into the loading dock. He could be a Transcendent success story released into the wild.

"The Richard Simmons of charter schools," I said. We unloaded the loose tools to clear a path for the larger machines. Baxter and I walked the workbench to the tailgate and then lifted it beyond the rubber bumpers onto the concrete floor. Eduardo propped open the back door with an anvil, then pushed a dolly and pulled a hand cart behind him. The four of us unloaded the truck in less than a half hour.

"It's not a Bridgeport, but it works pretty well," I told him as we assembled the milling machine along a wall next to a drill press. The workbench found a home nearby along the same wall and we stacked small tools on top for later dispersal.

"Many of these kids watch screens and drink soda all day, can't hammer a nail when they come in," Eduardo said as he gave us a tour. "We're not trying to turn all of them into machinists or 3D artists, just grow some level of empowerment, agency. You start to appreciate geometry more when the flashlight you built doesn't fit together."

"Where are the kids at?" I asked.

"The grand opening is next year. We currently host two days a week of science and shop classes for our sister campus. We'll be at full capacity this spring with all subjects, enrollment is really picking up. Grades 9 through 12."

"Cool workspace. That laser jet cutter could have come in handy for this," I said, pulling up videos of the hydraulic difference engine and explaining its function as a quasi-analog computer. Eduardo seemed intrigued, but this was his default state. "I built it with the guy that owned this stuff. We were originally trying to make a water computer, ever heard of those?"

I attempted to explain how the original Russian article may have worked, integrating liquid flows to simulate a physical phenomenon. I showed him an online photo of one the size of a refrigerator. "This is a compact unit, some of them filled up entire rooms."

"That is wild. I like yours though, people can visualize the flow. I'll always pick the solution that lets you see it, touch it. This could be simulated right?" he asked.

"Yeah, in a spreadsheet or with code, maybe making a prediction and then running the experiment." We kept talking about using it as a frost depth calculator, creating custom inserts for the input tank, and he seemed genuinely interested. Theresa gathered up the straps and wheeled her dolly back to the truck, swinging the tailgate up against its latch emphatically.

"We need to head out, but I could come back later and help you set the rest of this up," I said.

"Stick around, Maria is dropping off tamales at noon. I'll give whoever stays a ride back."

We unboxed more of the tools after Theresa and Baxter left, Eduardo regaling me with stories from his career from when he was a retail architect through his time as a Maker workshop leader to his new gig as the High Plains Academy principal. With slightly different settings on the knobs of virtue, he could have been a con man or cult leader, someone people wanted to believe in.

"Some sort of engineer, right? Software?" he asked while we torqued down a vice on the workbench.

"Between jobs. Taught math overseas for a long time."

"High school math?"

"All types." I had recently dredged out an old calculus book and had been playing around, sparring with some integrals. "High school included."

"I'm filling out your application today, physics too right, a real unicorn?"

"I need to get certified in the state."

"We can work with that. No pension here though. Pay is ..." Eduardo hesitated. "Pay is reasonable."

We finished assembling the mill, shimming the base and mounting the two-axis platform, turning it on and running the handwheels, and installing a key lock safety box over the power plug after making sure it turned on.

"The man who owned this equipment built some chaotic machines, ones that start with simple motion and display complex behavior. His brother Leo designed them in post-Cold War Russia then disappeared before any were built," I said and showed Eduardo videos of completed machines and notebook excerpt photos that Pierre had sent over.

"Where can I see these?" he asked while scrolling through the content.

"They're being restored to be shown at the Museum of Contemporary Art early next year."

"The kids will love them. Definitely putting a field trip into the schedule. Art museums are usually snooze-fests but these look beautiful, not to mention the engineering angle and this gorgeous notebook."

"I should be able to help arrange something," I said, thinking of a private viewing.

Eduardo continued talking up the school while we replaced a blade on a donated bandsaw, explaining that Xmundio pledged to provide each student with a laptop and would be installing the IT network over the next month. He had lined up a few of their managers to speak at assemblies and work directly with students on projects.

I sat on a wooden table in the middle of the workspace while Eduardo stepped outside to take a phone call. The shop was a rehab facility of donated equipment. These new machines would be connected to other machines and students, all productive and consumptive in their web, completing the sought-after return loop not in a single brilliant hydraulic pathway but through chaotic and branching capillaries – a dispersed reflective machine greater than any water computer. Any one agent's contribution is only some short lifetime packets of material and information. Like pollen and seeds carried by the wind, some would fertilize and recombine, carve out new territories, climb out of potential wells, and under the right sequence of collisions, escape out of the center hump to a tail end of the distribution for a while. We could continue to push against the central limits of our experience, carry on the spirit of Victor and his machines, try to affirm life working with but not reliant on a technological savior.

The list on my phone started with textbooks and grew to include whiteboards, springs, used bicycles, gear pumps, a toolbox of experimentation. Sun from the south-facing windows started grazing the western wall of the workshop. It was only noon.

Made in the USA
Middletown, DE
16 October 2022

12907610R00166